I0681181

Moment of Truth

Marcus McGee

PEGASUS BOOKS

Copyright © 2010 Marcus McGee
All Rights Reserved

Copyright © 2010 Marcus McGee. Printed and bound in the United States of America. All Rights Reserved. No part of this book may be produced or transmitted in any form or by any means, electronic or mechanical, including photocopying, recording or by an information storage and retrieval system—except by a reviewer who may quote brief passages in a review to be printed in a magazine or newspaper—without permission in writing from the publisher. For information, please contact Pegasus Books c/o Ms. McGhee, P.O. Box 235, Neptune, New Jersey, 07754.

ISBN – 978-0-9826936-9-8

LCCN: 2010930835

Comments about *Moment of Truth* and requests for additional copies, book club rates and author speaking appearances may be addressed to Marcus McGee or Pegasus Books c/o Ms. McGhee, P.O. Box 235, Neptune, New Jersey, 07754, or you can send your comments and requests via e-mail to marcus.media@yahoo.com

This is a work of fiction. The events described are imaginary, and the characters are fictitious and are not intended to represent specific living persons. Even when the settings are referred to by their true names, the incidents taking place there are entirely fictitious; the reader should not infer that the events set there ever happened.

For Elaine

"Who is this? And what is here?"
And in the lighted palace near
Died the sound of royal cheer;
And they crossed themselves for fear,
All the Knights at Camelot;
But Lancelot mused a little space
He said, "She has a lovely face;
God in his mercy lend her grace,
The Lady of Shalott."

There have been and will be many and diverse destructions of mankind, of which the greatest are by fire and water, and lesser ones by countless other means... The truth of it lies in the occurrence of a shifting of the bodies in the heavens, which move around the Earth, and a destruction of the things on the Earth by fierce fire, which recurs at long intervals.

The priest of Sais, to Solon,
Greek statesman

The sun shall be turned into darkness, and the moon into blood, before the great and notable day of the Lord come.

Paul of Tarsus, Acts of the Apostles

Moment of Truth
by
Marcus McGee

Chapter 1

"Jack of spades, two of hearts, five of hearts, king of..."

Adam Smock opened his eyes, sighed and shook his head.

"King of diamonds? How many is that?"

JR answered as he counted the remaining cards.

"This is a double deck, and there are only six left. So that was ninety-eight."

"How many wrong?"

"Only the last two."

Adam sipped the tequila, the frustration evident in his demeanor.

"When I was in college, I could do a triple deck with no mistakes. I'm losin it."

JR laughed.

"I'm sure when you were doin that back then, you hadn't downed four and a half tequila shots in twenty minutes. And that's the high octane stuff."

Adam Smock had become a regular bar customer at Jackie O's. When he decided to volunteer for the Lazarus Project, he forfeited life on the surface. Because he had no wife or kids, it was easy enough for the Lazarus Project's logistical team to arrange his earthly demise. Accessing airline computers, the team inserted his name on the passenger manifest of a small jet that crashed in Detroit shortly after takeoff. From late October on, Adam Smock ceased to exist above ground.

"So, were you born with this 'static memory,' or are you a government project?"

"Both. I was born with it, and because it's very rare, I *became* a government project."

"Short version. How does it work?"

Adam thought for a moment and responded.

"Short version? Ninety-four percent visual recall, seventy-six percent audio, eighty sensory, eighty-two olfactory and palate."

"And the rest of us?"

"For your basic good memory? In the thirties. Forties would be a great memory. A lotta people make the mistake of thinking having a static memory makes you smarter, but it's not true. You just remember more. And believe me, I'd call it a curse before I'd call it a blessing. Sometimes it's good to forget. It's why I drink. I drink to forget. As humans, we go through a lot of bullshit out there that we're *supposed* to forget so we can learn new things, common sense things. So that's why I'm here. I have no common sense. Short enough for you?"

JR chuckled.

"I'm probably in the teens. I can't even remember what I had for dinner last night."

Adam took a table in a secluded corner of the restaurant. As he sat alone, he opened a two-inch-thick report and read for a little more than twenty minutes before his guest arrived. Adam and the woman sat in silence for the better part of an hour as both pored over reports.

In the meantime, JR seated Davis Franklin and his assistant, Baldev Heir, at a table on the other side of the restaurant. Paranoid, the men talked in whispers for fifteen minutes until a third man arrived. Everyone in the restaurant recognized the third man as Eaton James, head of Crypt security. Two specially trained guards joined James at the table and sat as he gave them instructions.

Across the room, Adam Smock put the report down.

"Just what is Davis Franklin doing down here anyway? Hasn't he got enough money to build his own Crypt somewhere?"

"What? And live in a hole in the ground for the next thirty, forty years longing for the past? Live in a place where all his billions mean nothing? Down here he can help shape the future."

"And he isn't going on the Ark? Maybe he knows something we don't know."

Isabel put the report down and removed her glasses.

"Actually, I offered him a place, but he's got a wife and daughter down here. He and the wife separated recently, but he's not going to leave her or the daughter."

Adam set his report on the table and leaned back in the chair.

"Can't argue that, but it wouldn't hurt to have a computer expert like him on the other side."

After dinner, Adam began with the first of three questions about the project that had been nagging him throughout the day.

"So what about Cheyenne Mountain and NORAD? Why didn't the government just refit one of those places to accomplish what you're doing here?"

"The current administration didn't know we even existed until the Nostradamus threat. Our objectives, and therefore our capabilities, are entirely different. Cheyenne Mountain and NORAD were built specifically to work as *military* command centers in the event of global thermonuclear war. The Crypt was built for the preservation of life on Earth in the event of a global life-threatening *asteroidal* or cosmic impact. People locked in Cheyenne Mountain and at NORAD might very well survive the initial August 7th impact, but they won't be expected to live beyond twelve or so years, and they sure as hell won't be in any position to re-establish human or animal populations on Earth."

Isabel stopped and sighed.

"All that's really out of my scope. Your *father* would be the person to answer questions in that area. You'd think a person with such a celebrated memory would remember I'm Life Ark, not the government."

The insult rankled the twenty-eight-year-old, who still wasn't used to Isabel's sarcasm.

"Page one hundred seventy-seven, third paragraph down, you say: *In the past two months, the advances we have seen in cryogenic preservation and subsequent life restoration techniques have been reassuring, if not phenomenal. Cold sleep has gone from theory to reality. Already, we have managed to reduce the expected cryopod/recovery failure rate down to a single digit number. Currently, the expected failure rate is seven percent, but we hope to reduce it to four percent before the launch in March.*"

He had quoted verbatim from the closed report on the table before him. While such a display of static memory was enough to amuse a woman in his experience, Isabel never even raised an eyebrow.

"I know what you can do. I'm not impressed. If there isn't a question in there somewhere, you're wasting my time."

Adam smirked, cleared his throat and continued.

"Seven percent of forty-four is what? Three point zero eight? And four percent is one point seven six. So that means that, under even the best of circumstances, between two and four of the forty-four selectee-volunteers are as good as dead before launch time?"

She contemplated before conceding.

"Statistically yes, but it's an acceptable risk, considering the percentage of the human population expected to die after the impact. I think that's about *one hundred* percent."

"Yes, but these three or four selectee-volunteers will be forfeiting six months they could be living on Earth just to die in a cryopod in space."

"That's why they're volunteers."

Adam thought a moment before responding.

"Does position matter? I mean, does it matter *where* on the Ark the cryopods are positioned? Are some pods more at risk than others?"

Isabel sighed, nodding.

"It's not in the report, but actually, position does matter."

"Does anyone know which pods are at risk and which ones are the safest?"

"Well, yes."

Adam's eyes narrowed as he put the next logical question.

"And who chooses where the individual selectee-volunteers are positioned on Life Ark?"

She turned away from Adam, took up and opened the thick report, half-smiling.

"You disappoint me, Adam. You *really* have to ask?"

****

News of the Earl Krebbs suicide was greeted with mixed reviews. The media characterized Earl's death as ancillary to the Echo Valley tragedy. "He took his own life," a news anchor eulogized, "because he was overcome with profound grief over losing his son in godforsaken Echo Valley."

America's national day of mourning included an hour-long television news feature on Colonel Earl Krebbs and his dream of a New American Republic.

According to National Security Advisor Jett Turner and others in the Whitmore administration, the piece was a blatant propaganda campaign initiated by a loose confederation of interests across the country. Its purpose was to legitimize the New Republic and to ratify its claim to legitimacy.

Turner believed the governors of California, New York and Florida, as well as key American military personnel and several multinational corporations were involved. He warned that if someone could sway American opinion to support the New Republic's asserted right to independence, then it would be easier for the larger and more powerful states, banks and corporate entities to assert their autonomy in the coming months.

"Three months ago," Jett asserted, "the New Republic was a fuckin joke. Now they've got F-18s, tanks, well-trained divisions and some of our best military minds. If they somehow manage to get the support of the American people, we're not just lookin at some little crazy, redneck militia group hidin out in Wyoming! We're lookin at the end of the Union, the end of the United States of America!"

Even within the New Republic, where many hated Earl Krebbs and scoffed at notions he was the nation's founder, he became an instant hero of folklore. Reporters excused his racial hatred, blaming it on his father and his troubled family history.

Others glazed over his savagery, recalling the necessary bloodletting and violence of the the Bible and the American Revolution. Some historians even likened Earl Krebbs to the heroic General Washington and patriot Thomas Jefferson.

The New Republic scheduled the funeral for four p.m. on Thanksgiving Day. The diminished National Football League, operating with only fourteen of its previous thirty-two teams, played its last symbolic "Turkey Day" game at ten a.m., pitting the Dallas Cowboys against the Washington Redskins.

It was the last NFL game ever, as neither the public nor the players in the league felt motivated about the rest the season. Eight of the fourteen teams left were planning to announce their dissolution on Monday. After the game, the network aired a retrospective of the NFL, covering its eight-decade history.

Later, the two remaining major networks carried news stories on the history of the New Republic, features leading up to live coverage of the Krebbs funeral. In various interviews conducted around the country, it became clear that, contrary to Jett Turner's assertions, many Americans still viewed the New Republic as a threat to U.S. security.

Many continued to consider the New Republic to be America's number one enemy. In a sound bite replayed throughout the day, CNN political talk show host Titus Coffee, a hard-line critic of the New Republic and its founders, shared his opinion.

"The very thought that this ignorant, immoral racist could go from being America's most wanted criminal to an American folk hero makes me tremble to think where we're headed from here. There is no greater threat to America, no greater affront to freedom and equality in this great country than the New Republic and all the evil it represents. God bless America!"

In stark contrast to Coffee's suggestion, residents of the New Republic's capital city, New Lexington, still blamed the federal government for the mass poisoning at Echo Valley. In attempts to influence American opinion, several New Republic officials warned that the Whitmore administration poisoned Echo Valley to set up a pretext for bombing, "which Whitmore has on more than one occasion suggested he wanted to begin after Thanksgiving."

In front of the funeral procession was a mule-driven cart with Earl's casket displayed on a hay-covered trailer. It traveled slowly down a bumpy, gravel road and stopped in front of the makeshift cemetery in the northwest corner of Echo Valley.

Behind the wagon, young children walked along with baskets, tossing fresh flower petals, collected from the thousands of condolence bouquets sent by friends from across the demarcation line. In some places, the frozen path was lost, covered with flowers. It was a testament to the fact that some of the New Republic's children had lived.

Under bleak gray skies, thousands of mourners stood shivering in the freezing cold, bundled in coats and blankets, as Earl's wife stood at the microphone and read his favorite Bible passage:

Yea, though I walk through the valley of the shadow of death, I will fear no evil: for thou art with me; thy rod and thy staff they comfort me. Thou preparest a table before me in the presence of mine enemies; thou anointest my head with oil; my cup runneth over. Surely goodness and mercy will follow me all the days of my life: and I will dwell in the house of the Lord for ever.

Despite Jett Turner's warnings, the president allowed reporters and cameras to cross over into the New Republic to cover the funeral. Whitmore did insist, however, on a discreet one-minute tape delay as a fail-safe for purposes of editing out inflammatory remarks. Although the feed seemed live from Echo Valley, it was delayed. The lag was imperceptible to viewers.

"New Republicans, Americans, and whoever else might be out there watchin, as ya look around at the valley surroundin you, maybe you'll understand why we chose this place as a transfer station for the children and everbody else we was sendin back. We thought it was a very safe place. We thought it was a well-protected place, from the weather and our enemies. It's a unique valley. From some places in here, ya don't even need a microphone to be heard by everbody. And believe it or not, it's about ten degrees warmer in here than it is outside the valley, with virtually no wind."

Robert E. Lee wore his gray military uniform as he stood on a platform above the crowd. During the Bible reading, he had removed his hat. His thick, black hair hung down past his shoulders, giving him an unmistakable Native American look.

"In one night, Echo Valley went from bein a little oasis in the mountains ta bein Hell. Please observe a moment of silence with me for the forty-two thousand New Republicans who lost their lives here."

Robert bowed his head, and the crowd followed suit. After about one minute, Robert raised his head and took out a handkerchief to wipe his eyes.

"I lost ma dear wife, Becky, and ma eight-year-old son, Dayton, that night. I buried their bodies out there. May all the dead rest in peace in Echo Valley."

He closed his eyes and sighed before resuming.

"And now we're here ta pay our last respects ta ma dear uncle, Colonel Earl Krebbs."

He glanced down at his notes.

"Earl Krebbs was a good man. He had a good heart. Sure, he had a temper sometimes, but that was because he cared. Earl Krebbs cared about the New Republic. As he was so fond of sayin, Earl was the founder of the New Republic. He was a good American. He was a national hero."

Frustrated with the notes, he abandoned them, looking up.

"There's been alotta good and bad stuff said about Earl Krebbs. Well, none of that stuff matters now cuz he's *dead*. He's dead all right. I watched im put his own gun in his mouth and pull the trigger. He didn't wanna go on after he lost his son. So all we have left is what Earl stood fa and the way thangs are."

The crowd was silent.

"Earl believed in the idea of America, which means freedom and justice and bein the best in the world. That's why he didn't trust the federal government. The federal government lied ta Earl, and he called em on it. They lied ta me. They lied ta forty-two thousand people who died here in Echo Valley last Friday mornin. An they're lyin ta alla y'all about the so-called asteroid threat."

He raised his hands.

"Now whether any of ya believe me or not when I say the federal government's lyin, we all gotta admit that there's always things they jus kinda decide not ta tell us. They call it classified information, they call it top secret, and because of it, the federal government ain't never gonna be on the up and up. They ain't never gonna tell us the whole truth. They ain't never gonna give us the whole story. We all know that."

There was sporadic applause from the crowd.

"The federal government is *using* that poor colored gal, that Brenda Brown girl, ta tell ya that it was Earl Krebbs who poisoned the water supply at Echo Valley. But don't put it past em ta have set that whole thang up. Ms. Brown seems like a nice enough girl, real pretty, and smart. I think they brought that gal in here, scared her, made her think Earl and his guards was behind the poisonin, and then they saved er so she could go testify before the church and the American people. None of us should put that kinda duplicity past the federal government."

Robert hesitated as he thought through the rebuttal.

"But that Brenda Brown story don't make no sense. Just think about it. Why would Earl poison his own son and cause imself so much grief? Why would he do that and cause himself so much grief that he would put a gun in his mouth and pull the trigger? What did he have ta gain by that? Why would I let anyone poison ma wife and son for any reason?"

Robert looked down at Tyler, who stood at attention. The boy fought back tears as he stood tall among his Uncle Earl's pallbearers.

"Truth is, we was sendin all them kids home as a gesture of goodwill. We told the federal government we wasn't interested in no fightin. We know that woulda been a losin proposition. All we ever wanted was the right ta deal with this so-called asteroid threat and any otha threat ta America in ways *we* felt was right and proper, from out *here.* We don't trust the federal government. We just wanna be left alone out here."

He nodded toward his personal guards, who allowed cameramen to close in on his position.

"America was born ta be a free country. The American people were born to rule America's destiny. The fate of America should never be left up ta the beliefs and reasonin of a single man or a single administration."

He paused as his eyes searched the written text before him to find his place in the script.

"Today we face a crisis unlike any we have ever faced before— the collapse of our government and the end of our liberty. Whether or not any of ya believe in that asteroid is of no consequence. Frankly, I think it's all government bullshit. But there's only one set of questions we need ta ask. At worst, even if there *was* an asteroid and it was gonna hit us, do we just lie down and die? Show the world how nobly we can do it? Or do we, like so many brave Americans before us, fight it out ta the end? Do we bravely struggle against whatever odds we thank we're facin an find a way ta beat em? How do Americans wanna *deal* with this crisis?"

He let the question reverberate through the valley and dissipate.

"Well, I know how the people of the New Republic of America wanna deal with it. Whatever the situation might be, we ain't givin up. So I'm appealin ta all Americans ta join us in our battle ta save the soul of America. What can you as individuals do? Call your senators. Call your congressmen. Tell em it would be wrong for em ta bomb us, wrong for em ta treat us no better than they did that gaddamn bin Laden and Saddam and otha enemies of freedom. Tell Whitmore and his cronies the people of America won't put up with em tryin ta wipe your last hope for America, your last American militia fightin for freedom, off the face of the planet. It's what Earl Krebbs died fer."

He looked heavenward.

"Earl, if ya can hear us now, we swear ta ya taday, ya didn't die in vain. The New Republic is still dedicated ta those principles ya held so dear. We still believe in freedom and we still believe in our God-given right ta protect ourselves. We only hope we'll have the support of the American people as we continue beyond this day. Without it, we don't stand a chance. God bless Earl Krebbs! And God bless America!"

Robert stayed on the stage until a black teen-aged boy came up and began *God Bless America* in a clear, haunting tenor voice. With the crowd chanting the words of the song, Robert went down and followed the casket as pallbearers carried it to its final resting place. As the minister performed graveside rites, Robert pulled one of his aides aside and whispered.

"I need someone ta get in touch with Whitmore. Tell im with Earl gone, it's a whole new set of rules. Now it's 'leave us alone or else.' Let us be, or risk a civil war so divisive that the whole country'll go ta hell. That asteroid won't make a damn bit of difference."

Chapter 2

"It was a night from hell!" one injured woman, identified as Ayet Abdullah complained. "The bombs fell all night for four, five hours! All the people dead! All the children dead!"

Although the region had been beset by violence for many years, never before had the carnage been so great in a single day. After one night of heavy, deafening bombing by U.S. B-52s, entire villages and camps were leveled. Huge, smoking craters in the earth replaced military installations held by both sides. Irregular chunks of concrete, some measuring over twelve feet long, were spread out over many miles.

Religious differences had made them ancient enemies for over two thousand years, but death and desperation had finally brought them together. Ancient injuries were forgotten as fire rained down indiscriminately from the heavens, consuming Palestinian and Jew alike.

Young, able-bodied men from both sides worked to save children and the elderly from burning buildings. Doctors from both sides, working together, attended to the wounded. The curses shouted into the skies, against the Americans, and the supplications to Almighty God, were spoken in Hebrew and Arabic.

The Israeli government scrambled fighters into the skies, but the American bombing contingent was well protected by F-18s. In the end, all that Israel, Palestine and the world could do was watch as the Americans bombed indiscriminate targets in the West Bank in retaliation for the Central Park concert bombing on November 1.

Outraged, the Israelis, the Syrians, the Jordanians, the Egyptians and the Iraqis voiced their protests and condemnation to the U.N., but by Sunday morning, December 1, American vengeance had been exacted, and the bombers were already headed back to the United States.

The American people en masse supported President Joe Whitmore and his decision to bomb the West Bank, though there were angry protests across the country by Jews, Arabs and Muslims, who considered the action as cruel and a crime against humanity. An ad hoc conference of Jewish and Muslim clerics resulted in an official posture and public statement.

"We must not forget that even at its worst, the front-line soldiers and suicide bombers in the Israeli-Palestinian conflict never killed so many innocent civilians in a single incident. America has in one night redefined the evil and inhumanity associated with the term terrorism."

The American people assumed a defensive posture, referring to Whitmore's warning issued back on August 7. He had put the world on notice when he said that America would answer any act of violence against Americans in America or abroad with excessive force.

Although Whitmore and his administration hadn't provided clear and convincing proof that a combination of *Mossad*-trained Palestinian Israelis and Palestinians were responsible for the November 1 Central Park bombing, they assured the American public that the proof was there. The bombing and all the resultant pain and suffering were justified in the minds of the American people. America had no choice but to make good on its promise.

The Israeli prime minister, in powerful, condemning language, called Whitmore a traitor and a coward, adding that American-Israeli relations would be "frosty" through August, though he indicated the two nations would remain partners in the Middle East for strategic purposes. He assured the world that *Mossad* had nothing to do with the Central Park bombing in New York.

Islamic leaders took specific umbrage at the timing of the strike, which had occurred during the holy month of *Ramadan*. The Egyptian leader, however, quoted in an Arabic newspaper, remarked that America had, for the first time in modern history, dealt evenhandedly in the Middle East.

"If the evidence indeed proves that the perpetrators of the Central Park bombing were Palestinians and *Mossad* working in league, and the facts can be corroborated, then I believe the attack can be justified. The destruction of innocent Palestinians and Jewish settlers is unfortunate, but Whitmore had put the world on notice."

Whitmore's secretary of state explained at a press conference that civilians were not targets in the assaults, though he confirmed reports that thousands of Jewish settlers and thousands of Palestinian civilians were dead. The majority of the civilian casualties, he indicated, were the result of stray bombs and mistaken targets. Without accusing Israel directly, the Secretary hinted at *Mossad*'s possible motivation for participating in the Central Park bombing, which had shrewd pre-emptive objectives.

Israel had legitimate concerns about an increase in Palestinian attacks against Jews in the West Bank and in Jerusalem, especially as the months would wind down through August. It was known that some local Palestinian leaders were calling for a *jihad* in July.

Many young Palestinian men were outspoken about their preference in light of the world's predicament: A quick death in a war against Israel was more honorable than an ignoble end after an earthquake brought on by the asteroid, a swift demise suffered while avenging innocent Palestinian blood better than a slow death punctuated by fear and uncertainty. Martyrs held more esteemed places in heaven than victims.

The Israelis had the military capability to take out the Palestinians, but doing so would have infuriated and incited the Arab world against them. Key Whitmore administration officials, speaking under condition of anonymity, suggested to the media that *Mossad* wanted to set the Palestinians up.

If the *Mossad* connection had never been determined, the United States would have punished the Palestinians alone, wiping them out. The Americans would have eliminated the Palestinian threat against Israel, and *Mossad* would have achieved its ultimate pre-emptive objective. Whitmore's retaliatory strike was a measured response that symbolically punished both sides, though it intentionally left Palestine and the Palestinians intact.

One day after the West Bank bombing, British military forces invaded the Irish Republic, beginning a tenuous occupation purposed to ensure peace and security on the war-torn island. As expected, British forces met with fierce resistance from the Irish Republican Army, who vowed to topple England in response to the occupation attempt.

The IRA threat drew an immediate military response from the prime minister, who stepped up attacks on IRA strongholds and positions. According to news correspondents reporting from Belfast, Ireland was "the most violent and bloody place on Earth."

The Chinese continued to occupy parts of southern Japan, pushing as far north as Kyoto. A month earlier, Korean cities Pyongyang, Seoul, Inchon, Taegu and finally Pusan yielded to the advance of the People's Liberation Army. The North Korean government and the Korean Peoples' Army were surprised by the invasion and slowed China's advance for five days, but the sheer number of PLA conventional forces rolling across the border was overwhelming.

Han-guk, or South Korea, was better prepared for the invasion, and yet with surprising swiftness, city after city fell. After six days of fierce fighting, the remainder of the bested South Korean Army had retreated to Pusan, where the last pocket of resistance in Korea was crushed.

When the American government completed pulling military forces out of Seoul in mid-November, political analysts predicted an escalation of hostilities all along the 38th Parallel, the demarcation line separating North and South Korea. Some even warned North Korea would utilize the low-grade nuclear weapons it had been developing for over twenty years. No one imagined the pullout would precipitate an unexpected Chinese invasion.

At the bay at Pusan, the Chinese continued to build up forces and summoned battleships up to the Korea Strait, where the Japanese offensive began. The Japanese Prime Minister appealed to the United States and the United Nations for intervention and protection, but both President Whitmore and the U.N. Council were at a loss for a quick resolution to the anxious and desperate petition.

As days passed, the Chinese landed on the southwest coast and began capturing cities still occupied by Korean forces. Within one week, the estimated number of PLA ground forces occupying southwest Japan exceeded one hundred twenty thousand troops.

For China, the invasion of Japan was a calculated risk. Chinese leaders gambled the threat of civil war and domestic revolution would so preoccupy America that the idea of a protracted war with a superpower on the other side of the world would be unthinkable.

More significantly, the invasion struck a mortal blow to the United Nations Council, who, from the first day of the attack, ceased to be a relative factor in world affairs. For much of the world, December came to mark the official beginning of "The Last Days."

****

"I know you're gonna think I'm bein a little silly, but I always wanted kids. I always imagined a little boy or girl who was part me and part you."

She narrowed one eye and raised the alternate eyebrow as she shot an incredulous on Reggie's direction.

"Well, I think in order to have that little boy or girl, you'll have to do a little more than just imagining."

He sighed, saddened and hurt by the reference.

"Now that was just plain *mean*, Layla."

She cringed as she realized what she had blurted out and knelt next to the wheelchair.

"I'm so sorry, Reggie. I didn't mean it. I'm, I'm really sorry."

He didn't bother to wipe the tear that streaked down the left side of his face. After a full minute, he spoke.

"No, I'm sorry, Boo. It's my fault. I'm the one who went out there and got myself all blown up."

She held his face in her palm and kissed his forehead.

"You were trying to help because you're a good person. You're a *hero*! I was being selfish. I guess I'm frustrated."

In the discomfort and silence that followed, she decided to be direct.

"You know how I am. When I feel a lot of pressure, I just want to have sex. I need it. I need it and I haven't had it. I haven't had any since Halloween night. That's a whole month!"

Reggie nodded.

"I know. And you've been so good to me through all this. You know I want you, but it's all the medication and the injuries. Doctor's said I'll be up to speed around March or April. We'll have at least from April to August, and then you *know* I'm gonna tear you up. We'll make up for all the lost time."

She smiled, her nostrils flaring.

"Really?"

He leered, whispering.

"Come here."

When she neared, he clutched her shoulders in his hands, drawing her close.

"Mornin, afternoon, night, before we go to sleep, when we wake up, all through the day. You know what I can do."

Her hand was in his lap, caressing, stroking, but as before, nothing was happening. Straining to smile, she pulled away.

"It doesn't matter. I'll get over it."

She was crying.

"I love you so much, Reggie. With all that's happening in the world, I just want you to know that."

"I love you, too."

"No. I mean the sex isn't the important thing. I love you for who you are. Don't ever think I was disappointed in you because you couldn't. I love you for you. No matter what happens to me, I want you to remember that, okay?"

He studied his wife's nervous agitation as she dithered there.

"You make it seem like something bad's gonna *happen* to you. You ain't thinkin about takin one of those pink pill things, are you?"

She snapped out of the daze.

"Oh, no. It's, it's just hitting me."

"What?"

She scanned the decorated living room of the upscale Jersey City high-rise apartment.

"In a way, I've been in denial these past few months, but now it's starting to really sink in. This is all going to be gone, everything! It's December already. We're only nine months away."

The thought of Nostradamus caused Reggie to withdraw, reflecting on his own morose thoughts. Layla pulled back the curtains, revealing a clear nighttime sky. The stars were bright. The heavens seemed no different than on any other night.

"I mean look at the sky out there. Isn't it hard to believe there's something out there getting closer every second, something that's going to wipe out all life on Earth? It's so hard to really *believe* that."

"So *you* don't believe it, Layla?"

She sighed.

"Yes, I believe it in my mind. It's coming. We're dealing with the physical laws of the universe. But I'm still having trouble believing it in my heart. It seems wrong. This wasn't supposed to happen. You and I were supposed to have a family, kids and grandkids. We were supposed to grow old together. It's Whitmore's fault. He should have never told us about it."

"Why?"

"Because it was more information than we needed. He could have said it was going to hit and there was going to be some damage, but he should have held out some hope, if even just a sliver. You know, hope, something for us to believe in, and we all need that. It would have been something positive to carry us through till that day."

Reggie wheeled over to the couch where she was sitting, gazing toward the sky through the huge window.

"I was more pissed off at Whitmore than you were after that speech, but I don't get it. You're always the one who talks about how important it is to be honest, and now you're sayin you wish he had *lied* to us?"

She wagged her head, acknowledging her incongruity.

"Okay, we all know we have to die someday, and we accept it, but no one wants to know the day. No one *should* know the day. To tell someone the day they're going to die is cruel."

"I don't understand. What difference does it make?"

She turned to Reggie.

"Answer this question: If you knew I was going to die on a specific day in February, and there was nothing you or anyone else could do about it, would you tell me?"

Reggie deliberated before answering.

"Well, I guess I probably would at some point."

"Why?"

"Cuz maybe you'd wanna know?"

Frustrated, she sighed.

"Why would I want to know? So I could spend my last days in agony or depressed thinking about it? I'd be *pissed off* if you told me!"

"So you'd want me to lie?"

"Yes! Lie and let me live out my last days the way I've lived the rest of my life. Let me *feel* that I'm the captain of my soul and the master of my fate. Don't take that *away* from me. Don't ever take that away from me. Because if you do, my spirit dies, I give up and my life is already over."

As Reggie nodded, thinking, Layla finished.

"Let's make it real, Boo. You want to have a baby, right? So if we know it's all going to be over in August, nine months from now. And if your pipe won't be working until April, you have to give up all hope of having a baby. That's because Whitmore told you it'll all be over in August. If he didn't tell you, you'd still have that hope right to the end."

She crossed her arms. Careful not to strain the broken ulna, she took his hand in hers.

"That's why I'm telling you time is precious, especially now. I just want us to love each other and enjoy each other, because from here on, we have no guarantees. Let's enjoy each and every moment we're able to spend together."

She was leaning over the wheelchair, looking into his eyes. She placed her lips on his and kissed. After three minutes, he held her face in his hands, speaking.

"You do realize that, when I'm able, I'm gonna make love to you like I never have before, because I'll be thinkin about how much I love you and how incredible you are."

She hugged him, tears streaming down her face.

"I know you will."

She had lied to protect him. Cringing at the thought, she knew, according to the agreement she signed with Dr. Benoit, she'd be leaving in mid-February to participate in the Life Ark project and she would never again make love to her husband.

Chapter 3

From the guard tower, two inmates took pot shots at Army Apache attack helicopters that were flying by to assess the validity of the group's claim that one hundred and forty correctional officers and more than two hundred of the prison staff and others were being held hostage. Six guards and twenty inmates were lying in the yard, apparently killed during the initial rebellion. It was evident the prisoners had complete control of the facility.

"Tell those *cholos* ta knock that fuckin shootin off—they're gonna get us bombed!"

Bernardo Gomez, the revolt's charismatic leader and organizer, had been the president of his senior class at Lincoln High School. He had a 4.34 grade point average in honors classes. He had even attended college classes for a year at UCLA before he met Sara Miles, the woman who ruined his life. Every significant person in his world—including his mother, his older sister, his college counselor, Father Martinez and Eduardo Jimenez, his best friend—warned him about Sara.

They said Sara was jealous of his future. She was a pretty blonde with a "Baywatch-type" body, but she had issues stemming from her dysfunctional childhood, and she was a cocaine abuser. Friends and family said she commented occasionally that Bernardo's eventual success would spell the end of their relationship.

"You watch—he's gonna get all educated and uppity, and then he's gonna kick me ta the curb. I *know* him."

Bernardo's mother, Sandra Ayala, believed Sara set the whole thing up just to make things bad for her son.

"If she couldn't have him, she didn't want the world to have him. He was going to be a great leader, you know."

His mother was right. At age nineteen this *pachuco*, who through sheer will and brilliance had defied the odds, committed a single act that transported him from his distinguished position as one of East Los Angeles's greatest hopes to a disappointing rank in California's prison system, where he became just another sad statistic.

"Tell them we're not talkin to any low-level administration negotiator on this. Tell em we got three hundred and fifty hostages who are gonna start dyin in six hours if I don't get a call from either the Governor or the President. We want one million dollars cash and safe passage to Mexico. We're not spendin these last ten months in this prison waitin for that thing ta hit!"

Sara told Bernardo she hated his best friend Eduardo on numerous occasions, and it was clear that Eduardo disliked her. Much of Eduardo's contempt for her stemmed from the fact that Bernardo had dumped Cecilia, Eduardo's younger sister, in order to be with Sara. Sara accused Eduardo of being a racist who didn't want to see his best friend with a white girl.

Sara and Eduardo were also jealous of each other. Both competed for Bernardo's attention and loyalty. They couldn't even exist in the same space without the scene becoming ugly before long. That's why Bernardo was so shocked when he stopped by Sara's apartment one Sunday afternoon and surprised his best friend and the girl he loved in bed together.

Eduardo was rushed to the hospital with a slash wound to his abdomen. There was a dark half-circular bruise under Sara's right eye, indicative of physical violence, and the left side of her face was beginning to swell. Bernardo was led away in handcuffs and locked down at the county jail. He was charged with two counts of attempted murder. When Eduardo died two days later, the district attorney modified the charges to murder one and aggravated assault.

Apparently, California Governor Creighton Dobbins and the Whitmore administration had differences relating to how they would deal with the prison hostage situation.

The Richard J. Donovan Correctional Facility was located in San Diego, less than twenty miles from the Mexican border. Although California's official prison policy insisted, "hostages will not be recognized for bargaining purposes," Governor Dobbins said he saw the event as an opportunity to rid himself of one of his thirty-one overcrowded prisons and its liability to the state. And he could save hostages at the same time. His negotiators were hoping to grant the inmates safe passage to Mexico, but there would be no million-dollar pot at the end of the Tijuana rainbow. Negotiators were authorized to offer no more than fifty thousand dollars.

To complicate matters further, the state's lieutenant governor and other valuable people were among the hostages. The lieutenant governor had been working with the state's correctional system on the challenges presented by the unique combination of factors facing California's prisons: overcrowding, dwindling custody and support staff numbers, and the threat of Nostradamus.

Bernardo's mother had a lawyer friend with the Mexican American Legal Defense and Education Fund who worked hard to beat the conviction, but the jury sided with the prosecution. Sara testified that Bernardo found out about her sexual liaison with Eduardo weeks before the murder and that he had told her he was planning on "killing Eduardo the first chance I get."

She said Bernardo was lying-in-wait outside her bedroom and that he slashed Eduardo's stomach wide open when Eduardo exited in the nude.

"Eduardo was standing there in shock, looking from Bernardo's face to the sight of his own blood and guts lying on the floor in front of him. He was squeezing what was left of his guts in his hands, he said *Lo siento* to Bernardo and then he fell on the floor. I dialed 911."

Although Bernardo took the stand and tried to convince jurors that the killing of his best friend was a crime of passion, Sara's testimony was enough for eight women and four men to return a verdict of guilty after six hours of deliberation.

The prisoners had been planning the revolt for two months. The Mexican Mafia took the lead by declaring a truce between the Norteños and the Sureños and by making peace with the Bloods, Crips and Black Gorilla Family gangs, all longtime rivals in the southern and central state. Even members from the Aryan Nation and Eastern bloc gangs were enlisted.

The plan, according to leader Gomez, was to pick a day when staffing no-shows were critically high. The trustees—convicted felons who were allowed outside their cells to assist with low-security functions of the prison—were to kill three key guards who had high security clearance and capture four others.

Another set of trustees would take out prison personnel involved in communications within the prison and with the outside world. The key to the revolt entailed not killing skilled prison staff, but rather coercing them to provide key information and codes needed as the quiet insurrection grew.

Then staff could be used as hostages during negotiations. The abduction of the lieutenant governor was a fortuitous turn and served as an omen to leaders that their insurrection and the quest for freedom would be successful.

Bernardo Gomez's cellblock was the first to be freed. The guards in the area were killed and their weapons taken. Bernardo first took his prisoner army to the prison's communications control center, where after fierce fighting, they overcame the guards outside the locked room.

Inside, trustees had the Donovan Correctional Facility communication staff bound, gagged and piled in a corner. Three dead persons were lying next to the door and a fourth was critically wounded, bleeding from a deep slash wound in her neck.

One of the communications operators managed to get an emergency call out to the guard station, and the desperate call had brought more guards to the area. The battle at the communication center drew guards from other areas and left detention areas short on security.

Thus the trustees, in possession of keys and door codes, were able to free block after block with little resistance until the prisoner army grew to twenty-five hundred men. Trapped and outnumbered, the guards and staff began to surrender. They were all bound and taken to the cafeteria near the center of the facility. Only after the perimeter and all areas of the prison were secure did Bernardo place the initial call to the Governor.

At sentencing, the judge and jury gave Bernardo twenty-five years to life for the murder of Eduardo Jimenez. It was at Corcoran State Prison in Kings County that Bernardo earned his manhood and respect.

One guard in particular didn't like Bernardo's smugness and his seeming air of superiority. He rough-handled Bernardo every opportunity he got. Then one night he put Bernardo in a cell with a known rapist and told the man to "have at it." The raping and the problem with the guard continued until Bernardo joined the Mexican Mafia, though the protection of the powerful brotherhood came at a price.

Javier Escobar, the Sureño leader at Corcoran, liked Bernardo right away and handled Bernardo's initiation himself, something he had never done for a new member before. In order to prove himself and to show he was leadership material, Bernardo had to kill a certain Norteño leader.

The assassination would have been much more difficult at another prison, but Corcoran had instituted an integrated-yard policy, wherein rival gangs were placed together in small yards, ostensibly to teach them to get along. The nervous guards watched the yards, careful to step in to pre-empt any threat of a conflict. Yet there were opportunities, and Bernardo was patient.

When the staged fight in the yard broke out, Bernardo went for the Norteño leader, steel shank pressed against his forearm. Ironically, on the way over, he bumped into the guard who had persecuted him for two years—the same man who watched, laughing, the night Bernardo was raped for the first time. He swore to himself that he would kill the man the first chance he got, but he proved loyal to his mission and the shank found its mark between two ribs in the back of the Norteño leader.

Bernardo spent that whole night and the next day in the hole, hoping and worrying, but by morning it was confirmed—he had made his first kill, and the status and reputation of the dead leader embellished Bernardo's own reputation in the Latino gang. He had earned his respect.

Black Gorilla Family leader Larry Jones, the selected spokesman for the black gangs, handled most of the negotiations with the Governor's representative, though Bernardo sat at the table, listening. Having once been an elected official, Jones had the political experience and education.

No, the lieutenant governor and three other persons would not be turned over as a gesture of goodwill, and fifty thousand dollars was a joke! Yes, hostages would be put to death to underscore the urgency of the matter, and yes, the lieutenant governor's name would be in the lottery selection process. Governor Dobbins had until midnight to decide. Otherwise half the hostages would die in the morning.

At eleven p.m., one the Governor's top aides called Bernardo and read a prepared statement into the receiver.

"Mr. Gomez, although State policy related to your takeover of the Donovan Correctional Facility calls for non-recognition of hostages, I am willing to make a carefully considered exception in this case. Without detailing any specific reasons for my decision, I hereby grant your request to leave the facility and travel to Mexico, provided assurances can be made regarding the security of the three hundred or more persons you are currently detaining. If any of the civilian hostages are killed or harmed, I will personally make certain that you and all the prisoners in the facility will die. I require proof that your hostages are alive and uninjured. Furthermore, the State will give you seventy-five thousand dollars and not a penny more. This is my final offer. You have ten minutes to accept it."

What Governor Dobbins failed to disclose and what Bernardo failed to recognize was the fact that the Governor's brother and another family member were among the hostages. As fate would have it, the Governor's brother and his eldest son were accompanying the lieutenant governor on his visit to the prison. When the insurrection began, the two discreetly discarded their IDs and kept their mouths shut, hoping they would not be identified by any of the inmates.

The assassination of the Norteño leader increased regional tensions at Corcoran Prison and caused the warden to re-institute a policy segregating rival gangs. Javier Escobar and other Mexican Mafia leaders, recognizing Bernardo's intelligence and loyalty, moved him through the ranks until he became the gang's third-ranking leader at Corcoran.

That November, after Javier killed a Blood leader, he was transferred up north to the secure housing unit at the Pelican Bay facility in Crescent City, leaving Bernardo second in rank to Mike Perez. Then in May the next year, the Bloods exacted revenge, killing Perez and seriously injuring Bernardo. Thus Bernardo emerged from the infirmary as the undisputed Mexican Mafia leader at the prison.

The Corcoran prison guards were attuned to the Norteño-Sureño rivalry and the racial tension between African American gangs and Mexican gangs at the institution.

During the year Bernardo rose to power, some guards had even begun exploiting the existing acrimony for purposes of entertainment and gambling. In numerous instances during the following year, corrections officers would set up gladiatorial battles between prisoners from rival gangs and bet on the outcome. But if the violence got out of hand or the combatants failed to stop when so ordered, the guards would shoot them.

According to a story from a San Francisco newspaper after the scandal broke, "the result has been countless fights and dozens of unjustified shootings by guards—seven of them fatal." An FBI investigation resulted in the arrests of several guards, a lawsuit brought by one victim's family and relocation for Bernardo, who testified against the guards. In January the next year, per one of the conditions that brought his testimony, he was relocated to the Donovan facility in the south.

"The Governor thinks it best that you start out at 2:30, in the cloak of night. If you can cover five miles an hour, you'll be in Mexico before sunrise. The hostages you take for insurance will have to be guards, and you're to release them once you get to the border."

It was a done deal. Bernardo Gomez and his prisoner army would get seventy-five dollars in cash and would receive immunity during their passage to Mexico. Once in Mexico, they would be on their own, so Bernardo and other leaders made sure their men completely emptied the armory of all weapons and devices.

The seventy-five dollars in cash in twenty-dollar bills arrived in a heavy lockbox shortly after midnight. It wasn't the million dollars Bernardo originally wanted, but the rebellion, for all intents and purposes, promised to be a success.

That is why it was such a shock when fire began to rain down from the sky shortly after one o'clock a.m. The first incoming missile hit the tall guard tower, causing a loud explosion that shook the ground under the startled and scrambling prisoners. Huge sections of the tower tumbled to the ground and burned in the freezing darkness.

"What the hell was that about, Bernardo? What's goin on?"

Bernardo stood, brushing the powdered cement from his face and hair.

"He lied ta us! Get the Governor on the phone. Tell him the hostages are gonna start dyin! Now!"

Larry Jones, the black leader, yelled his response across the room, a cellular phone in his hand.

"He's already on the line! Wants ta know what's goin on over here!"

"No *shit*! What does he think's goin on? We're under attack!"

Another explosion rocked the complex, causing Larry to reel and swagger as he described the blasts to the person on the line. Bernardo looked up just in time as a portion of the roof collapsed above him, crashing down to the floor. He reached for the phone.

"That's the Governor?"

"Yeah!"

"Let me see that."

He put the phone to his ear.

"Okay Governor, what the *fuck's* goin on here? I thought we had a deal!"

He cringed as he felt tremors from another strike on the other side of the complex.

"Whadaya mean? If you're not behind it, then who the fuck is?"

Bernardo's eyes grew large in reaction to the response.

"Goddammit! They can't do this! How can they *do* this?"

The shock of the next deafening blast blew Bernardo, Larry and everything on the desk against the wall. The cell phone was lost in all the mess, but neither bothered to look for it. Instead, they staggered to their feet and made for the door. Bernardo's voice was loud, because he could barely hear himself as he yelled toward Larry.

"The federal government's behind this! *Big* bomb's comin, he said!"

Dazed, Larry nodded, but Bernardo wasn't sure he understood. Bernardo figured Larry was probably deaf as he watched a trail of blood run from Larry's left ear. He shouted while pointing.

"Main housing—gotta be the safest place!"

As Bernardo and Larry hurried in the surreal glow of fuel burning on the rubble, Bernardo wasn't sure if he himself hadn't gone deaf. The sound of the fighter jet was gone. The sound of the explosions had stopped. Even the sound of wounded men screaming aloud had ceased. The silence was eerie and foreboding.

That is when Bernardo realized why the skies had grown so suddenly silent. The fighter had come in to stall the prisoners at Donovan until the bomber arrived. There wasn't much time.

"We have to get outa here! Right now!"

He rushed into the complex where the inmates and hostages were huddled in the middle of the room.

"Okay—this goes for everyone! The government's got a bomber headed this way right now—it'll be here any minute. They're gonna kill us all! We gotta go! We gotta get outside the prison or we'll all be dead!"

Within seconds, the door was clogged as the panicked men scrambled out into the yard, prisoners and hostages alike. In the sky, a faint light blinked in the east, perhaps twenty miles away.

When the commotion cleared, only one person remained in the room. Chad Dobbins, the Governor's eldest son, sat on the floor, unfazed by the spirit of desperation that pervaded the place. He withdrew a cell phone from his pocket, dialed a number and held the phone against his face.

"Hi Dad. They say a bomber's coming. How much time?"

Chad closed his eyes and nodded.

"That's what I thought."

He took a deep breath, listening to his father.

"What am *I* gonna to do? Well, nothing. What *can* I do? I'm just gonna to sit here and accept it, I guess. Make my peace with God. Try'n find serenity within. I don't wanna die a desperate man, running and scared like the rest of em. I wanna die with some dignity."

A tear ran down Chad's cheek.

"I love you, too, Dad. Please tell Mom and everyone I love them too. You'll all be with me in my final thoughts."

Chad lowered the phone, closed his eyes and bowed his head. He could hear the panicked men screaming outside. The bomb was obviously on its way down. When he heard the explosion, instead of bracing himself, he relaxed and waited.

True to his desire, his last thoughts were only of the people he loved. He drew in a deep, wonderful, cherished breath as he felt the hot wind rushing past, and he raised outstretched arms. One second he was there, and a second later, he had disappeared in the instant firestorm.

Chapter 4

"Mr. President, the com link is ready. Connection will be active in thirty seconds."

Joseph Whitmore sat down at the desk and stared at the bright blue monitor, waiting. Advisor Jett Turner stood in a place to his far left, peering over a pair of glasses that had slid down to the tip of his nose. General Lucas Draco, chairman of the Joint Chiefs of Staff, was also in the room.

"The connection is active now."

The blue screen dissolved to the image of Robert E. Lee, who also appeared to be seated at a desk. When he turned his head to speak to someone off-screen, it became apparent that the audio-video connection was live and in real time.

"Mr. Lee, while I'm glad you agreed to this conference, all this added protocol and equipment were hardly necessary. We could have met like we did before."

Uncomfortable with the technology all around him, Robert hesitated before responding.

"Well, things was different before. I don't trust ya as much anymore. Not since y'all sent that Barnes guy in here ta kill Earl."

Whitmore seemed dumbfounded.

"Kill Earl? What are you talking about?"

Robert wagged his head.

"Oh, don't play dumb with me. Guys like Barnes don't do political assassinations unless they got orders from the top."

Uneasy, Whitmore glanced toward Jett and then back toward the screen.

"Waitaminute! Are you trying to tell me that Krebbs' death *wasn't* a suicide?"

Growing more accustomed to the technology-assisted dialogue, Lee studied Whitmore's face and demeanor on the screen.

"Either you're shittin me or you're completely outa the circuit, Whitmore. And frankly, I don't know which is worse. If you're puttin me on, then by lyin you're startin off on the wrong foot. But if ya ain't in the know about a political assassination ordered by your *own* government, then maybe I should be talkin ta someone who *is*."

The President didn't flinch.

"I'm not here to talk about Krebbs, but if you want to discuss the honesty issue—it does seem, after your little pitch at the funeral, that you're not any better with the truth than I am. You're the one who advanced that Krebbs suicide story. If it was an outright lie, then that makes you a liar."

After a long, silent staring contest, Lee blinked and began.

"But we're not here ta talk about me."

Whitmore nodded.

"I suppose we're not. So what is this urgent matter that you said you needed to discuss with me?"

Lee leaned forward.

"President Whitmore, I called this meetin to discuss the terms of your surrender."

Ignoring the profanity in the background, the President smiled in derision.

"Now that's ludicrous. I'm a very busy man, Mr. Lee, and I don't have time for your foolish bravado. You have exactly fifteen seconds to come up with a legitimate purpose for this meeting or I'll terminate this com link. Fifteen seconds."

Lee raised a hand toward the screen.

"Hear me out. Maybe you're gettin the wrong idea here. Now I'm not talkin bout surrenderin *all* the states. I just want the western states."

Whitmore glanced over at Turner and then at Draco before signaling the technician.

"Terminate the link."

"Wait! I don't think ya wanna do that! There's somethin ya gotta know!"

There was a serious expression in Lee's eyes that made Whitmore hesitate.

"I'm listening."

"Well, I just spoke ta the governor of California last night—that Dobbins fella. He called ta inform me that California is gonna leave the Union on January 1st. Wanted me ta know the New Republic would have the unwaiverin support of the California Republic."

Lee smiled and nodded as he watched Whitmore's countenance flush with concern.

"Yeah, so now if you're plannin on bombin out all who resist ya, it's gonna take a lot more bombs. And I suppose I should tell ya it's only befittin that Washington State ain't gonna take the capitulation of America lyin down neitha. Governor Adams up there says if California goes, the Republic of Washington'll follow her lead."

Whitmore did not respond. He was still reeling from the gravity of Lee's revelations, if true. Lee continued.

"North ta south, I want Montana, Wyomin, Colorado, New Mexico and everthang west from there..."

Angry, Whitmore broke in.

"And I can already tell you—that's not going to happen."

"I'm not finished—"

"Yes you are. All you've done today is convince me that you and your New Republic are threats that America can no longer tolerate."

Whitmore stood.

"California and Washington I'll deal with separately, but you, Lee, and everyone in your New Republic, are going to die. So make your peace with God. Do whatever you have to do. Here's one presidential promise I'll keep: You and the New Republic won't see the beginning of the New Year."

****

If it had been a military mission, an Army general would have occupied Dr. Don Smock's leadership role at the Crypt. However, Lazarus was a top-secret government project, and Smock had made a career overseeing clandestine government operations.

By all accounts, his special area of expertise involved "surviving cosmic winter." As a noted cosmic winter expert, he was the majority shareholder and board chairman of the New Millennium Construction Corporation, a conglomeration of contractors and developers of underground caves, fortresses and asylums. Beyond mere planning and construction, Smock wrote the instructional and survival manuals for subterranean operations.

The New Millennium Construction Corporation had worked with nearly all of the world's developed nations, secretly engineering underground shelters of varying complexity and scope in strategic locations since the early 1970s. The company performed specialized jobs in the Middle East during the 1980s and 1990s, including vast networks of underground caves in the mountainous regions of Afghanistan, Iran, Iraq, Pakistan, Turkey, China and Russia. During the year 2002 alone, annual revenues for NMCC exceeded $11.2 billion.

According to Smock's manuals, the expected lifetime for shelters, once sealed, was ten years, more or less, depending on how close shelters were filled to recommended capacity. No shelter on Earth was expected to last more than fifteen years until the Crypt was completed, and no long-term live-in capacity had exceeded fifty persons.

The Crypt represented the culmination of Don Smock's thirty years of work and experience with subterranean survival technology, and it exceeded his greatest ambitions. Given a virtually unlimited budget and a fleet of engineers, Smock was encouraged to indulge his imagination.

During the spring of 1976, Dr. Don Smock, an avid spelunker and a geologist by discipline, found the ideal site for an ambitious U.S. facility in the heart of the pinkish Sangre de Cristo Range of the Rocky Mountains of south central Colorado, sixty-nine hundred feet above sea level. It was a huge, conical-shaped natural cavern that stretched almost seven hundred and fifty feet high and measured a mile in diameter. He named it the Crypt and began drawing plans for a shelter that could comfortably house one hundred persons for one hundred years.

The overall project wasn't approved and funded until 1979, and construction did not begin until 1980. It took four years to put the outer shell and pilings in place and another two for the inner shell. The infrastructure, which included electricity, plumbing, life-support, seven levels and twenty-two subdivisions, was completed in 1994.

"Initial Operational Capability," or "IOC," was achieved in November 1997. Thus in 2001, twenty-five years after Don Smock first stumbled upon the Crypt, it became fully operational as Earth's best hope for the human species ever surviving prolonged cosmic winter.

An adjacent cave nearly a mile away had been modified to house the machines and other supplies that would be needed by the Life Ark volunteers who returned to re-establish human populations on Earth. It contained tractors, earthmovers, cranes, trenchers, building materials, power tools, a hermetically-sealed seed warehouse, the chemical ingredients necessary for the manufacture of explosives, prop planes, a heavy-duty transport helicopter, fuel, spare parts and instruction videos, among other supplies.

When Life Ark was first proposed, Dr. Benoit asked Don Smock to volunteer for the project. His extensive knowledge of geology and environmental systems, she insisted, would be invaluable as humans ventured into a wild new world, full of challenges.

Yet both Benoit and Smock knew that he was too old, that his failing health would put him at risk in cold sleep, and that even if he survived the three hundred and fifty years of stasis in space, he'd only be good for ten or fifteen years after that at best.

And then, while being one of only five men on Earth responsible for repopulating the Earth sounded exciting, he wasn't certain he'd be able "to keep up with thirty-nine horny women who haven't had sex in almost four hundred years!"

His son Adam, he asserted, was a much better prospect. At twenty-eight years old, he was one of the youngest persons to ever co-pilot a space shuttle mission. His distinguished career as a Top Gun Navy pilot included strikes against targets in Iraq in 2005 and against Afghan installations during 2007. Furthermore, Adam was a Rhodes Scholar with a near-photographic memory. And finally, he was brave, handsome, charming, and women loved him.

While Isabel resented Adam's unabashed playboy attitude and lifestyle, she had realized, after working with him over sixty days, that he had talents that were indispensable to Life Ark.

Besides, after the collision with Nostradamus brought on cosmic winter, Don Smock would best serve humankind by directing earthly operations in the Crypt until the initial smoke cleared.

"You know, after it was finished, I actually wanted to change its name. The Crypt was the natural cave. Once the shelter went in, I wanted to rename it."

Davis looked up from his notes at Smock, who was interfering with productivity by lingering there.

"What did you want to name it?"

"I wanted to call it GOD."

Davis stopped working, eying Smock with suspicion.

"God? Why God?"

"It's an acronym for 'Grace Or Damnation.' Over the years, I guess I've had second thoughts about what we're doing here. For me, it always comes back to this question: If the cosmic clock was set and Nostradamus was destined to collide with Earth from the beginning of time, then did the Crypt come into existence by the will or grace of God? Or is the Crypt a modern-day Tower of Babel, standing in defiance and opposition to God and his purpose?"

Silent for a moment, Davis stared before commenting.

"All I know, Don, is that I have a job to do here, and I personally would prefer to leave God *out* of it."

Smock's gaze was fixed in the distance. He didn't even consider Davis's response as he continued his rambling thoughts.

"Then you have to think about the Noah character in the Bible and the master plan for the Ark—did God spell it out to him literally—hand him a blueprint? Or did he plant the *idea* in Noah's head and let Noah use his own intellect to work out the details?"

"Don—"

"And right back to us—is God working through *us* to bring about man's salvation or are we, like Nimrod at Babel, working against God's ultimate purpose for the Earth?"

Davis was becoming irritated.

"Ark, Tower of Babel—I don't care. I have a job to do here. The thought of any god working through me is ridiculous, basically because I don't *believe* in God. There's no god out there that has anything to do with any of this. This all just happened! It was destiny."

Taking a deep breath, Smock nodded, resigning.

"The government's sentiment exactly. That's why it's still called the Crypt."

Sensing Davis's perturbation, Smock stood, smoothing the waist area of his pants.

"Of course, being the worldly man you are, Davis, you *do* know what happened at Babel, don't you?"

Davis looked up.

"No I don't. Refresh my memory."

"Babel means confusion. Chaos, Davis, utter *chaos* is what happened."

****

"Stop right *there*! Yeah, there. Can you enlarge that?"

The image grew larger in stages as the technician across the room worked at the computer.

"Can that be cleared up? Can you sharpen the focus?"

National Security Advisor Jett Turner drew a long drag from the cigarette and blew the smoke skyward toward the fluorescent lighting fixture. Three persons sat at one end of the long mahogany table in the huge, dimly lit conference room.

At Turner's left sat General Lucas Draco, chairman of the Joint Chiefs of Staff, while at his right sat Barbara O'Connor, director of the Office of Homeland Security.

The young technician was placed at the far end of the forty-foot-long table so that he was not privy to the sensitive conversation taking place at its other end. Jett directed him by speaking into a microphone suspended from the communications headgear he wore. For a moment he had two cigarettes in his mouth—one nearly gone and a much longer second cigarette that had been lit from the first.

He turned the microphone on with a hand-held device.

"Okay. Now crop it all and leave just the face."

The fifty-five-inch monitor sat on the table before the three. The young woman's face grew huge on the screen.

Draco sighed.

"Okay. So now we have a face."

Jett raised his hand, signaling for patience.

"Just wait and watch."

He continued to the technician.

"All right—now split the screen and pull up the close-up of the image I gave you this morning."

Seconds later, there were two remarkably similar faces displayed on the monitor, though the face on the right seemed more distinctly familiar to all three.

O'Connor squinted as she commented.

"I know I've seen that one on the right before. Who is that?"

Jett spoke into the microphone.

"Split it again. Four images—two right there at the top and the two originals on the bottom."

O'Connor gasped after the images were displayed.

"I knew it! I never forget a face. Susan Whitmore!"

Draco cut in.

"Isn't she dead? Didn't she die in that plane crash in Washington State?"

Jett stood, answering.

"Apparently not. Photo on the right was taken about two weeks ago."

O'Connor broke in.

"Does Joe know? Where, where was the photo taken?"

Jett smiled as he blew another cloud of smoke.

"Remember that Brenda Brown speech in that L.A. church on November 24th? Right after Echo Valley? Well, some private person who was videotaping it sent us a tape with a note voicing suspicion that the woman there looked a lot like the President's daughter."

He shrugged.

"We naturally checked it out, and it's her. The young woman you are looking at is none other than Susan Whitmore, the President's daughter."

Draco muttered to himself, nodding his head before speaking.

"Do we know where she is?"

"Yep. Ironically enough, she's living in the Reverend's home with his family—a wife, a teenage son, and believe it or not, a rabbi."

O'Connor interrupted.

"Do *they* know who she is?"

"Don't know, but we have to assume they do."

"Does the President know?"

Jett wagged his head, dismissing the technician as he responded.

"Not yet. Figure there's no need to tell him until we deliver her to NORAD or Cheyenne Mountain. Once she's there, hopefully we can use her to lure the President down there. Once we got him there, we'll make sure we keep him there."

O'Connor studied Jett's face.

"So it's true? You really want to get Whitmore out of the picture so you can put someone in who'll do your bidding?"

Jett sighed, resigning.

"Joe's the fuckin president—it's what the people elected him to be, and he's good at it—but we can't afford anyone being 'presidential' right now. I told him to take out the New Republic early on, but he waited too long. Now we got California pulling out of the Union in January. I told him to bomb all the prisons in the country, but once again he wouldn't listen, or we could've poisoned all those criminal bastards. So now we got real prison problems all over.

"As the months start rolling by an America's enemies start training their sights and scopes on us, we don't need a fair-minded president of The People, for The People. We need someone who's going to go out there and kick ass and take numbers."

He raised a hand, as if he was trying to shield himself from culpability.

"Don't get me wrong. Joe and I have been friends for years, but when he rushes to Cheyenne Mountain in order to reunite with his long-lost daughter, I'm going to do everything in my power to persuade him to stay there. What do you think?"

O'Connor closed the folder before her and stood.

"Well, besides sounding like you're perfectly willing to commit high treason, it seems your second priority is to completely use up our entire stockpile of bombs and missiles."

She looked over at Draco.

"I take it you agree with his plan to take Joe out of the picture?"

"He's the president. He has a right to early retirement."

Draco stood.

"But I'm not altogether convinced that he's too indecisive. I think we should wait to see how he handles Lee and the New Republic situation. He's popular with the American people, and that says something."

O'Connor persisted.

"And bombing or poisoning over four hundred thousand people left in the prisons? I suppose that's all right with you? I think Jett mentioned anthraxing them at one time."

Jett answered for the General.

"Look, either we're going to release them or we have to keep them locked up. The ones where it's been iffy, we've already let go. That means the ones we still got are going to stay locked up till the asteroid takes us all out in August. So I ask, what difference does it make? They can die now or they can die in August. It's not like there's any quality of life for them in there anyway—it's Death Row with no appeals. And in the meantime we have to feed them and guard them and deal with their shit."

He looked toward Draco for support, but the General remained stoic and silent.

"These are extraordinary times, and with each day that passes, the situation gets more and more desperate. So we've got o get out of all these conventional ways of thinking about things. Prisons are a liability—they serve no useful purpose except to keep dangerous criminals off the streets. Bombing serves the same purpose, with added benefits—it frees demoralized guards who don't show up for work anyway an wipes out any possibility of a bloody revolt like the one at Donovan."

O'Connor wagged her head.

"And California? If Dobbins and the state try to secede, you want to take California out too?"

"The New Republic, the prisons and even California if we have to. This is about national security. We can't tolerate even the mere mention of secession. If Dobbins tests us, we've got to make an example out of him. We've got to make Dobbins and every other governor understand that either they all hang together *with* the federal government, or they'll hang separately."

Chapter 5

Dr. Levin's face wasn't the first indicator. No, it was the emotionless phone call and the extraordinary wait once David Blum arrived at the office. There was also the feeling of malaise he had suffered through every morning since early November.

Initially, he was certain the weight loss was the result of the heartache and loneliness that were ever present since Lynda and Stephen went to Rhode Island to be with her parents. But somehow he knew there was something more, something that seemed to be sucking his life away.

Even in the mirror, David's once chestnut-colored eyes seemed gray and languid. Strangely, his eyes made him remember the black and yellow California king snakes he caught when he was a boy. He remembered how they had a sort of gray, torpid, deathly look right before they shed their skins.

Just before it happened, they seemed to die, and then from that dry and ghastly grayness emerged a supple, vibrant, bright colored, fresh and reborn snake.

At his right sat his good friend Jonah Williams who, ignoring David's protests, insisted on accompanying him to Dr. Levin's office. As they sat in the lobby, David still grumbled.

"Ya know, I gotta lotta *Jewish* friends that coulda come if I really *needed* someone ta be with me through this. I didn't need my one *black* friend ta come down here."

Jonah wagged his head.

"And I gotta lotta black friends who I could be hangin out with right now. I didn't need to come down here to be with my one Jewish friend. I *wanted* to be here for you, David."

Dr. Levin approached, smiled toward Jonah, turned and spoke to David.

"I'm afraid it isn't good, Rabbi. Tests indicate the cancer is localized in your pancreas, but we think the caudal lobe of your liver and a portion of your colon might also be involved. It's malignant and it's inoperable. I'm sorry."

David bowed his head.

"How long?"

Dr. Levin closed his eyes and sighed, ruing his responsibility.

"It's slow growing. If we do nothing to treat it—maybe six months."

His arm around David's slumped shoulders, Jonah looked up at the oncologist.

"What, what kind of treatment are you talking about, Doc?"

"Well, that would be up to the Rabbi after we've explained all the options, benefits and risks associated with our proposed form of treatment. Even this early, it's safe to say treatment would involve chemotherapy and possibly some mild radiation. Surgery of any kind would be pointless."

"And how long if he goes through treatment?"

"A year, hopefully longer. Depends on how his body responds. God willing, we may be able to cure this thing."

An enduring, uncomfortable silence followed. David's head was still bowed. His eyes were closed as he spoke unintelligible, foreign words in an undertone.

Dr. Levin placed his hand on David's shoulder.

"Rabbi?"

David looked up.

"Take whatever time you need to think about what you would like to do from here. Maybe talk it over with your wife and family. If you do decide to pursue treatment, we'll need to get started as soon as possible. We'll need to pursue it aggressively. Maybe you and I can sit down and talk about things on Monday?"

David nodded. The doctor extended a hand toward Jonah.

"Thanks for coming, Reverend. See that he—"

Jonah stood, nodding.

"I will."

After the doctor had gone, Jonah looked down and noticed that David was weeping in silence.

"David?"

David raised his head and stood, his reddened eyes still flowing. Despite his tear-blurred vision, he could see the strain on Jonah's face and in his demeanor. Jonah looked as if someone had just slugged him in the stomach. Throwing his arms open, David gestured and the two men embraced.

Still holding his friend, Jonah patted David's back.

"I'm sorry, David."

"Don't be sorry. I'm not. I've lived a wonderful life. It fills me with joy to think about that."

"But—"

David interrupted.

"You have to understand—when I weep, I don't shed a single tear for me. I'm not feeling sorry for myself. I'm filled with the joy of God."

He held Jonah at arm's length.

"My tears are for Lynda and Stephen, who I might not be around for, when and if the end does come. I was so sure we'd be together."

****

"I thought it was a bad idea three hours ago, and I think it's an even worse idea now. What are we doing out here?"

Dexter opened the car window and craned his neck outside, straining to get a better view of the dimly lit house.

"I'm sorry. I thought she'd be home by now. I can't believe it. She's out past curfew."

Megan motioned toward the clock in the radio console, which indicated it was nine o'clock p.m.

"And so are *we* in case you've forgotten. We're stuck in this car. We won't be able to drive until the morning. Your folks'll be pissed."

"Not if they know I'm with you. Besides, they're in New York till Tuesday. They won't even know."

Earlier in the day at 5:30, Megan yielded to Dexter's constant begging and borrowed Aaliyah's Lexus. They took the 405 over to Inglewood. Traffic was heavy between 5:45 and 6:30 as drivers hurried to reach their destinations before the vigilantly enforced seven o'clock curfew was imposed. By 6:45, Megan had parked down the street from the Brown's home in a position where she and Dexter could see the front of the house.

Since three o'clock that afternoon, Dexter had been calling both her home and cell phones at fifteen-minute intervals, though she hadn't answered a single time. He left messages until her message boxes were full.

It had been almost a month since Brenda Brown returned from the New Republic, and during that month, Dexter had only spoken with her once, and only then to relay a message to his father. When he saw her at church, she was always too busy making plans with "grown-ups" to talk with him.

Brenda Brown was a mature teenage girl when she left Los Angeles in early November for the New Republic, and yet within mere weeks she had become not just a woman, but also a young woman many in America admired. Her poise and grace during the nationally televised speech about her experiences at New Lexington had brought her instant celebrity and media attention.

Her actress mother, acting as her agent, worked hard to get Brenda booked on the right shows, involved in America's pre-eminent issues and surrounded by the world's most influential people. In fact, during early December, Brenda was a featured guest during President Joe Whitmore's *Eight O'clock Hour*, his daily address to the nation.

"Megan, wake up! I see a car! There's a car in front of the house!"

Complaining all the while, she managed to sit up and checked the car's clock.

"It's 3:30 in the morning!"

"Yeah, I know. That's why it's so surprising—that car was driving after curfew! No one's supposed to do that."

Megan rubbed her sleepy eyes as she peered down the street.

"It's a limo—probably got some special pass or immunity. No one's gotten out?"

"Not so far. It's just pulled up."

Fifteen minutes later, the door opened and Brenda and a man stepped out of the limousine and stood next to it, talking. She was wearing a formal gown, and he was wearing a suit. He was tall, thin and much older—probably at least in his thirties. He gently stroked Brenda's face as she gazed up at him, and then he kissed her.

"No Dex! Don't—"

Megan's protest went ignored. Dexter was already out the car and running toward the limo. As he neared, a huge driver/bodyguard stepped out and stood between the closing boy and the car. Seconds later the driver had Dexter detained, his arms pinned behind his back.

Dexter called out.

"Brenda? What are you doing with *him*?"

Embarrassed, Brenda turned her face away from the boy. The man spoke something into her ear and she returned a whispered reply.

The driver looked toward the suited man.

"Whadaya want me ta do with im, Boss?"

The man smiled.

"Release him. He'll be okay."

He walked toward Dexter, extending his right hand.

"Hi Dexter. I'm Congressman Billy Elders from the state of Tennessee. Your cousin here tells me you're a remarkable young man. I'm honored to meet you."

From a place outside the congressman's view, Brenda pleaded toward Dexter, beseeching him to uphold her lie. Halfhearted, Dexter shook hands with the man, saying nothing as Billy continued.

"I'm not sure if she's told you, but we're getting married in January—big wedding in Nashville. And I'm not exaggerating when I say I feel like the luckiest man in the world right now."

Dexter looked toward Brenda with an expression of betrayal and sadness, his eyes begging for contradiction.

"Is it true, Brenda? You're going to *marry* him?"

She nodded.

"Yes. I hope you can be happy for me."

She never saw his response. He had turned away. She watched him walk toward the car in the distance, stiff, as if he had been stabbed, his shoulders slumped. He seemed like such a little boy!

For a fleeting moment she remembered how much they loved each other, she remembered the innocence, excitement, the smiles and the laughter. She remembered all the promises they made to each other, before each other and before God.

And yet within a month, she had broken every one of those promises. She realized she had broken Dexter's fragile heart, a heart he had dedicated to her. Her mouth and lips pronounced his name, but no sound emerged. Tears flowing down her face, she strained to keep him in her sight as his wilted form disappeared into the darkness.

****

It was the third straight night that high-flying B-1 bombers droned overhead, dropping leaflets and supplies. During the second and third weeks of December, skirmishes broke out in several places along the border, leaving miles on the western side in the control of U.S. forces, who welcomed a steadily growing flow of New Republic defectors and refugees.

Officials at New Lexington initially sent a division to the area to prevent a mass exodus, but the division was recalled two days later to prepare for the possible defense of the capital against an imminent ground offensive.

The leaflets contained messages encouraging citizens of the New Republic to abandon "a perilous course and return to America and to your families." The leaflets promised immunity to those who returned and warned that anyone who still remained at New Lexington on January 1 would be destroyed during intense bombing campaigns. At several stations on the breached western border, U.S. soldiers welcomed defectors with hot food, blankets and bus rides over to the Army's Dugway Proving Ground in Tooele County, Utah.

Temperatures and heavy snow continued to fall throughout the month of December. Shoshone elder and shaman Captain Clyde said it was the worst winter he had experienced in seventy-eight years. According to Clyde and his Indian stories, the ancient demon of cold and confusion, who left a tiny crack in a boulder near the summit and came down the mountain once a year, would mark the end of time by defeating the spirit of light.

This demon of cold and confusion would rule the earth until the spirit of light was reborn. The other terrestrial spirits would hide the reborn spirit deep within the earth until it was strong enough to challenge and defeat the demon of cold.

Clyde insisted that the demon, who fed on the dead and dying, was growing stronger with each morning as dozens of bodies arrived at the New Lexington morgue. Most were victims of exposure or disease brought on by the combination of freezing temperatures and malnutrition. By the third week of December, the demon had claimed almost eighty thousand, nearly doubling the tragic loss at Echo Valley.

Robert Lee and his generals saw the cold and the defections as a definitive winnowing process. The weak would die and the cowardly and faint of heart would defect, leaving the New Republic's strong and loyal guard behind.

After heated debate among his top advisors, Robert Lee conceded that capital city New Lexington would be abandoned before the bombers and ground troops arrived. The New Republic army would then fall back to secure strongholds in the mountains where the severe weather and terrain altered by heavy snowfall would hamper

the search and destroy teams and Special Forces the U.S. Army would
no doubt employ.

Many of the Special Forces units on both sides had gained
valuable search and kill experience in Afghanistan and Iraq during the
wars. Units on both sides had received the same training, utilized the
same tactics and employed the same weapons.

Yet the New Republic Special Forces had a distinct advantage,
resulting from their knowledge of the terrain under the snow. They
had spent late summer and fall charting and exploring every
outcropping, every hill and valley, every cave and crag. They had even
logged the locations of the larger snow banks in the northern Tump
Range.

While the Tump Range of the Middle Rockies contained many
natural caves, the New Republic Army Engineering Corps spent late
summer and fall constructing a cave and tunnel network in the
mountains. In early September, Anton Bunch had spent almost six
million dollars on four state-of-the-art tunnel boring machines.

Once complete, the cave and tunnel network was stocked with
weapons, supplies, food and liquid oxygen. Abbreviated tunnels in the
extreme north contained the tank division, while the artillery was
spread across the network. Four of the F-18s were contained in deep
grottoes, but the balance remained outside New Lexington at the
ready, awaiting scramble orders.

The main objective of the New Republic's recently finalized
plan, called Project Hidden Light, was to conceal and protect troops
and assets through the long, severe Wyoming winter.

New Lexington would be surrendered without resistance, and
families living outside the threatened city were encouraged to remain
while the army retreated to the mountains. Surrender would save New
Lexington while the presence of a hundred thousand or more unarmed
non-militia settlers would help preclude the threat of indiscriminate
bombing and military aggression.

Essentially, the plan involved putting to sleep the threat posed
to the federal government by the New Republic army—it involved
making the problem go away. Robert Lee likened it to hibernation.
The year's heavy snowfall would serve as a great, flowing blanket,
insulating troops and assets from the world. Thus while the New
Republic army slept, Lee and strategists were counting on the severe
Wyoming winter and unrelated domestic and global events to

discourage the federal government from pursuing the inconsequential and difficult-to-reach army sleeping under the mountains and snow.

Then, when the New Republic army re-emerged in April, Robert Lee would be dealing with a weakened and weary federal government. It would be a government weakened by the secessions of California, Washington and possibly Texas. It would be a government under increasing pressure to protect its external borders and to guard citizens against terrorist cells and independents acting within its borders and it would be a government afflicted by the cancer of corruption and by instability as world government after world government collapsed or changed hands.

Inside analysts predicted that if the New Republic could sleep safely until April and retain the majority of its assets, then Robert E. Lee, after a challenge and a possible civil war, could wrest the mantle from Whitmore and become first in America.

Chapter 6

"Honey, you should come out here for this. I think they're about to air the video."

She glanced sidelong at the face in the doorway and nodded, her concentration barely broken.

"Five minutes. I'll finish this entry within five and I'll be right on out. I promise."

It had been forty-five days since she started writing in the journal. Writing had become a ritual with her. She began at five o'clock a.m. and wrote until noon. In the evenings, she always managed to get in another couple of hours.

Nighttime sex wasn't a distraction, after all. Until November, she never considered herself much of a writer, but as she looked back on written reflections and musings, she realized she had not only real talent but also a genuine *desire* to write.

She wrote about the events of her day. She wrote about Reggie, about her mother and about her family history. She reflected on her life as she grew up, describing all her ambitions, successes and disappointments. She related the learning and growing experiences in great detail.

She was just finishing a narrative of events leading up to her first menstrual cycle. She was a twelve-year-old seventh-grader at a new school. When her lower abdomen started cramping after lunch, she thought it was gas until she felt an uncomfortable wetness *down there*. Intuition told her the time had come, and she confirmed it when she went to the bathroom and saw the blood in her panties.

She remembered sitting in the office, waiting for her grandmother to come and her grandmother's story about a girl's journey into womanhood in the car on the way home. In fact, Layla was just finishing the story when Reggie knocked, asking her to come out. She reworked the last set of lines three or four times, but it still didn't sound right. Frustrated, she sighed, shut down the computer and headed out to the living room.

"I don't know why we haven't bombed them already. All we have to do is fly over and do like we did in Afghanistan and Iraq. End of story. No more New Republic."

A dish of carrot sticks in her hand, she plopped down on the couch. Reggie sat in a wheelchair next to the couch, absorbed in the explanation of the video detailed by a CNN analyst. With Reggie's superficial wounds healed and the swelling gone down, he looked like himself again. Irritated for having been invited out only to be ignored, Layla threw a carrot that hit the side of Reggie's head.

"So what's going on with all that?"

Reggie turned, smiling. He was glad to have Layla with him and off the computer.

"Well, they *say* Lee's surrendering the New Republic. At least that's what the video he sent is supposed ta be about. They say he's dismissing his army and returnin to private life. Personally, I think he cut a sweet deal with Whitmore."

A minute later, the CNN anchor's shoulders and face came onscreen over a subtitled announcement.

LATE BREAKING DEVELOPMENT: NEW REPUBLIC SURRENDERS

With unmistakable disappointment and grave seriousness, the anchor announced that the Whitmore administration had sent marshals to Atlanta, confiscated the tape and ordered the station not to air any footage already extracted from it for related stories.

Station managers took the government order seriously, though literally. Jett Turner's edict prohibited the station from airing any portion of the Robert E. Lee videotape, but it did not proscribe reporters and analysts who had already watched it from being interviewed and from discussing it.

Coverage cut to *The Titus Coffee Show* and a quick lead-in by the host. On a quickly assembled panel sat a reporter and two analysts who had worked hard to prepare the story about the video only to have it canceled by the government.

Coffee began with questions.

"So first of all, how did the tape come to CNN?"

Reporter Jane Saget, the woman on the panel, answered.

"Perfectly logical manner. With all the people leaving the New Republic through Utah—and with the U.S. Army's help, mind you, Lee apparently made the tape and gave it to someone headed back to Atlanta. A nineteen-year-old from Decatur hand delivered it to us."

"And it's an authentic tape?"

"Lee himself does the speaking in the single camera, uncut tape, though he is flanked by a group of advisors and cabinet members, which interestingly enough, is racially diverse."

Ignoring Jane's tacit invitation to discuss racial issues about the New Republic, Titus stayed the course.

"What does he want to tell us in this tape?"

She glanced down at her notes and nodded.

"Basically, he says he's dissolving the New Republic. He says that he's still dedicated to the cause of saving America and all the New Republic ideals, but when given the choice to surrender or die, he surrendered to save the lives of New Republic Americans who have decided to settle in Wyoming. He said, despite the mass exodus of at least six hundred thousand New Republicans, at least twenty-six thousand American families were determined and committed to remain and live in the area around Mount Isabel. He said his government would dissolve and leave New Lexington, and that would be the end of the New Republic."

"And did he say where he would go? Would he return to Alabama? Fountain, Alabama, is it?"

"He didn't say. He actually said he would go into hiding because the federal government had a bounty on his head. He said time would tell if he was right about insisting that the Nostradamus threat is a hoax perpetrated by enemies of America. He said, and I quote, 'When you all finally realize the real purpose of the Nostradamus threat, which is the collapse of America and the rest in favor of their New World Order, you'll remember me then, and then I shall return.'"

Next Coffee introduced former magazine editor David O'Shea, who indicated the true intent of the video was to persuade the American people to oppose the bombing of New Lexington and other targets inside the New Republic.

"His appeal to the American people is explicit. He says that the threat of the New Republic is over, that the only people who will be left on December 31st will be the non-militia settlers who have decided to stay, along with their wives and children. The suggestion is that once the New Republic government is dismantled and New Lexington is abandoned, then bombing serves no real objective and only risks the lives of innocent American families."

Rounding out the panel was Capitol analyst William Parker, who took the suggestion one step further.

"Just last Sunday Joint Chairman Draco said the military had pictures of Lee's army tunneling into the mountains northwest of Mount Isabel last summer. By now, a good part of his army and their weapons could be in place in caves under mountains and heavy snow, waiting for Lee to join them. And if that's the case, then the settlers around Mount Isabel might be there to serve as a human shield against bombing and other military aggression."

O'Shea nodded, agreeing.

"That is absolutely correct. So the real question here is: Does Whitmore proceed with the bombing of New Lexington, and after that, does he bomb the non-militia settlers outside the capital city?"

Parker cut in.

"Once again taking that thought process a step further—does he send in ground troops to try and search for the New Republic's army in the mountains? And if so, would he have the support of the American people for such a monumental and risky undertaking? Is going after Lee even *worth* it?"

Coffee cut in.

"Jane? Your comment?"

"I think the fact that Whitmore let Turner come in here and confiscate the video sends us a clear sign. I don't think Whitmore and Turner *want* the American people to know what they're going to do, which is in itself insidious. Of course they want to bomb! If they shut out the media, they can do anything they want—kill over one hundred thousand non-militia men, women and children, torture people—and this is America, mind you, not Afghanistan."

Coffee sat back in his seat, musing, looking over his notes.

"Reflecting back to Whitmore's warning's on August 7th, he said, 'America will answer any threat or action against her with immediate and brutal vengeance.' I have to ask: Do any one of you believe that the mere *possibility* that the New Republic's army might be still intact, sleeping under the mountains and snow, do you believe the mere *possibility* of their existence gives Whitmore justification to start bombing and launching a ground offensive?"

Jane answered unprompted.

"Absolutely not. We're talking about more than one hundred thousand innocent Americans in Wyoming who would probably die. They've already started the cover-up. So what happens when Jett Turner starts on Governor Creighton Dobbins in California and on

Governor Adams in Washington State? He's already goaded Whitmore into bombing out half the prisons in America, killing over four hundred thousand innocent people. I just think the American people have to get involved here. They've got to let Whitmore know that, despite the Nostradamus threat, this is America and not some twentieth-century fascist state."

Parker wagged his head, responding.

"While I'll agree that Americans must press Whitmore for accountability, especially where the lives of Americans are involved, I must point out that Whitmore is in a difficult position. He's in an almost impossible position. If the New Republic army still exists, its mere existence represents a clear and convincing threat to America. And I think whatever it takes—short of harming the non-militia settlers and their families—Whitmore must *eliminate* that threat. And finally Jane, you might be able to convince me that there are a few innocent people in prison, but not four hundred thousand, and those prisons were sealed shut and bombed only after the prisoners staged revolts against the guards."

Jane's nostrils flared as she forced a smile and responded.

"All that according to Jett Turner, who by the way, wants to bomb California and the rest of the world."

Coffee raised his right hand to signal a stop to the argument.

"Let's get back to the issue of the government taking their quest for control of the media one step further. The confiscation of the video is truly unprecedented. While government officials have occasionally *discouraged* media coverage in matters that compromise national security or in matters that might endanger U.S. troops in sensitive areas overseas, never before has the government confiscated a news agency's property and issued orders in a blatant attempt to control the message and public opinion. It seems we're heading down a dangerous path. David?"

The television screen went black. Layla was let down and baffled until she saw the remote in Reggie's hand, pointed toward the screen.

"Why'd you do that?"

"They ain't showin the gaddamned video. Just a buncha talkin heads. I wanted ta see what Lee had ta say."

"What does it matter? Lee's a nut, and he's a bigot besides."

Reggie sipped from a bottled water while he wagged his head in disagreement.

"No, *Krebbs* was the bigot—that's why the New Republic had ta take him out—ta make themselves legitimate."

He held up a pamphlet titled *The Truth About The Nostradamus Threat*, written by Robert Lee and circulated by the New Republic.

"Lee's a smart man if ya ever lissen ta him talk or read what he writes. And I wouldn't be surprised if the government's tryin ta take im out because some of what he says is the truth. Cuz the real truth is, if that asteroid's really comin, *it's* gonna take the New Republic out anyway, so what are Whitmore and the government so worried about?"

Layla stood, angry for having seen the pamphlet.

"What is wrong with you, Reggie? Robert Lee and the rest of them are dangerous people! How dare you bring that literature in this house!"

She went over, snatched the pamphlet from his hand and ripped it twice. Reggie watched in disbelief.

"Now you trippin. What you do that for?"

"No, you're trippin. You think the government doesn't keep track of who *orders* this stuff? You don' think the fact that you ordered it puts us on some kind of government list now?"

"Who cares?"

She leaned over to look into his eyes.

"I care, and you better care."

She stood upright and continued, looking down on her husband.

"Look, I don't claim to know anymore about this Nostradamus threat than anyone else, but in the end I sure as hell don't want to cast my lot with a loser like Lee. He's already quit. He's given up. All any association with him or the New Republic can do for us is *hurt* us."

She sat beside him and took his hand.

"I hate to bring this up, but haven't I been right in the past when I've warned you about threats to our family?"

He bowed his head.

"Yes."

"Then you have to promise me you'll never visit that website again. You have to promise you won't even talk about Lee or the New Republic ever again. You have to promise me that, Reggie."

He nodded.

"I promise."

She kissed his mouth.

"Thank you."

"But I'll be watchin. I'll keep my promise, but I'll be watchin ta see what the government's gonna do when the snow starts ta melt in the spring and they realize they're dealin with somethin more powerful than they ever imagined."

Chapter 7

Together, they watched the flames creep along the bottom of the log from left to right. The fire was already in the wood, peeking out at them occasionally with red, glowing, sinister eyes, like a penned-up wild tiger, waiting for a momentary lapse of diligence, seeking any random opportunity to exact vengeance on its captors. Sitting deep in its red-orange chamber, it used the flames to hypnotize the two into a catatonic trance so that even as they watched the graceful pyromantic ballet, they had no idea they were also being watched.

Dexter sat at one end of the chocolate brown leather sofa, his eyes lost somewhere in the flicker of the hearth, while Megan sat at the other end, her face blank, her eyes glazed. A soulful rendition of *Silent Night* played in the background.

Thirty minutes into the thought-provoking fireplace feature, Megan sniffed and wiped a tear that had run down to her chin. Seizing upon that cue, Dexter unleashed a silent stream of tears, though he batted his eyes in a futile attempt to dam the source.

Glancing over, Megan smiled, and then she laughed.

"What? Are you crying?"

He shook his head in the negative, wiping away tears all the while.

She continued.

"Aren't we a couple of pitiful souls? Here it is, Christmas Eve, Earth's *last* Christmas Eve—and the best we can do is sit in front of a fireplace and cry? Obviously, we're doing something wrong."

He nodded.

"You're right. I was just thinking about that. This is a special moment, and we're wasting it. I hear everyone saying it lately, and I really believe it. We have to start making the best of *every* moment. People spend most of their lives waiting for things to happen to them. Well, now something's *happened*. We've all got eight months left. Time to stop waiting and to start living."

She smiled, turning toward Dexter.

"Okay, I agree. So how do we start living?"

He turned toward Megan.

"Marry me?"

"Are you joking?"

"I'm not joking. Will you marry me?"

She laughed, turning away.

"That's funny, because aren't you the same boy who spent all last week crying because you got jilted by Brenda Brown? I mean, what about *Brenda*?"

Dexter sighed, embarrassed.

"That was ages ago. Well, it *was* when you think about how much time we've got left. I'm over her already. It's like you said last month: she never really loved me in the first place."

She wasn't convinced.

"Well, if that's the case, then why were you crying just a few minutes ago?"

He raised his hands in protest.

"That wasn't about her. It was about going all the way to August and not having someone to love and care about, someone who would care about me."

"You have your parents."

"And where are they now? In Washington hanging out with that annoying Whitmore instead of being here. My father has always belonged to the congregation and to God. I've never had him. And my mother belongs to him. Sure I have parents, but they're not going to care about me in the way I want to be cared about."

She sighed.

"That's because you're fifteen and horny. All you think about is sex."

"No, that's not it. What? You think I asked you to marry me because I wanted to have sex with you?"

"You mean you *don't* want to have sex with me?"

He hesitated, baffled about how to respond.

"No. I mean yes, but that's not why—"

"I think that proves my point."

He bowed his head in an effort to regroup.

"What I mean is I asked you if you'd marry me because I *care* about you. I've always thought you were nice, and pretty. And I think we could be happy together. And I'm sixteen now, not fifteen."

She smiled.

"Okay. So now that you're sixteen, as of *yesterday* mind you, you think you're now somehow ready to get married?"

"I'd marry you today if I could."

A gruff voice broke in from behind the young people.

"What's this about getting married? You two?"

Dexter stood, nervous.

"Rabbi Blum! I didn't know you were... How are you feeling?"

"I'm fine. Got room on the couch?"

Dexter surrendered his spot and took a place next to Megan. David Blum smiled, though his face looked thin and tired.

"You two? Married?"

Megan answered.

"It's his thing this week. Next week it'll be something or someone else."

Dexter grasped her hand.

"That's not true and you know it. I've never been surer about anything in the world. I want to marry you."

He turned toward the Rabbi.

"I'm not sure how it all works, but you're a man of God. Could you marry us even though we're Christians?"

Megan broke in.

"Waitaminute. Hold on, Dexter. Now I never said I *wanted* to marry you."

"Well, will you? Will you be my wife for the next eight months?"

She looked toward the Rabbi, explaining.

"Look, we, we never really *talked* about this. This sort of just came up just now."

David Blum shrugged.

"Well, do you wanna get married?"

Megan hesitated, looking into Dexter's eyes and then back to the Rabbi.

"I, I don't know."

"You kids got eight months left—that's not a lotta time. If you love each other and wanna be with each other, what's the point of waitin? But that's up to you. Life is short with no guarantees. What is it that all the young people are saying now? *Love is the only important thing.*"

Dexter had taken Megan's hand. He spoke to the Rabbi.

"I want to marry her if she'll have me. I'll talk to her. We'll let you know tonight."

The Rabbi stood, eyes rolling as he swooned and swayed.

"Good. You kids talk. After that revelation, I think I better go back up and get some rest."

He walked toward the doorway and stopped, turning toward the young people.

"Ya know this thing you're thinking about is a beautiful thing if you make commitments to each other, take them seriously and make God your partner. You remember, Dexter? I was against this sorta thing for Stephen, but I think I was wrong. I'll admit that."

His eyes watered.

"You know I was praying upstairs, and God directed me to come down here to talk to you. At first I thought it was for your benefit, but now I realize it was for mine. He was answering my prayer. Now I know what I've gotta do."

Both Dexter and Megan knew about the Rabbi's cancer. In fact, the entire Williams household was apprehensive, awaiting David Blum's decision about what method of treatment he would pursue, if any. Dexter stood as he asked the question.

"What? Are you going through with the chemo and radiation?"

The Rabbi answered and with an unmistakable self-assurance.

"No, Dexter, I'm not goin to do the treatment. I'm gonna try to be healthy and put my faith in God. If he wants me to stick around, we'll all know it soon enough."

David Blum smiled.

"This is all ironic. You asked earlier if it was possible for a rabbi to marry two Christians. Well, the way it seems things might end up, none of that will matter. Religion won't matter because it will become strictly a matter of faith. Either we'll put our faith in God, or not— whatever our religion. But we will all be forced to make that conscious decision. Like, like it was with the people and the prophet Elijah at Mount Carmel. Maybe that's what he meant for us to do. Then, who knows, maybe he'll make this thing go away and we'll all be stuck with whatever we chose. We've proclaimed our faith all this time. Now we have to act on it."

****

The three Special Operations MC-130Es flew in tight formation, flanked by an escort of six F-18 fighters. They had left Little Rock Air Force Base at dusk and been flying for one hundred and fifty minutes. During the day before, U.S. forces had invaded the New Republic and had stationed ground radar controllers a quarter-mile outside the capital city. The ground controllers would be responsible for positioning the aircraft prior to final countdown and release.

According to intelligence gathered through aerial photographs a day earlier, the city was only sparsely inhabited, because the majority of its residents had scrambled to get out by the January 1 deadline. It was no accident the bombs were coming on December 31, as Jett Turner convinced Whitmore to strike a day early in order to catch Robert Lee before he went into hiding. Jett was acting on information supplied by FBI operatives who had infiltrated the city. One source provided that Lee had been sighted outside his residence as recently as six p.m.

The bombs were carried aboard the MC-130Es because they were far too heavy for the bomb racks on any other bombers or attack aircraft. At fifteen thousand pounds each, the BLU-82B was the largest conventional bomb in existence. Many news agencies had erroneously reported the BLU-82B, or Lucifer's Hammer, was a fuel air explosive, though it was a conventional explosive incorporating both agent and oxidizer. The warhead contained twelve thousand six hundred pounds of low-cost GSX slurry (ammonium nitrate, aluminum powder and polystyrene).

The bomb was originally used to clear helicopter landing zones in Vietnam, where it was nicknamed Commando Vault. To that end, it was detonated just above ground level by a thirty-eight-inch fuze extender, optimized for destruction at ground level without digging a crater. It was called the Daisy Cutter in Afghanistan in 2001, where it was dropped as much for its psychological effect as for its antipersonnel impact. Released from over six thousand feet up, its lethal radius was seven hundred and fifty feet.

As the Special Operations MC-130Es entered the no-fly zone, Air Command instructed them to descend to a parallel formation during the approach to New Lexington. From that point on, the pilots adhered to instructions given by the radar controllers on the ground. Simultaneously cargo bay doors were opened and countdowns began. *Five, four, three, two...* And then the bombs fell on New Lexington. The flash was like lightning and the rumble like thunder in what eerily seemed to be the opening scene of *Ragnarok*. Lucifer's Hammer fell with three great blows on New Lexington, and all the unsuspecting souls who still remained in the city were blasted into oblivion.

****

They had been closing in on her for two weeks, though she hadn't consciously noticed. Once, about a week before Christmas, she thought a light brown Chrysler Park Avenue had followed her on the 405, through the city of Bellflower, and back north on the Santa Ana Freeway.

And Dexter had remarked that the two men who sat three rows behind them in church on Sunday didn't seem right. One was black and the other was white, and they just sat there through the service, never smiling, never even reacting. He remembered that each placed a dollar bill in the offering basket when it came around.

Jonah and Aaliyah Williams returned from an extended trip to the East Coast on December 29, just in time for Jonah to prepare the message for his midnight sermon on the 31st. During the sermon, he spoke of goodwill, especially in the last days.

He related touching examples demonstrating that, despite the state of the world, the goodness and unselfishness of God still abounded in the human heart. He appealed to the congregation and millions of listeners, encouraging them as they considered the coming year, to cultivate the fruit of the Spirit, which are love, joy, peace, long-suffering, goodness, mildness, faith, meekness and temperance.

He also described his Christmas Eve visit with President Joe Whitmore. He said the President was in a difficult position. Jonah described a man who was troubled about the mortal consequences of many decisions he had already made and still more concerned about the historic and far-reaching decisions he would have to make in the coming months.

According to Jonah's comments, Whitmore was a sensitive, caring man who had lost his wife and daughters in an unfortunate jet crash. Jonah said the President confided that each day he lived was diminished by the loss of his family and that what he missed most of all was the smile and impetuousness of his youngest daughter, Susan.

Curfew restrictions forced the congregation to spend the night in the church on New Year's Eve. When morning came, the sisters began to prepare and serve a light breakfast. Dexter scoffed at the portions and insisted on going out to get breakfast instead. His parents were "with their congregation" and would never leave, so he asked Megan if she would abandon serving on the food line to go out and get pancakes, bacon and eggs.

Megan hesitated. She was disturbed by Jonah's description of the President's predicament and mental state. It was ironic that the President had invited Jonah to the White House and that the two had met. She respected both men, but for very different reasons.

She admired the President for his charm and intelligence, for his sense of pride and loyalty and for the fact that he loved his family. She respected Jonah for his faith, dedication to God, truth, fairness and righteousness. Yet they were very much alike in that they were driven, dedicated men who could never belong to their families and loved ones. They belonged to the world and to history.

Languid on the food line, Megan bumbled for ten minutes until Aaliyah came over and relieved her. Aaliyah slipped her car keys to Megan and whispered, asking Megan if she would take Dexter out to breakfast at the Pancake House.

Wiping the tears that streamed from Megan's eyes, Aaliyah hugged her and made her promise to share whatever was bothering her when she got home. Megan nodded, kissed Aaliyah and embraced her for a full minute before leaving the church.

****

It wasn't intuition. It was rather the totality of a hundred different hunches. She knew that eventually they would come for her. She knew they would eventually find her. Why she looked up at the exact moment they walked in may have been accidental, but everything else—the brown sedan, the strange men at the church, Jonah's invitation to the White House, his message that morning, the strange sense that she was being watched and dozens of other little clues—everything else made her believe that they would come and take her.

They would take her to that cave in Colorado where she would be forced to live the rest of her life in an underground prison. The prospect of such a life was so ugly that her mother and sister had taken that pink pill to commit painless suicide. It would be life in a dark dungeon with no one who cared about her and no one she cared about.

The tall, muscular suited men in dark glasses walked toward the table.

"Young man, I'm Agent Timmons with federal Secret Service."

He flashed a badge and continued.

"We are here on official government business. My partner here will now escort you to the car of a fellow agent who will drive you home. Before you're released, you'll be briefed and debriefed. For your own safety and the safety of your family, I suggest you follow the instructions you receive very carefully."

Intimidated by the two large men and their demeanor, Dexter set down his fork, put his napkin on the table and began to slide out the booth.

"No, Dexter."

He hesitated for a moment. Undaunted, Megan spoke to Timmons.

"He's staying with *me*."

Familiar with reports and stories about the girl's bold antics, Timmons became frustrated as he sighed and set his jaw.

"I'm afraid that is *not* going to happen."

"Oh, I think it will. Apparently, you guys aren't as good at gathering intelligence as you thought."

Unable to see the eyes behind the dark glasses, she wasn't sure if she could intimidate the man.

"You know who he is, but you didn't know he's my *husband*. Dexter and I got married on Christmas Eve, and he knows everything. He knows about the staged plane crash, about the empty casket at the national funeral, about me, about my father, about the shelter in Colorado, everything. He knows government secrets even *you* don't know about, so how do you expect to debrief that? You can do all the briefing and debriefing you want, but I think you know you can't leave him out here."

While Timmons sighed, removing his glasses for a better look, Susan Whitmore reached for Dexter and clutched his left shoulder with her hand.

"And as the President's daughter, I'm insisting that my husband goes where I go."

When Timmons slumped, she knew she had him.

"So I suggest you get on your little squawk box and talk to someone who can make accommodation arrangements for an extra person."

Timmons's face was red. He nodded to his partner, pulled up a chair and sat at the end of the table. The other agent went out the front door. Megan slipped her fingers into Dexter's clammy hand and smiled to calm him as they waited.

Fifteen minutes later, Special Agent Timmon's partner returned, approached the table and sat in an empty chair.

"Ms. Whitmore. You were home all day on Christmas Eve and Reverend Williams was out of town. You couldn't have gotten married on that day."

She squinted her eyes, defiant.

"Most of the time, I think you guys are way overpaid, but this time I think you're bluffing. You know Rabbi Blum lives in that house. When you checked out my story, you know he could have married us. So why do you want to play games? I'm calling the shots here."

The serious agent responded.

"Ms. Whitmore, we all know you can be difficult when you want to be, and we realize you're a smart girl, but you're *not* calling the shots here."

She sneered at the man.

"Oh really? You guys want to look around? People are staring. Two big government goons in suits and dark glasses intimidating a poor, young married couple? What happens if I stand up on the table and start telling all these people who I am? You going to shoot me? You going drag me out of here and debrief my husband, take me to Colorado but leave him here? You going to brief all the people in this restaurant?"

The angry black agent leaned toward the table in a threatening posture. She sighed.

"Look, I'm not asking for much. I'm *cooperating*. I said I'd go with you, but I'm insisting that my husband here comes with me wherever I'm going. What's so hard about that?"

Just then, Timmons' phone rang. He answered and listened, nodding occasionally, for about a minute and a half. Snapping the phone shut, he rose, the resentment evident in his voice.

"Congratulations, Newlyweds. Looks like you'll be together after all. All I can say is I feel sorry for you, young man. You have no *idea* what you've gotten yourself into."

Chapter 8

It started back in late September. The sudden influx of middle-class populations from unincorporated suburbs and enclaves all over California resulted in the greatest housing shortfall in the history of the state.

With no protection from gangs and warlords in rural areas, many moneyed families flooded into the metropolitan areas of San Diego, San Bernardino, Riverside, Santa Barbara, Los Angeles, Long Beach, Fresno, Bakersfield, Monterey, San Jose, San Francisco, Marin, Stockton, Sacramento and Redding, prepared to pay competitive rents for whatever space became available. This profound demand for living quarters set off a series of events that resulted in the establishment of the California Militia and its rise to power.

The federal government, prompted by FEMA Director Jerrod Freech, anticipated the housing shortfall in California, a state with over thirty three million residents. Yet despite the emergency shipments of money and pre-fabricated housing, incentives for families to take on boarders and the transfer of over two thousand residents to lesser-populated states, the monstrous demand overwhelmed the inadequate, slowly creeping supply.

California Governor Creighton Dobbins and the majority and minority leaders of both houses of the Legislature met in an emergency session during early October to organize and approve a volunteer citizen guard intended to stem the surge across the state's southern borders.

The Border Patrol estimated that as many as twenty thousand illegal immigrants had crossed over into California from Mexico and Arizona in August alone. With the collapse of the Mexican government on September 4, state analysts predicted that, unless the southern borders were better protected, fifty thousand more would cross in September and perhaps as many as seventy thousand would cross in October.

Governor Dobbins appealed to President Whitmore for greater assistance with the southern borders, but Freech and administration officials responded that the government was already overcommitted in troop deployment across the United States and could not spare any more resources for California. Freech, in an acerbic, disdainful tone, told Dobbins that California was already sucking the nation's resources dry. The heated exchange between the two ended bitterly.

"There are forty-nine other states in the Union, Governor, and forty-nine other governors. You folks out in California seem to have forgotten that. FEMA doesn't exist solely for California's benefit. You're on your own with that southern border situation."

The Governor and legislative leaders responded by creating and commissioning the California Volunteers, which started as a group of citizens loyal to the California and to sealing off borders in the southern state. The act seemed to violate Article I of the U.S. Constitution, but Dobbins and many powerful Californians believed the federal government had left the state no other option.

The state furnished uniforms, trucks, badges, guns and training for the volunteers, while organizers within the group provided various incentives for enlistees. By the end of October, the California Volunteers boasted fifty thousand soldiers, who took orders directly from the Governor, while the federalized National Guard in California took orders from the President.

By mid-November, there were more California Volunteer soldiers in California than there were federalized troops, and tensions between soldiers competing under separate commands were mounting.

The primary reasons for the sudden swell in the ranks of the California Volunteers were money and unemployment. While the State of California provided nothing more than a fifteen dollar per day stipend and a food ration, the Volunteer's directors found other sources of revenue that they used to entice young men and women to join the pride of the state, the newly-named California Militia.

Depending on where troops were situated, some earned more than one hundred and seventy-five dollars a day in cash, in addition to the stipend and food ration. Initially, state officials wondered where the money was coming from, but then the funding mechanism began to become clear.

During late August, not long after President Whitmore, with the unanimous consent of Congress, suspended all credit and debt, the California Landlords Association held a meeting in San Francisco. The President's decree, they asserted, was unclear and subject to interpretation. Whitmore had promised, "No American family shall lose its home for its inability to make mortgage payments."

His declaration, they insisted, related only to American families who owned homes and were making mortgage payments. No such guarantee was given to renters and lessees. During a televised press conference following the meeting, CLA Chairman Drew Miles informed California renters that the President's decree did not apply to renters and that those who refused to pay rent, as well as those who could not pay rent, would be evicted forthwith.

The obvious problem would involve rent enforcement and physical eviction. Many of the suburban and rural refugees flooding into California's major cities made it clear that they had money to pay for rent and were willing to, in some cases, pay two or three times the August rents.

But in many neighborhoods, the renters organized themselves and vowed to remain in houses and apartments rent-free until Nostradamus came. A tenants' coalition traveled to Washington a week later and sought President Whitmore, asking him to extend his protection to renters, but the President was too busy to meet with them.

The true test came at the beginning of September when landlords demanded rents and were refused payment. Eviction notices were served, but renters ignored them, daring landlords to attempt physical evictions.

Up and down the state, California residents declared rent-free zones and rent-free neighborhoods. During August and September, landlords collected less than five percent of all rents owed. Appeals to the Whitmore administration by the CLA went unanswered. It was clear the federal government was loath to get involved in the matter, at least for the moment.

Undaunted, California Landlord Association Chairman Miles went to California Militia director Brian Archie and offered fifty percent of all rents collected to the militia if the militia would handle rent enforcement and evictions. The offer was made after California landlords, gauging demand, agreed to a comprehensive forty percent hike in rents across the state.

Concerned with his own interests, Miles miscalculated Archie's ambition and resourcefulness. Not only did Brian Archie and his forces begin enforcing rent payment and performing evictions, the California Militia hit the CLA with so many extra surcharges and fees that landlords considered themselves fortunate to receive twenty-five percent of rents collected. By mid-November, Archie and the CM were collecting sixty percent of all rents owed and paying most landlords a mere pittance, if paying them at all.

In the meantime, the California Militia grew in numbers and influence so that by early December, its ranks numbered over one hundred thousand and growing. National Security Advisor Jett Turner saw problems brewing in California early on and urged Whitmore to arrest Governor Dobbins, Brian Archie and other troublesome Californians, but other presidential counselors called for restraint and non-intervention in matters that should have clearly been settled within the state.

Yet when National Guard commanders announced concerns about overwhelming numbers of California Militiamen, about the California Militia's open contempt for Whitmore and the federal government and about their increasing challenges to the Guard's command, Whitmore realized he had to act immediately and decisively.

He first ordered Governor Dobbins to dissolve the California Militia, which by its very existence was in violation of Article I, Section 10 of the U.S. Constitution. Dobbins agreed to obey the order, but Brian Archie and militia leaders refused to stand down.

Whitmore then ordered the arrest of Archie. The militia director was arrested at the state Capitol on January 1, sentenced by a military tribunal on January 5 and executed for the crime of high treason on January 6.

The assassination of Archie did not diminish the resolve of the California Militia to oppose the dictates of a federal government they believed cared nothing for California and its unique needs. Rather, the killing proved to be a rallying point for the militiamen and women and more importantly, it polarized the population of California against Whitmore and the federal government. Whereas before Archie's death, the idea of secession from the Union was a fringe movement, it grew into a statewide obsession.

The Western Growers Association, representing many farmers and farming families in California, was quick to join the secessionist movement. Many of the federal troops deployed in the state were involved in the seizures of farms, crops and warehouse holdings. Disregarding huge losses and added requirements on growers, entire harvests of many of California's crops were seized and shipped out of the state for national distribution.

Beyond that, some farms would be forced to plant unfamiliar crops in the spring, according to directives from the U.S. Secretary of

Agriculture. The association, describing government actions as a "federal stranglehold on farms," went so far as to invite the California Militia onto farms to challenge federal troops.

Whitmore next moved to federalize the still growing California Militia, but his negotiators were rebuffed and sent back with a proposal from the newly formed California Republic. The proposal, signed by Dobbins and his new cabinet, called for the U.S. government to recognize the California Republic as a separate and sovereign nation.

The new California Republic sought status as a friendly though independent nation. As such, Dobbins, his new government and the California Militia were prepared to cede all previously held federal property within California back to the U.S. in exchange for continued military protection from foreign threats. The California Republic would continue to donate a percentage of its crops and resources to the U.S. on a voluntary basis, though the needs of the California Republic would be considered first.

Governor Creighton Dobbins and his new cabinet were charged with high treason and arrest orders were issued. When Dobbins became aware of the federal indictments, he and advisors fled the Capitol, fearing possible air strikes coming from Travis AFB in nearby Fairfield or from Beale AFB in Marysville.

In the meantime, the California Militia, at Dobbins' orders, demanded the surrender of all farms and all civilian posts held by the National Guard. Outnumbering the Guard three to one in some areas, the California Militia took over Guard posts and commands all over the state.

By January 15, the CM called for the unconditional surrender of all civilian areas within the California Republic. National Guard soldiers were required to either turn in all weapons or switch allegiances. In this way, the California Militia absorbed more than half the National Guard in the state and became the supreme military ground force in the California Republic.

In Washington, Jett Turner had been urging the President to rein in California since November, but top advisors could never agree on how to deal with the powerful state. If California succeeded at secession, it would be likely that other states like Washington, Texas, Florida and possibly New York would follow. In the end, it seemed Whitmore was left with two options: occupation or compromise.

Occupation would mean launching air strikes against northern California from U.S. military bases in the state, followed by a land invasion from Oregon and the Pacific Ocean. The strategy, proffered by Barbara O'Connor, director of the Office of Homeland Security, involved gaining control of the less populated northern state and then controlling the water supply to the south. This would be achieved by shutting down the California Aqueduct and taking control of key reservoirs in the south.

"We don't have to bomb southern California. If we can gain control of the water supply, we can literally thirst the people into submission. Believe me—I lived there for thirty years."

Jett asserted that O'Connor's proposal was too soft and lacked the necessary punitive value.

"California's got to be punished. We have to hit em hard and make an example out of Dobbins and that damned militia! I say we spend a week bombing militia positions, let a few strays hit central LA to create a slew of funerals. Then we make sure the media shows plenty of images of people suffering. It'll make any other state think twice about trying the same thing."

Compromise would have involved cutting a behind-the-scenes deal with Dobbins, perhaps letting him retain some of his power, money or whatever else he wanted. But it became clear that the California governor wasn't motivated by ambition or greed.

Whitmore had ordered the strike on Donovan prison that killed Dobbins' son and brother. Then Whitmore lied, claiming he ordered the strike against the facility only after the inmates had begun killing the hostages. It was a lie, and thus Creighton Dobbins would never cut a deal because he was obsessed with exacting revenge.

The Whitmore administration also considered aligning itself with the Governor's political foes in the state, but Dobbins had gained the overwhelming support of the people by throwing off the yoke of an oppressive government and declaring the state sovereign and independent.

One thing was certain, however: The New Republic army, sleeping under the snow-covered Rockies in Wyoming over a thousand miles away, was safe until the spring thaw.

****

"He's got so many security codes and protocols—I'll probably never get access. But I'm going to keep on trying. I've got nothing else to do down here."

Chardonnay was uncharacteristic for Asia, but she had given up vodka.

"Anyway, he's up to something. They got some kind of project under way, and I've got to find out what it is."

JR held an empty crystal brandy snifter up toward the light, squinted and polished the glass.

"Why? What difference does it make?"

She leaned toward the bar.

"Don't you ever wonder what this Crypt is all about? I mean the government didn't go through all this expense just so one hundred or so people could live an extra thirty years and just die. And they've got Davis working on some big project down here. He left Tomorrow Systems to come down here."

JR shrugged.

"He's *your* husband. Has he ever said anything?"

She paused in thought before answering.

"No. But I know he works on Level Four. That means this Crypt goes down at least four levels."

"It goes down five. I've heard they've got a new supercomputer on Five—the one that runs everything. That voice-command features in all the living units—is that your husband's?"

She nodded.

"Annoying, isn't it?"

"It's like having an invisible butler or maid, and I understand that in a few years there'll be robots in every room."

"Believe me, you'll learn to despise it."

JR checked over his shoulder to make sure the cook wasn't within earshot, and whispered.

"My friend Selena from over at Dubya's—she's been seein some presidential liaison-type person in the Northwest Quarter. Well, she said that last night this young girl arrives under heavy guard, and she's got this young black kid with her."

He leaned closer.

"Anyway, at first he told her we'd all find out who she was soon enough. But she kind of pushed him and he said it's supposed to be the President's youngest daughter, Susan."

"Didn't she die in that plane crash?"

"There's more. The young black kid with her—he's supposed to be her *husband*."

Asia sipped the last of the chardonnay and motioned for a refill.

"Nothing surprises me anymore. That's why I want to find out exactly what this Crypt is all about. Do you want to help me?"

"Not me. They might tolerate it from you. You're Davis Franklin's wife. You're a *somebody*, but I'm just a worker down here. Just let me get caught stickin my nose somewhere it shouldn't be. They'd throw me out in a second, or worse. I'd just disappear without a trace. I'm not the man for that job."

The refilled glass of chardonnay was empty. Asia was still learning how to *sip* wine.

"Just as well. I guess I'll just have to find someone else. But I will make you this promise: I'm going to find out what else is going on here, and when I do, I'll let you know."

****

Jett lit another cigarette, inhaled and blew a trail of smoke toward the lighting fixture overhead. He smiled toward the hulking figure sitting across the conference room table at the Pentagon.

"Told ya we'd get er."

The General nodded.

"You did indeed. And what are you going to do now?"

"I'm going to *tell* im when he gets here."

"And then?"

Jett stood, playfully ashing the cigarette in the circular glass tray as he answered.

"Then I make the offer. I've already had it approved by the council. I'll tell him he wouldn't have to give up command until March. We'll stage the assassination at the end of the month and blame it on someone we already want to take out. Then at long last he can be reunited with his sweet little daughter in the Crypt."

"And the Vice President?"

"He's already indicated that he doesn't want command. He'll resign."

"So that'll leave us the House Speaker Chuck Bentsen?"

Jett nodded.

"Yep, and he's one of ours. He'll do whatever needs to be done without a second thought. I say the sooner we get him installed, the better."

The phone rang twice before Jett answered.

"Jett. Yeah, thanks."

He mashed the cigarette and took a file from the black soft leather briefcase next to his chair.

"He's on his way."

Lucas Draco stood to show respect for the man who entered.

"If he decides to resign his command, I'll loyally support whoever replaces him. But if he doesn't and you and your council challenge his command, I'll have no choice. I'll make sure you're all arrested and punished if he orders it."

Jett stared for a few seconds, and then he smiled.

"Is that a threat, General?"

"Just a clarification. It's only proper you know who and what you're dealing with here."

"Point taken."

Jett's eyes lit up when Joe walked into the room. He walked toward the President with open arms, hugged him hard and held his shoulders at arm's length.

"Joe! I've got the most incredible news!"

The President seemed nervous.

"*Good* news for a change? Maybe I should sit—I'm not sure I can handle getting good news."

Whitmore nodded toward Draco.

"General—"

"It's very nice to see you, Mr. President."

Joe sat at the table and sighed. He seemed tired.

"Sit down. What's this good news?"

Jett and Draco seated, Jett pushed the file toward the President.

"I found Susan, and she's fine. Right now, she's right where she belongs—at the Crypt in Colorado."

On hearing the words, the president bowed his head, covering his face with his hands.

"Oh my God! Thank you. Thank you. Thank God she's *alive!*"

He opened the file and stared at the recently taken photograph. Tears streamed down his face.

"Where was she?"

"It's all there. She was the houseguest of the Reverend Jonah Williams in Los Angeles."

"Jonah? Son of a gun! Did he know?"

Jett wagged his head.

"No. She had em all fooled. Went by the name Megan McIntyre. You want to talk to her?"

Whitmore seemed incredulous.

"My God. Yes! Of course I'd like to speak with her."

Jett picked up the phone and dialed his secretary.

"You got her on?"

He smiled.

"She's all yours, Joe. Drake and I'll step outside and come back when you're done."

When Jett and the General returned, Whitmore was still at the table. He was reading from the file, occasionally dabbing his eyes. He looked up, smiling.

"I don't know how I'll ever be able to thank you, Jett."

"Seeing you two reunited is all the thanks I'll ever need. I'm happy for you."

The General placed a hand on Whitmore's shoulder.

"Congratulations, Mr. President."

"Thanks, Luke."

Jett wasted no time.

"Are you going to see her?"

"I, I don't know. I'm still numb right now."

"Did she tell you she got married?"

Joe looked up.

"What?"

"Yeah. She married that Reverend Williams' kid. She made the Secret Service agents take *him* too. He's there with her."

The President flipped through the folder toward the end until he found the photo and summary. It was a picture of Susan and Dexter asleep in Aaliyah's Lexus on the night they spent the night down the street from Brenda Brown's house. Dexter's arm was draped over Susan's shoulders and her face was nestled into his chest.

"How long?"

"Christmas Eve, though that photo was taken weeks before."

Joe Whitmore studied the photograph.

"I wonder why she didn't tell me."

"I'm sorry I mentioned it. Maybe she wanted to tell you in person."

Joe's eyes were glazed over.

"Yes."

Jett stood and walked over, placing a hand on Joe's shoulder.

"All this must be a big shock to you, Joe. But it seems to me you and Susan have got a lot of catching up to do. You need to go see her."

The President bowed his head.

"I don't know."

"Go for a day or two. The world will still be out here when you get back."

Jett finally caught the President's eyes.

"You owe it to her, Joe. She's been through a lot in these last few months."

Whitmore nodded.

"You're right. You're right—I need to go see her. I have to talk to her."

Employing a metal stylus, he checked his upcoming schedule on a digital device.

"This weekend and next week are shot. Soonest I'll be able to go will be a week from Saturday."

"Then a week from Saturday it is. I'll take care of the arrangements."

Still sitting, Whitmore sighed and smiled to himself.

"She's alive. God gave us a second chance. I lost her once because I was too busy to be there for her, Jett, but whatever it takes, I swear I'll never abandon her again. I swear I'll never lose her again.

Chapter 9

"You don't know me, but I just want to say thanks."

"Thanks for what?"

"For hot, steaming jasmine tea in the morning—just like my mom used to make—and all I have to do is call a command from my bed."

Davis looked up from the Tomorrow Systems documents he had been poring over for the last ninety minutes.

"Beverage component?"

"I've had it for a week. All I have to do is load it up once a month. Makes killer kamikazes too."

Davis had already gone back to his analysis. For him, there was no person standing by the table.

"Hey—mind if I sit down and join you for a minute?"

There was no response. Undeterred, the young man pulled out a chair and sat, sliding uncomfortably close to Davis. He withdrew a small notebook from his coat pocket and began writing, humming as he worked. It took ten minutes before Davis realized he was there.

"Excuse me?"

"Alan."

"What?"

"Chan. It's Alan Chan. I just got down here. I'm a mythologist. What's that?"

He reached over and grabbed one of Davis's pens.

"It's a White House pen? So I take it you've met Whitmore?"

Frustrated, Davis closed his folder.

"Yes. What is a mythologist?"

"Well, I'm actually an anthropologist, but myths are my specialty, especially doomsday myths."

Davis nodded, interested.

"Doomsday myths?"

"You know—Armageddon, Ragnarok, Judgment Day, Atlantis, The Great Flood, Kali the Destroyer, Götterdämmerung, dissolution into Chaos—every culture has one or another."

Davis backed his chair away, squinting as he tried to assess the strange young man.

"And why would anyone be interested in doomsday myths?"

"Well, in order to solve the Cosmic Riddle, for one."

"Cosmic Riddle?"

Alan nodded.

"Yes, it's incorporated in our genetic programming. It's worked its way out through our myths, our religious writings and even the science fiction we read, write and watch. Are you with me on this?"

Davis reopened the folder.

"No."

Alan reached over and shut it.

"The asteroid we're facing—this isn't the first time it's happened. According to the geological record, an asteroid like Nostradamus collides with Earth every one hundred million years, though that's an average. I mean, this one's only thirty-five million years early."

Alan smiled with satisfaction. At least Davis hadn't gone back to his reading.

"Sixty-five million years ago at Chicxulub on the Yucatán peninsula—the one that killed the dinosaurs—that was the last big one. It wiped out seventy-five percent of all species on Earth, but there were others before that. There was a bigger one, like Nostradamus, that hit two hundred and fifty million years ago near the Falklands. It left a crater one hundred and fifty miles wide and wiped out ninety-five percent of all species on Earth. Interesting stuff, huh?"

"Go on."

"Right now, the international science community out there is working to preserve human DNA and the DNA of other key species. Basically, they want to re-create the seeds of life that will lie dormant and sprout after cosmic winter so that in maybe another one hundred million years, *Homo sapiens* will again be around to deal with yet another asteroid. It's all cyclical—man moves over to the next *Yuga*, and that's where the Cosmic Riddle comes in."

Davis wagged his head.

"This, this is starting to become a little too esoteric for me."

Alan raised a pleading hand.

"I'm almost finished. It could be God or it could be scientists or sages from hundreds of millions of years ago, or it could just be a glitch in our DNA, but the answer is in our programming. Someone or something from back there is possibly sending us a message across time. Somewhere in our programming may lie the solution or answer to how humans can survive one of these huge collisions intact, or better yet, prevent one. The key to man's salvation, the key to this solution is coded in our doomsday myths."

Davis sipped from a glass of club soda on the table.

"And someone pays you to do this?"

"I'm actually department chair at the Princeton School of Anthropology, or let's just say I was. Now I'm here to pursue the riddle."

Davis nodded, raising his eyebrows.

"And Smock brought you here to study myths?"

"No, I'm on the Ark with Dr. Benoit. I think we'll all be gone in March."

Alan stood smiling, extending a hand.

"But until then, I hope to see you around. I've always admired you, you know, and now we're talking just like buddies. I thought I'd be bored here, but I'm amazed at how fast we became friends. See ya around, Dave."

Davis squinted in anger as Alan bounced away. He hated being called "Dave." Yet he smiled as he returned to his analysis. At least the kid had spunk.

****

The wilderness lay desolate and white. On the west end of the valley, where New Lexington had sat against the base of the mountains, the landscape was level, with no trace of the vast complex that had once been there. The bombs on December had flattened the city, and subsequent snowfall covered all the rubble. Thus the fallen city had disappeared beneath a blanket of snow. The settlers' encampments and houses further east were also gone: most flattened and burned during the explosions, others evacuated by the U.S. Army and still others abandoned after supplies were exhausted.

In the barren white expanse, a single figure trudged along a trail next to an embankment that blocked the swirling wind. He struggled under the weight of the frozen carcass strapped to his back. He walked along for eight miles, stopping twice to rest. He pushed himself to get home before sunset, when temperatures would plunge ten degrees. By three o'clock, he had reached the base of the mountain, ready to ascend.

The grade was steep and became slippery as the snow began to fall. He had hiked up a mile when he heard the howl of a wolf pack not far off. He loaded his rifle and hid behind a rocky natural wall for fifteen minutes until he was sure the yips and wails were moving away from him and down the mountain. An hour later, he reached the cave he had left at four o'clock that morning.

Ellie was waiting outside the entrance, watching for him, so she saw him collapse. She ran over and dropped to her knees, panicked.

"Please tell me ya *got* somethin!"

He nodded, his entire being yearning for a place beside the warm fire inside.

He continued as she helped him onto to his feet and into the cave.

"Yeah. Thought I wasn't gonna, but I got it right when I was ready ta give up."

He yanked the strap over his left shoulder with his right hand, freeing the load from that side. When he freed his right shoulder, the carcass crashed to the floor. He sighed, relieved.

"How's Katie?"

She glanced over her shoulder, toward the back of the cave.

"Not real good. She's sleep. I'm sure food'll help."

"And the boys?"

"Hungry. It's been eight or nine days since we all had anything ta eat but pine nuts. They're out gettin wood. Thank *God* ya got somethin!"

She hugged her husband Buck.

"What did ya get?"

"Young female. I sawed off the head and skinned er cuz I couldn't afford ta be carryin around the extra weight. In a few minutes, I'll go out and dress it."

An hour later, the cave was filled with the welcome aroma of stewing meat. Inside a pot on the fire, thin slices of cooked flesh churned in violent, frothy swirls that animated the broth. Occasionally, a leaf or piece of root roiled to the surface, dancing momentarily before floating back to the bottom. Six children waited next to the pot, eyes widened and stomachs growling.

Ellie served the children first. They ate from small wooden bowls, grunting all the while. Then Ellie took a bowl over to the corner of the cave and hand-fed Katie, who was too sick and weak to even sit up. Only after she was sure all the children were satisfied did Ellie fix a bowl for Buck and for herself. Buck ate squatting in a corner of the cave, chewing the tough slices of flesh, swallowing, closing his eyes and nodding his head.

"Mom, Dad—I know ya had ta do what ya did. I want ya ta know I'll never blame ya fer it, but I *know*."

Buck responded in rage to his teary-eyed, seventeen-year-old son, who had whispered from behind.

"Shut yer mouth, Boy! Ya don't know what yer talkin bout."

"I do, Daddy. I was just outside. I saw em bundled up where ya hid em."

Buck turned and leered toward Danny in a threatening way. Danny backed up.

"I wasn't spyin, Daddy. I swear. I just come across em, I swear! I thought it was maybe some pieces ya missed."

Ellie touched her husband's cheek to get his attention.

"What's he talking about, Buck?"

"Somethin ain't none of his business, somethin he shouldn'ta been lookin at."

"I'm sorry, Daddy."

A tall, stout man, Buck towered over the shivering teenager.

"It's all right, Boy. Now ya just need ta forget ya saw anathang at all. Ya didn't see what ya saw, ya undastan?"

Ellie insisted.

"What the hell are y'all two talkin bout?"

"Somethin between me and him. Somethin that's gonna *stay* between me and him."

He spoke to his son.

"What ya do with em?"

"I, I left em where they was."

"You stay with yer mama and the kids. I'll be back in a coupla hours."

The snow swirled in the wind so thick that Buck could hardly see his hand in front of his face, and yet still he made his way up the mountain. He wasn't sure where he was going, but he knew he would find a proper place.

While he walked, he thought of the process he had just gone through. He remembered peeling the skin off, filleting the flesh from the bone and slicing it into wafer-thin pieces. Most of it he wrapped and larded under a frozen rock pile, but the rest he brought in to Ellie.

He told her it was a young, inexperienced bear, hungry and stranded away from her mother. He told her how he had crept up on her and dropped her with a single shot to the back of the head. He described how he had dragged the body away and hid it in a snow bank until the desperate mother and family had gone. He even told Ellie he had sawed her head from her frozen body and hauled the stiff body up the mountain.

But it was what he *didn't* tell Ellie that bothered him. It was what had bothered his son. Sometimes it was just better that people *didn't* know. Honesty had its virtue, but sometimes lies were what desperate people needed to hear or believe; sometimes even a lie had virtue. *She was going to die anyway.*

He saw the place. It sat maybe six feet off the trail. It was blanketed with snow, but he knew it was perfect. He broke a branch from a lodgepole pine and used it to brush the snow from the surface and from around its bottom edges. After five minutes, the entire rock lay exposed.

For five minutes he banged at its base with a six-foot-long iron pry, chipping rock away to create a plant point. Beveled edge securely under the rock, he used a smaller stone as a fulcrum and pushed down on the end of the pry with all his might. As the edge of the rock lifted, he slid the iron bar farther under it and adjusted the fulcrum stone closer to the rock. Steam flowed from his sweaty face as he repeated the process three additional times, raising the rock a little more with each thrust and adjustment.

In this way, he was able to pry one side of the rock eighteen inches off the ground. He knelt low to make sure he had adequate clearance.

Limping on near-frozen joints, he went to his backpack, unzipped it and removed the bundle from there. Tears froze on his cheeks as he took the bundle to a spot in front of the rock and knelt. He prayed in silence for five minutes.

At last, he reached to place the bundle under the raised rock, but he stopped. Something made him stop. Something made him stop to look on the horrific display that disturbed his son so much, the vision that was no doubt etched in the boy's troubled soul.

Placing the bundle on the snow-covered ground before his knees, Buck unwrapped the folds covering its contents. When the bundle was finally opened, Buck cringed and turned away, glancing sidelong at the ghastly collection before him, all covered with blood: the dismembered hands, feet and butchered heart of a poor little girl.

Desperate to escape a vision that had began to burn itself into his memory, he swept the hands, feet, heart and cloth under the rock, stood and strained as he struggled to pull the pin. Grasping the pry bar, he leaned forward with all his might, lifting the rock higher, and then he yanked the bar out, sprawling to the ground with it in his hands.

The rock slammed down, covering at once the glowing guilt, shame and horror hidden beneath it. Buck rushed over and touched the mighty rock, stroking it with seeming gratitude. *It was a young bear. There was no little girl.*

He used the beveled end of the pry to scrawl a faint, imperfect cross on the face of the rock, stood back apace and stared. Minutes later, through his tears, Buck fancied he saw the cross become perfect and bright and then he saw a tiny, radiant, exultant soul ascending into the heavens.

****

"Susan, do you realize what you've *done*? You know he can't go back now."

"It was his decision too. He doesn't *want* to go back."

Joe Whitmore looked at the nervous young man sitting next to his daughter.

"How old are you, Dexter?"

"I'm sixteen, Sir."

"And at sixteen, do you think you're mature enough or experienced enough to make a choice like this, with so many profound consequences?"

Dexter knew the question would be asked, so he was prepared with an answer.

"I'm old enough to know that last August 7th, I realized I have just as much at stake here as anyone else, if not more because I'm younger. Please realize that it was my decision, Sir, and I'm plenty mature enough to make it. I want to be with Susan for the rest of my life."

Whitmore smirked, sarcasm flavoring his voice.

"Doesn't seem you have much of a choice now. So you two are married? By a rabbi?"

Susan interrupted with an answer.

"We've decided that we're going to spend the rest of our lives together, yes."

"And you two are in love?"

Dexter answered without hesitation.

"Yes."

Susan faltered as she stared into her father's discerning eyes.

"We're getting there. It's going to work. I'm sure of it."

The President sat at the table across from the young couple.

"Don't you think you're being a little selfish, Susan? Did you choose him just so you wouldn't have to come down here alone? Just so you would have someone down here your own age?"

She answered.

"No. We chose each other after we had a long talk on Christmas Eve. That night, we talked about life, and what's important—things people sometimes take for granted. We agreed that what matters most is the love you're able to give and receive. What's important is being true to yourself and the people you love. We're young, Daddy, but it doesn't take years of experience or marriage or even gray hair to realize that. We know we love each other, and that love will grow as we continue to grow."

Nodding, Whitmore looked toward Dexter.

"Your parents must be worried sick about you."

"I left them a note. I told them I loved them. I said I was going away with Megan... I mean Susan. And I said I probably wasn't coming back. I said goodbye."

"And I suppose a *note* is going to make them feel better? They're going to really miss you. Don't you miss them?"

Dexter only bowed his head, tears in his eyes.

Whitmore sighed in frustration and glanced toward his daughter.

"So you said you wanted me to *do* something?"

She took a breath and nodded.

"Yes. I want a wedding."

"But I thought you were already married."

"We are. But I want a wedding. I want a wedding with a white dress and guests and a fancy dinner and the works. And I want you to perform the service."

Chapter 10

Jonah tiptoed into the room and eased into the leather armchair. He tilted the light toward his lap and read from the Psalms of the Bible in an undertone while David slept in a bed three feet away.

"I waited patiently for the Lord; and he inclined unto me, and heard my cry. He brought me up also out of an horrible pit, out of the miry clay, and set my feet upon a rock, and established my goings."

This time, David had been asleep for thirteen or fourteen hours. He had lost more than thirty pounds during January.

Lynda seemed suspicious the last time she called from her father's at 7:30 that evening. She asked Jonah in confidence if David was feeling well. She said he seemed strange on the phone over the past few weeks.

She said she was certain he was hiding something from her. When she told David she was returning to California to check on him, he got angry and insisted she stay in Rhode Island. Lynda was becoming desperate, but then again, so was Jonah.

"Blessed is that man that maketh the Lord his trust, and respecteth not the proud, nor such as turn aside to lies. Many O Lord my God, are thy wonderful works which thou hast done, and thy thoughts which are to usward: they cannot be reckoned up in order unto thee."

January had been a difficult month for Rabbi David Blum. He told Dr. Levin on December 25 that he had "after much prayer" decided not to pursue recommended medical treatment for his cancer. A month earlier, he had been diagnosed with inoperable pancreatic cancer and was told that he would be dead in six months unless he began immediate treatment. He worded the decision to the doctor as well as to himself.

"And all along, I thought the asteroid was the true test of my faith, but then *this!* And as I struggled through this decision, I remembered Satan's taunt to the Lord: *Skin over skin, and over his person a man will give everything he has. But put out your hand and hit his bones and flesh, and see if he will not curse you to your face.* This cancer is *my* test. For me, as you know, the asteroid's irrelevant. I've decided to put my trust in my God."

Two other specialists and three other rabbis tried to persuade David to change his mind and pursue radiation treatment and chemotherapy. Dr. Levin went so far as to assure David he would be "definitely dead" in months if he didn't submit to treatment, but David's faith proved steadfast, although to his detriment.

With each day that passed in January, he grew weaker, felt lousier, slept longer. By January 15, he had lost seventeen pounds, and by February 1, he had lost another twenty. He looked gaunt and frail. His eyes became gray and hazy. It seemed his body was dying, but he remained positive in spirit.

One week earlier, he had asked Aaliyah to journey to an herbal store to pick up some blue violet, chickweed, cleavers, coral, red clover, sorrel, virgin's bower and goldenseal. He also asked her to bring fresh tomatoes and freshly squeezed vegetable juices. His favorite was the carrot juice.

Aaliyah made David teas from the herbs, according to his directions, and she kept him supplied with fresh fruits, vegetables and juices. He ate no meat. Yet with every day he felt fainter and closer to death.

The Reverend Jonah Williams was not without his share of trials and tribulations either. In December at a convention of Christian ministers in Atlanta, he was denounced by the association's chairman and vice chairman in vitriolic speeches that were aired on national television.

The chairman identified him as a false shepherd and a minister of the apostasy. The ministers warned that true Christians risked alienation from God by watching Jonah's broadcasts on television or by listening to his sermons on the radio. They called Greater Faith an apostate church and labeled all its adherents false Christians.

These ministers maintained that the Rapture would occur on August 6 or 7—that on that day, Jesus Christ would return to the Earth a first time to *snatch away* all good Christians, or Saints, who would be united with him "in the air." According to their doctrine:

> *No matter what we are doing, we will be suddenly taken out of the world. The Rapture of the Church will be an event of such startling proportions that the entire world will be conscious of our leaving. Some have suggested that there will be airplane, bus and train wrecks throughout the world when Christian operators are suddenly taken out of the world. Who can imagine the chaos on the freeways when automobile drivers are snatched out of their cars!*

And then the tribulation would come, marked by the arrival of the asteroid on August 7. After the tribulation, Christ would return to the Earth a second time to establish his kingdom and begin his millennial rule.

Instead of encouraging his congregation to prepare for the Rapture and the destruction of the wicked, Jonah had suggested since the president's announcement about the asteroid that God would somehow deliver fleshly Christians in the world from the judgment purposed for mankind.

The December rebuke by the United Association of Christian Ministers caused an immediate decline in Greater Faith's Sunday attendance, in its television viewership and in its radio listenership, though in February many of the straying sheep began to return to the fold.

During a sermon on the first Sunday of February, Jonah addressed his separation from the association. In doing so, he encouraged freedom of thought, tolerance and acceptance over separatism, condemnation and persecution.

He preached that the Lord was God of all men and all women, God of the righteous and unrighteous, God of Christians, Muslims, Jews and Gentiles, God of the living and the dead. Without condemning or returning insults and injuries to those who had abused him, Jonah continued to extol the virtues of faith.

In January, Jonah also had to deal with the sudden and curious disappearance of his son, Dexter. He and Aaliyah came home from church on New Year's Day and found a short note from their son explaining that he was going away with houseguest Megan and he wouldn't be coming back. Dexter assured his parents he loved them and cited Genesis 2:24.

Aaliyah was distraught from the moment she read the note. She cried for days, and when she was finished crying, she began to assess blame. At first she blamed herself for being such a busy mother and then she blamed Jonah for being too hard on the boy.

Throughout January, a rift grew between Jonah and his wife so that they hardly spoke to each other. As the division continued to grow, she spent more and more time away from home with her mother and other relatives.

For Jonah, it was the second time he had lost a young son. A year earlier, he had mused upon his resemblance to the restored Job:

his family replaced, his station in life renewed, his respectability restored. And yet those blessings had been taken from him a second time in an instant. For him, this second trial was far worse. He feared in his heart that in the end he would be left with nothing, except for his faith.

"For innumerable evils have compassed me about: mine inequities have taken hold upon me, so that I am not able to look up; they are more than the hairs on mine head: therefore my heart faileth me. Be pleased O Lord, to deliver me: O Lord, make haste to help me."

Lying still in the bed, David was able to hear the last passage Jonah read. Summoning strength, he turned toward his friend.

"Fortieth Psalm. Are you reading that for me or for you?"

"For both of us."

"Water!"

His extreme thirst quenched, David grasped the bed railing on each side and pulled himself to a reclined sitting position.

"You know how they've always said the Lord moves in mysterious ways? Somehow I can't help but think he's acting on us now. This is no accident."

"What?"

"This whole situation here. I mean, look at us. We're very different, you and me. We come from different corners of the world, from two different religions. And here we are together in our trials. I'm actually dying in your home."

Jonah closed the Bible and adjusted the light as David continued.

"Some of my friends from the synagogue—they don't understand it. They wonder why I'm in your home dying when there are plenty of good Jewish families that would gladly have me die in theirs. It's funny. Some of them even get mad with me about it. Say it disgraces them, not because you're black, but because you aren't Jewish. Well, I tell em I don't know. I don't know, but I think it's no accident. I think God brought us together to show us something, or to show each *other* something. What it is, I don't know yet."

David poured more cool water from the pitcher and drank.

"How're things with Aaliyah?"

"Still drifting apart. I'm trying my best to be patient. She just misses him so much."

"She's an angel. She's really gone out of her way to take care of me."

Jonah smiled, thinking of his wife. She really was a sweet person. Yet he felt powerless to ease her grief.

"Tell me again. Dexter wanted to *marry* her on Christmas Eve?"

"I came out while they were discussing it. He wanted to do it that night, and in the end, so did she, but they both backed out at the last minute."

Confusion registered on Jonah's face as he analyzed the words.

"And eight days later, two big government types in dark glasses came to the door and asked if they were married?"

"That's right."

"And you said yes?"

David raised a finger in protest.

"I told them, 'If they told you they're married by me, then they're married by me.' I wasn't sure what was going on or if they were in some kinda trouble, so I didn't want make matters worse."

Jonah wagged his head, confused.

"So you think they were in *trouble?*"

"I didn't say that. Like I said that first day, when Dexter brought the note, I realized they were okay. They're both good, smart kids, but there was obviously something going on. I'm sure they'll be back when they work it out."

Jonah nodded.

"I just wish he would call to say he's okay. It would mean the world to his mother."

Aaliyah knocked four times and pushed the door open. Her forehead and eyes appeared in the aperture.

"How are you feeling, David?"

David raised his right shaking hand, thumb pointing up. She smiled and got to her purpose.

"Jonah, can you come downstairs for a few minutes. I need to talk to you right away."

When Jonah entered the living room, Aaliyah was seated on the couch at right. Her eyes were fixed on the armchair a few feet away. The chair had been swiveled in such a way that all Jonah could see was its back. Aaliyah whispered something to a person seated there.

Jonah approached, hoping his prayers and supplications had at last been answered. To his profound disappointment, he recognized the voice that answered his wife, and then he saw her.

Aaliyah reached out to her husband.

"Jonah, sit down."

He sat next to Aaliyah, across from a person whose presence of late had brought great turmoil to his life. He sighed and forced a smile.

"Hello Brenda."

She seemed embarrassed.

"Hello Reverend Williams."

Aaliyah took her husband's hand.

"Honey, I've invited Brenda to live with us for a while."

His face and demeanor protested as he responded.

"Oh, really? I, I heard she was... I heard, I heard you were getting *married*?"

Aaliyah answered for the girl.

"That's all changed. You know I've never been one to beat around the bush, so I'll just say it. Brenda is pregnant, and she's pregnant with Dexter's babies. She's pregnant with twins. When the congressman she was engaged to found out about the pregnancy, he ordered her to get an abortion. When she wouldn't, he dumped her."

Brenda bowed her head to avoid Jonah's eyes as Aaliyah continued.

"And I don't know how that Alexis Brown can call herself a Christian parent! You know she told Brenda if she didn't get an abortion, she was going to have to move out. I told Brenda she was going to stay right here till she has those babies and as long as she wants after that. I should have talked to you about it first, but I hope you don't mind."

His eyes studied the nervous young woman whose fingers fidgeted from clasped hands.

"And we're *sure* they're Dexter's babies?"

She looked up.

"Yes Sir, Reverend. He's the only one I was ever with. I'm going to have these babies. I won't give them up."

Jonah nodded, leaning forward.

"We'll be here for you. Have you seen an obstetrician? Do you have a due date?"

She smiled.

"Yes I do. The babies are due on August 7th."

****

"The truth is, birds do it, bees do it, and it's no different with humans. At the end of the season, all species go at it with reckless abandon. It's in the programming, meant to preserve genes through winter."

Twenty-one women and three men sat in rows of chairs in what seemed like a college classroom. Some read from thick information packets, while others tried to take notes.

Dr. Isabel Benoit, wearing large glasses, an oversized white lab jacket and her hair pulled back, was in her element before the group. She acknowledged a young woman who had raised a hand.

"In Trinidad, where I'm from, I never in my life have seen people so horny. That's all everyone's doing—sex, sex, sex. Are you sayin it's gonna get worse?"

"Or better, depending on how you look at it. From a purely genetic point of view, the more sex, the more pregnancies, or fertilized eggs. The more fertilized eggs, the better odds for the genetic code to survive the winter. This *horniness*, as you call it, is actually our genetic survival instinct kicking in."

Another woman raised a tentative hand.

"And this is because our governments told us Nostradamus is coming?"

"Well, I don't know. Does anyone have to tell dragonflies that summer's coming to an end? Does anyone have to tell birds when to begin migration in order to avoid winter? Does anyone have to tell salmon when to begin their journeys?"

Isabel smiled at the Pakistani woman who flirted from the front row before resuming.

"It's all instinctive. The truth is, humans are just as beholden to genetic programming as any other creature. In answer to your question—some creatures of Earth might be capable of sensing that Nostradamus is coming instinctively. After all, it's not the first time an asteroid has come and wiped out the majority of Earth's species. Meteors from before have wiped out seventy-five to ninety-five percent of every genetic code. We, as humans, are the highest result of the genetic code that has survived those impacts. The progenitors of our genetic code have survived every cosmic winter that Earth has ever experienced, or else we wouldn't be here."

For a second time, she ignored Adam Smock's request to interrupt.

"And thus the argument can be made that perhaps the organisms that have survived are the ones equipped with some innate sort of sensing mechanism—the ones that are able to sense the coming of cosmic winter in order to avoid extinction. If it's a part of our programming, then all our telescopes and satellite surveillance systems are merely an expansion or extension of that sensing mechanism ingrained in our genetic code. Makes you wonder why our philosophers first looked toward the heavens."

With reluctance, she acknowledged Adam.

"Yes, Doctor Benoit, getting back to the issue of increased sexual urges. In your book of directives, you strongly discourage sexual contact between selectees prior to departure from Earth, but that's not for over a month. Do you expect us all to just be celibate for the next month when it's the end of the world and there's a chance our cryopods might fail?"

There was a hint of cruelty in her smile.

"I do not prohibit sexual contact. I merely *discourage* it, strongly. The purpose of bringing you here early is to help prepare your minds and bodies for four hundred years of cold sleep, which contains significant risks. For some of these women, the distraction of libido or any other distraction now could result in their never waking from sleep. There will be plenty of opportunity to engage in sexual pleasures, and that is on the other side. For now, I'm asking all of you to exercise a modicum of restraint. Find your pickings elsewhere if you can, Mr. Smock, or learn the art of self-satisfaction. But leave these women alone."

She checked her watch and sighed.

"Mr. Chan?"

"I'm sorry, but I understood there would be thirty-nine women on the Ark. Where are the rest? And where is this Matrix?"

Isabel gestured.

"All the women you see here are surrogates. They are perfectly balanced, healthy women who've each agreed to carry seven pregnancies to term. I brought them in early so that doctors here can perform necessary ovariectomies and begin hormonal injections prior to departure. The two obstetricians, who will also serve as surrogates, and their nurses are here elsewhere. The breeders and the Matrix will be along in early March. Any other questions?"

This time, Adam Smock did not wait to be acknowledged. His tone was sarcastic.

"And what will you be on the other side, Dr. Benoit? A surrogate or a breeder? Or are you this Matrix, this queen bee?"

She answered.

"I'm a surrogate. And just so you know, we haven't completed genetic screening on you yet. If you don't meet the breeder requirements, you'll never be more than a pilot on this project, you'll never be anything more than a drone."

Her briefcase repacked, she adjusted her jacket and turned toward the door.

"Unless of course we can find some clever way to make *you* a surrogate."

Chapter 11

The two New Jersey state troopers arrived at 7:41 p.m., just as he was preparing to call her mother. It wasn't like her to be out-of-pocket for so long. She had phoned at 2:30 to say she was on her way and asked if he needed anything from one of the supply warehouses. Even in bad traffic, she should have been home at 3:30—4:00 at the latest.

"Mr. Reed?"

"Yes?"

"Mr. Reginald Reed?"

He sensed it coming.

"Yes."

"We're sorry to inform you that your wife, Layla, was involved in a serious automobile accident at about 3:00 this afternoon. She was rushed by ambulance to Memorial Hospital where she was pronounced dead on arrival. We're very sorry."

It was as if someone had slugged him in the solar plexus. His crutches buckled and flew from under him as he collapsed to the floor doubled over.

"No! No! No, it can't be! Please God, no!"

The compassionate troopers helped him up and guided him to the couch.

"We're sorry, Mr. Reed. Maybe you shouldn't be alone. Would you like us to call someone for you? A minister? A friend? A brother or sister?"

He wiped a tear that trailed down his face, his lips trembling as he answered.

"No. Please just go. Just leave me. I need to be alone right now."

The clock struck nine. It was the first time Reggie had earnestly prayed to God in twenty years. First, he humbled himself. He apologized for all the years of resentment. If he hadn't married Layla, she might be still alive. Once again, he pleaded with God. *Please make them wrong! Please make her not dead! I'll do anything you want me to do!*

He must have fallen asleep sometime after midnight. Layla's older sister, Shayla, woke him up at nine by banging on the door. She wanted a copy of Layla's life insurance policy and insisted Reggie accompany her to the funeral home to make necessary arrangements.

Once again, God had either ignored his prayers or worse: he had reneged on an extremely crucial deal.

****

It was a full-scale invasion. As dawn broke, the skies above San Francisco were blackened with companies of U.S. Army helicopters and other Army and Navy aircraft flying back and forth in a seeming frenzy. The USS Ronald Reagan, a huge new aircraft carrier, sat in the bay, and according to television reports, another such aircraft carrier, the USS Nimitz, was situated seventy-five miles south in Monterey Bay. For the first time in history, Army tanks and armored personnel carriers rolled down Mission Street.

At 3rd, convoys turned left, proceeded through Market before veering onto Geary on their way to Golden Gate Park. For the first time in history, Pier 39, with all its shops, restaurants and boutiques, became a satellite Army post with armed guards stationed outside.

The Army set up its official command at Pier 41. For the first time in history, the Golden Gate Bridge and the Bay Bridge fell under Army control. Until San Francisco was secure, traffic in and out of the city was shut down.

Initially, a regiment of uniformed California Militia soldiers battled the advancing U.S. Army from rooftops and strongholds in the financial district, but it became clear that direct resistance was futile. Militia soldiers discarded their uniforms, fell back and regrouped in Yerba Buena Park to discuss organized resistance tactics and to establish the nature of the militia's command in the city.

Early on, the U.S. Army took out San Francisco's communication links to the rest of California, cutting Bay Area militia members off from former Governor Dobbins, who was calling shots from an undisclosed location in southern California. Land telephone links were severed, and cellular communication towers were shut down. Even television broadcasts fell under complete federal control and censure.

Although California Militia members scrambled to avoid arrest, the U.S. Army combed through neighborhoods, conducting interviews, seizing weapons and arresting alleged "terrorists" and "seditionists." By noon, over six hundred persons were in custody, awaiting eventual transport to the Presidio, where a detention center and tribunal had been established.

By one o'clock p.m., Sacramento, California's capital city located ninety miles east, was declared captured. Oakland in the East Bay and sprawling San Jose further south were a little more difficult to secure, but federal troops had established posts in the downtown areas of both cities.

In Berkeley, citizens staged mass demonstrations, opposing unwanted and "fascist" government presence and intervention. Protestors blocked key routes being used by the Army and videotaped unprovoked acts of aggression by federal troops.

At six o'clock p.m., U.S. Army General Webster Hutchinson came on statewide television with a message to Californians. In severe language, the stern General set the tone for the capitulation of California by its citizen militia.

"Citizens of California, it is truly unfortunate that it's had to come to this, but you must all remember—you brought it to this. You gave us no choice. Right now, the United States Army is in control of every metropolitan area of the northern state. We have secured the areas of Redding, Chico, Sacramento, Stockton, Merced, Richmond, Berkeley, San Francisco, Oakland and San Jose, and we fully expect to take control of Fresno and the central state by tomorrow afternoon."

He glanced toward the cameras.

"Tomorrow morning, we will begin to shut down the California Aqueduct, one of the major water supplies of southern California's water system. That, in addition to the fact that our Special Forces have already taken control of every significant reservoir in the south state, presents southern California with a very big problem. You'll have no water. You'll be completely shut down until you're ready to comply with the demands of the U.S. government."

He nodded as he paused, seeking to clearly establish the government's growing advantage.

"To Governor Dobbins and the leaders of the California Militia—the government's demands are clear. Turn yourselves in and save your people. If you truly love our California and its citizens, spare them from any more stress and hardship than they've already had to endure. You made a profound error in judgment, but it was your mistake. Don't make innocent, loyal Americans in California pay for it."

General Hutchinson, a native Californian, was chosen because he was well known and well liked in the state. In fact, he had planned to run as a GOP candidate for the U.S. Senate seat in California that would have been up in the next general election. Whitmore and advisors had already decided that Hutchinson should be appointed acting governor of California once the attempted secession was quelled.

"To California Militia members who have been misled by Dobbins and other treasonous leaders: turn in your guns, surrender your weapons. Return to your senses. The federal government is prepared to grant amnesty to all militiamen and militiawomen who surrender and are prepared to help us defend the United States of America and its Constitution. The government has reassessed several of the issues that are uniquely important to southern Californians, such as border control, overcrowding and food distribution. President Whitmore is planning an emergency trip to California within the next two weeks in order to iron out those very issues."

He extended his arms and hands, symbolizing the government's willingness to support the state and its citizens.

"To all the loyal, patriotic Americans who reside in California: reject this nonsense about secession. It is treacherous, unnecessary and only serves to divide our nation, making America and Americans more vulnerable to outside threats and insidious terrorist plots.

"Reaffirm your faith in America, the greatest nation in the history of the world, a nation of the people, by the people, and above all, for the people. Let us as Americans, like our fathers before us, work together to establish justice, ensure domestic tranquility, provide for the common defense, promote the general welfare and secure the blessings of liberty for ourselves and for our posterity. Therefore, reject secession and its advocates. In these difficult times, let us embrace America and all it stands for."

He paused to signal transition and conclusion.

"I, too, am a proud and concerned Californian, but before all else, I am an American. Many of the soldiers who serve under my command are Americans from California. But make no mistake about it. We will *not* allow California to secede. We will do whatever we have to do to defend America, regardless of the consequences for our fellow Californians. It's the only way it can be. That's why it's so important for you to reject secession and turn in its leaders. Once that is done, we'll all sit down and deal with California's concerns, and I promise you, we *will* deal with those concerns."

His tone signaled conclusion.

"I have great faith in the good people of this state, and I am confident that you'll do the right thing. Let's save California from those who would do her tragic harm and from traitors and terrorists in our state and the world who would do America an even greater harm. The choice, people of California, is yours. Will you reject secession and remain loyal Americans, or will you follow the traitors and thereby declare yourselves enemies of our great nation?"

****

It may have been a glitch in security protocol. It may have been a communication *snafu* (an American military term for situation normal all fucked up), but early on, close sources were certain there was coordination from the inside. The entire grounds had been confirmed as secure.

Nonetheless, a huge explosion rocked the Presidio golf course clubhouse at precisely 18:00, lighting up the sky and igniting the old Presidio forest ablaze. Hummers and jeeps zipped about while panicked soldiers scrambled in every direction. When gunfire erupted from the other side of Lincoln Boulevard followed by several mortars, every soldier at the venerable military headquarters knew the post was under attack.

The Presidio, established in 1776, had a distinguished military history. Over the years, it had served as military headquarters for Spain, Mexico and the United States. It had been a major command post during the Mexican War, the Civil War, the Spanish-American War, World Wars I and II and the Korean War. According to historians, though it had become a national park, it remained a symbol of authority in the Pacific. It may have been the reason Hutchinson chose the location.

Once again, television broadcasts statewide were interrupted for a patched-in emergency message. The face that dominated the screen this time was familiar to more Californians. While his face appeared anxious and stressed, Dobbins forced himself to speak slowly.

"Fellow Californians, I come before you with heartening news: The federal government's attempt to subjugate California, has failed.

The arrogant asshole general who came before you thirty minutes ago spewing threats, intimidation, extortion and slander—he's confirmed dead. He was killed in an explosion fifteen minutes ago at the Presidio in San Francisco."

His face stern and serious, Creighton Dobbins nodded.

"I won't be able to say much before they find a way to kill this broadcast, but all Californians must understand that our new nation must not be surrendered. We are the fourth largest economy in the world, the fourth most powerful nation on the planet. We are thirty-five million strong. If we stick together, we cannot be defeated. You must all understand that. We will not lose!"

He took a deep breath to calm himself.

"Don't get me wrong. They'll hurt some of us. They'll even kill or torture some of us, but we must not let that deter us. We must fight on. We must endure the pangs associated with the birth of a new nation. We must—"

Simultaneously, television screens all over California went dark and eerily silent. It was a silence that, for the good and bad of it, endured for the rest of the night.

****

There's a sayin old, says that love is blind
Still we're often told, seek and ye shall find,
So I'm going to seek a certain girl I've had, in mind.

The soulful tenor's voice reverberated in the cold, thin air of the voluminous, crowded church, its vaulted ceiling stretching to the heavens. The congregation, family and friends filled all the seats.

Many more observers stood in the back of the church, packed against the walls. The doors into the church were wide-open, allowing still more to hear the service from the huge atrium.

She had many close friends, and many of them were in the choir where she used to sing. One of her former best friends, Brandy, sang in her place that morning.

Brandy was the soloist during *Soon We'll Be Done with the Troubles of this World*, the song Mahalia Jackson sang in *Imitation of Life*. It was ironic that Brandy had taken her place. This was the same backstabbing friend who had slept with Reggie when Layla was on the road with the Sacramento Monarchs.

Reggie sat up front at center, surrounded by his and Layla's families. His head was bowed. Tears flowed down his face. He was remembering Layla. He was remembering their last time out on a date.

They had celebrated Valentine's Day at the Ritz-Carlton New York Central Park. Layla spent over twenty-seven thousand dollars on the room package for the night. Reggie balked at the price, but she insisted it was worth it, that he was worth it. The room was a palace.

They had dinner at Bobby Vans on Park Avenue, where Reggie had the best porterhouse steak he had ever eaten. Layla had a scampi dish she raved about. Then they went to Rockefeller Center for a performance of *Romeo and Juliet* by the Royal Shakespeare Academy from London. It was an incredible night.

> *There's a somebody I'm longing to see,*
> *I hope that she, someday will be*
> *Someone to watch over me."*

When they got back to the room, Layla put on a sexy red negligee with delicate white trim. She wore red silk stockings, a red lace garter and red silk marabou slippers. Her spicy perfume warmed the darkened room. The gentle shadow ballet played against the walls, reflecting the flames from one hundred tiny candles, lit all over the room. Luther Vandross sang *So Amazing* in the background.

Reggie was already in bed, sitting up, watching her playful dance as she approached. On hands and knees, she crawled from the foot of the bed toward him and kissed his mouth. She kissed his neck and shoulders. She kissed his chest and stomach. Her face in his lap for thirty minutes, she made a valiant effort to wake the sleeping beast.

It stirred, reacting to the distraction, but then it returned to its slumber. Reggie apologized and volunteered to return the favor, but it was just an appetizer. There would be no main course.

> *Won't you tell her please to put on some speed,*
> *Follow my lead, oh how I need*
> *Someone to watch over me.*
> *Someone to watch, over me.*

After the service, Reggie was too weak to stand, so he remained in his seat as the line of family and friends passed by him, offering condolences. His red eyes cried behind the black glasses. He nodded and thanked a few people for coming.

His four brothers and two of Layla's cousins lifted the casket and walked toward the hearse waiting outside the church. A parent at each side, Reggie struggled to his feet, crying.

"Layla! Boo! Layla come back! Please come back!"

Only one person remained after Reggie, his parents, his family and Layla's family left the church. It was a woman who sat in the back of the second tier.

She wore a baggy black dress, a huge overcoat and a gray wig. The shape of her head and facial features were obscured because she wore a black hat and a black silk veil. She cried silently through the entire service, her eyes always returning to Reggie.

She wanted to go to him, to comfort him, but it was impossible. She also realized that, as he exited the church, it was the last time she would ever see his face. Weeping, she sat alone in the peaceful, hallowed space. Until that moment, it really hadn't occurred to her.

She had realized that her life would change, but she had not imagined that her sense of self-identity would be so affected. She had thought she would always be Layla, but that wasn't true anymore. For all intents and purposes, Layla Reed was dead. Now she was simply the *Matrix*.

****

"We are gathered here today to celebrate one of life's greatest moments, to give recognition to the worth and beauty of love and to add our best wishes to the words which shall unite Dexter David Williams and Susan Poindexter Whitmore in marriage. Should there be anyone who has cause why this couple should not be united in marriage, they must speak now or forever hold their peace."

The small, non-denominational chapel was located on the west end of Level Two. A gentle, non-denominational minister usually performed ceremonies, but this day was different.

"Who is it that brings this woman to this man?"

Davis Franklin, in a black tuxedo, escorted Susan, who wore an elaborate white-lace wedding gown, to the front of the room where Dexter stood.

"I do proudly, on behalf of her father, Joseph Scott Whitmore, president of the United States of America."

Davis stepped back as Dexter took Susan's hand. On Susan's right, Asia Franklin stood posed as her matron of honor. Little Blake was the flower girl. Asia, sensing her husband's glance, turned to look into his eyes. She could tell he was missing her. *Why was he being so damn stubborn?*

"Dexter and Susan, life is given to each of us as individuals, and yet we must learn to live together. Love is given to us by our family and by our friends. We learn love by being loved. Learning to love and living together is one of the greatest challenges of life, and is the shared goal of a marriage."

Adam Smock stood at Dexter's left as his best man. He was handsome in his dark blue, Italian-tailored Brioni suit. Standing there, his eyes monitored Asia's every movement.

"A marriage ceremony represents one of life's greatest commitments. But it also is a declaration of love. I want to read to you what Paul wrote of love in a letter to the Corinthians. I believe it is a true model of love, and I hope you pursue it in your marriage."

All the seats in the small chapel were filled while many stood, as Susan had invited everyone in the Crypt to the wedding. The only Cryptites missing were Dr. Benoit and the secret group she kept segregated from the rest of the population.

"Love is very patient and kind, never jealous or envious, never boastful or proud. Love is never haughty or selfish or rude. Love does not demand its own way. Love is not irritable or touchy. Love does not hold grudges and will hardly notice when others do it wrong. Love is never glad about injustice, but rejoices whenever truth wins out. If you love someone, you will be loyal to that person, no matter what the cost. You will always believe in them, always expect the best in them, and will always stand your ground in defending them."

Joe Whitmore didn't expect it, but he couldn't hold back the tears that trailed down his face. It was the totality of the event. This was his youngest daughter, a daughter he thought he had lost.

Here she was getting married in an underground shelter where she would have to live for the rest of her life. It was sad, and yet it was wonderful as he looked on her.

Susan was beautiful and strong, and so optimistic. It made him think of Jean and his own special wedding day so many years ago. The true advantage of youth was optimism. Despite the condition of the world, Susan had changed her destiny. She had defied convention, went out, found happiness and brought it back with her.

"Do you, Dexter, take Susan to be your lawfully wedded wife?"

"I do."

"Do you promise to love, honor, cherish and protect her, forsaking all others and holding only unto her?"

He responded, smiling.

"I do."

"Do you, Susan, take Dexter to be your husband?"

"I do."

Embarrassed by his tears, Joe Whitmore removed the handkerchief from his pocket and wiped his eyes.

"Do you promise to love, honor, cherish and protect him, forsaking all others and holding only unto him?"

She took Dexter's hand.

"I do."

"Dexter and Susan, as the two of you come into this marriage uniting husband and wife, and as you this day affirm your faith and love for one another, I would ask that you always remember to cherish each other as special and unique individuals, that you respect the thoughts, ideas and suggestions of one another.

"Be able to forgive, do not hold grudges, and live each day that you may share it together. Live each day and year as if it were your last, as from this day forward you shall be each other's home, comfort and refuge, your marriage strengthened by your love and respect for each other."

Joe Whitmore bought the rings at Tiffany's in New York. Susan's was a 1.5-carat marquis-cut diamond set in platinum, while Dexter's was an etched platinum band studded with diamonds.

"Wedding rings are an outward and visible sign of an inward spiritual grace and the unbroken circle of love, signifying to all the union of this man and this woman in marriage."

Taking Susan's hand, Dexter placed the ring on her finger. JR, standing in the front row, approached with the video camera to get a close-up of the event. Smiling, Susan held the shiny ring out for all to see, and then she took Dexter's ring and placed it on his finger.

"Dexter and Susan, in so much as the two of you have agreed to live together in holy matrimony, have promised your love for each other by these vows, the joining of your hands and giving of these rings, I now declare you to be married. Whom God hath joined together, let no one put asunder. By the authority vested in me as president of the United States of America, I now pronounce you husband and wife.

He nodded toward Dexter.

"You may now kiss your wife."

Nervous, Dexter looked toward the President.

"Really?"

"Really. She's a handful, Dexter, and now she's all yours."

Chapter 12

CALIFORNIA HELD HOSTAGE

SAN FRANCISCO – Sporadic though intense fighting continued for the sixth day as U.S. armed forces fight to liberate millions of Californians from the oppressive control of a homeland terrorist group that calls itself the California Militia, or Cal Mil. Recent estimates suggest Cal Mil armed fighters number more than 75,000, with perhaps as many as 125,000 more covert adherents and supporters dispersed throughout California's massive population.

The California Militia is led by former California Governor Creighton Dobbins, who fled Sacramento in February and commands loyal forces from an undisclosed location in southern California. Cal Mil is composed of an unlikely coalition of separatist groups, street gangs and extremists who advocate California's secession from the United States.

Six days ago, Dobbins and Cal Mil took responsibility for two deadly bomb blasts at the Presidio, which killed General Webster Hutchinson, eight officers, and 21 other armed services personnel.

"The Presidio attack, if nothing else," stressed acting Governor George Steffes in Sacramento, "demonstrates the savage extremes to which these terrorists will resort to coerce Californians into secession. It also tells us they've got operatives on the inside."

Three days after the Presidio blasts, nine Army servicemen were tried and convicted of sedition and/or treason against the United States of America. According to an anonymous Army spokesperson, all nine were involved in either providing classified Army intelligence to Cal Mil operatives or in planting two large bombs at the Presidio golf course clubhouse, where General Hutchinson and federal strategists had convened for a top-secret meeting. Despite rumors that the arrested servicemen had been tortured into confessing by Army interrogators, all nine were executed yesterday at an undisclosed location on the Presidio grounds.

President Whitmore called for military intervention in California on February 22 in response to pleas for help from Californians all over the state. In a CNN poll conducted late Tuesday, an overwhelming 75% of Californians oppose secession from the Union in any form.

More than 2,000 California residents from San Francisco and Los Angeles were asked a series of questions about secession and their views on Cal Mil. More than 40% considered Cal Mil a homeland terrorist organization. Many in the entertainment industry took the occasion to speak out against Dobbins and his "thugs with guns." [See "Movie Industry Speaks Out Against Cal Mil," page A27.]

Americans in other states were outraged by the news of the attack on the Presidio. During an emergency session of the U.S. Senate on Monday afternoon, California Senators Billy Towne and Antonio Villa were nearly lynched by a group of angry colleagues from the southern

United States. Several of the senators called for the wholesale bombing of all metropolitan areas of the state.

BELEAGUERED IRELAND APPEALS TO U.S. FOR RELIEF

WASHINGTON – Irish political leaders from Dublin and Belfast along with a united coalition of ministers have asked American President Joseph Whitmore and the United States to intervene in what many independent observers are calling "ethnic cleansing" and "crimes against humanity" by renegade British soldiers who have occupied both Northern Ireland and the Irish Republic since early December. Catholic Bishop Fred McAllister and Protestant Minister Benjamin O'Rourke led a delegation of local community leaders and clergymen to Washington yesterday, seeking relief from an "insufferable, inhumane and illegal occupation." Since the collapse of the United Nations in early January, many countries and people of the world have appealed to Washington to settle disputes.

Thomas Hyde, Northern Ireland's governor, was uncharacteristically emotional as he described atrocities committed by undisciplined and unmanaged British soldiers against helpless citizens from Londonderry to Armagh. He brought with him Amber, a 12-year-old girl who described being beaten and raped by the soldiers who savagely murdered her father and brothers.

Sinn Finn leader Keith Brennan insisted that the British government and military were intent on turning Ireland into a great brothel in order to spare British girls at home the humiliation and degradation of rape and sexual violence.

"I can offer the world irrefutable proof," claimed Brennan at a Capitol press conference yesterday, "that the British Army has made it a practice of sending its worst sex offenders and biggest perverts into Ireland to run amok. They're killing all the men and boys and raping the women and girls. If that isn't ethnic cleansing, then I don't know what is."

A spokesperson from the British embassy admitted there were widespread problems in Ireland related to raping and pillaging by military personnel, but she said these were not limited to British soldiers stationed there. She added that just last month, the British government had launched an investigation into the matter.

The delegation met with President Whitmore behind closed doors and emerged from the three-hour-long meeting with a reason for hope. The United States will be sending its own investigation team to Ireland in two weeks.

ONE MILLION STARVE TO DEATH IN KAZAKHSTAN

SEMIPALATINSK – Over the past week, International Red Cross workers have found bodies, sometimes thousands at a time, rotting or burning in cities and towns across Kazakhstan, formerly a part of the Soviet Republic. Kazakhstan, an emergent democracy resulting from the dissolution of the USSR, borders the Russian Federation in the north, Uzbekistan in the south and China in the east.

Officials in capital city Almaty blame the famine on nuclear pollution produced by Soviet atomic tests performed in the region. Many food suppliers assert that the diversion of waterways that normally empty into the Aral Sea has ruined the farming and fishing industries, causing the severe food shortages.

"The cause is not important now," lamented head of state Nursultan Mogzhan. "There is no food and thousands die every day. We don't need more talking. We don't need more pity or money. We need food."

Facing mass starvation in September, the government appealed to the affluent nations of the world for assistance, but none came. By November, alarming numbers of casualties began mounting. It wasn't until January, when a Red Cross task force traveled to the region to document the famine, that the plight of Kazakhstanis received international attention. In Kazakhstan, a nation of 19,000,000, more than one million are confirmed dead. Thousands more will starve before the Red Cross and the world are able to decide what manner of assistance and how much aid the region will receive.

FIRST IMAGES OF NOSTRADAMUS

HOUSTON – NASA officials today will reveal the first pictures of Nostradamus, captured by cameras on board the *Helios* spacecraft. Images of the 13-kilometer-wide asteroid reveal a solid, oblong object with a smooth, sculptured, metallic surface.

"It's just an ordinary rock in space," said noted NASA astrophysicist Louis Anapolsky. "It's not unlike literally billions of other rocks out there. Only this rock has Earth's name on it."

Employing ultrasonic and scanning devices aboard *Helios* from a parallel course toward Earth 1,800 meters away from the asteroid, NASA scientists are hoping to determine the exact physical composition of Nostradamus and its approximate weight in order to better judge what effect Earth's gravity will have on the asteroid and to gauge the sheer physical force of its impact on our planet.

The *Helios* spacecraft, launched last year on October 21, is a joint project involving corporations from the United States, Britain, Israel, Syria, Russia and Turkey.

DATE SET TO PROTEST PROPOSED SLAUGHTER OF PARK ANIMALS

NAIROBI – At an emergency meeting held on Monday, more than 3,000 of the world's most vocal animal activists, conservationists and naturalists assembled at Nairobi National Park to plan an international day of protest against the slaughter of park animals for meat. The conference was convened only four days after nations supporting the International

Hunger Task Force endorsed a broad plan that would ultimately harvest the rich wildlife resources of Kenya and Tanzania to feed millions starving in east Africa and elsewhere on the continent.

Nairobi National Park is home to four of the Big Five: lion, leopard, rhino and buffalo—only the elephant is missing. Of these, the buffalo and rhino would be harvested along with wildebeest, giraffe, zebra, eland, gazelle and other ungulates. Ostrich, warthog and monkey would also be slaughtered and packaged. By early summer, water would be diverted from the Athi River, allowing the park to harvest the region's hippo and crocodile for meat. A similar plan is underway for Kruger National Park in Johannesburg, South Africa.

In America, Yellowstone National Park officials are considering a plan that would harvest more than 3,500 American bison, 5,000 elk and thousands of moose, deer and black bear to help feed the starving in the United States, Mexico and Central America.

"Conservation and ecology are moot points today," said International Hunger Task Force Chairman Mekatilili Kenyatta last week. "To conserve these animals when people are starving! When August comes, the animals will all die anyway. When the world blows up, it won't matter that we have no more rhino."

In answer to Kenyatta's statement, Nature First spokesperson Linda Redmond responded, "All Earth's starving people are going to die in August as well. Will it matter in the end that they were able to eat a few more meals? It's *Homo sapiens* arrogance to the highest degree. *Nature* chooses which species survive and which become extinct. It's never been our choice."

"Let the starving people die!" Redmond shouted later in a 45-minute keynote address. "Natural selection *must* occur if man is going to have any chance for survival, and there is nothing natural about wiping out the last of a species to fill the stomachs of people already doomed to death. The world must stand up to protest this unnatural, ungodly proposal."

The international day for protest against the slaughter of park animals has been set for April 22, just two days before the Kenyan government is set to begin harvesting animals at the former wildlife reserve.

Chapter 13

"Midgarde is the world of man, or Earth. Anyway, according to the myth, at Ragnarok the Fimbul Winter will come, a time of famine and pestilence and earthquakes, a time when brother will turn against brother and peace and goodness will pass from the world. Ragnarok, the end of the gods, will result in the destruction of the universe: the heavens will disappear, the earth will be swallowed up by the sea and fire will consume the elements.

"From the cold will come Loki's children—Jormungand, a huge serpent from the bottom of the sea, Fenris, the wolf, typifying man's guilt and Hel, queen of the dead. There will be a great spiritual battle that the gods will lose. Then Loki's children, along with their father and his forces, will set about destroying the heavens and the Earth."

Davis sipped from his coffee cup, his eyes never averting from the animated young man sitting across the table in the dining room at Dubya's restaurant on Level Two.

"So in the end, everyone dies?"

"All the gods—each in a separate, ironic fashion—and all the mortals, except two."

"Two?"

Alan Chan nodded, his manner matter-of-fact.

"One man and one woman, and these will live on to re-create a human race that will exist in a universe without the interference of gods."

Davis still studied Alan's demeanor.

"So this Loki person—is he Satan? Is he the Devil?"

"Loki represents disorder, or chaos. His name means destroyer. Chaos destroys order, and by contrast, order destroys chaos. The Devil, on the one hand, is perceived as wicked, but Loki lacks the *moral* aspect common to Christianity. He merely represents the other side of the balance. Chaos and order balance each other in a great, repetitive cycle."

"And you favor chaos?"

It was obvious that Alan was enjoying the discussion.

"I favor the balance between the two, and that means *both* must exist. Time is the relative measure of the process that goes from order to chaos and chaos to order. Think about it. From the Big Bang ultimately came Davis Franklin and all the order he brought to the world we know. And now, where are we headed? Back to chaos as a planet, but in the big picture, the entire universe cycles back and forth between the two."

Davis hesitated, uncertain about how to structure the question. Finally, he simply blurted it out.

"What does the name or word 'misanthrope' mean to you?"

Alan smiled.

"Ah, a good word. From the Greek *misanthropos*—means a person who hates mankind, a person who would destroy all humans if he or she could."

Davis's pause was deliberate, as were his next words.

"And how do you feel about that? Would you destroy all humans if you could?"

"It's inconsequential how I feel, personally. If humans are destined to disappear from existence, the actual instrument or cause of their demise will be irrelevant. They'll just be gone."

Alan thought to himself for a moment before continuing.

"Of course, all the doomsday myths suggest that there will be *survivors*, reminiscent of Noah, Lot and their families from the Bible and reminiscent of Ziusudra, Untapishtim and their families from the Gilgamesh Epos."

Davis would not let up.

"So if there was a delete button, and let's say by pushing that button *you* could destroy all flesh on Earth, would you push the button?"

Alan's face took on an ominous character as the implication of the question registered in his mind. Smiling, he answered.

"Of course, destroying man means destroying the conventional god he worships. For what is God without man? In answer to your question—I wouldn't know. Not until the time came for me to make that decision. I mean, could you say right now whether or not you would push the delete button or not?"

Davis ignored the question.

"Do you believe in God, Alan?"

"No. I'm just like you. Science is our god. People like us are too rational to believe in any supernatural God. We don't believe in any Christ as our savior. For us, there's only order and chaos. For us, there is a scientific rationale for every event that has ever occurred since the beginning of time, even for the doomsday myths."

"And the scientific rationale for the doomsday myths?"

Alan closed his eyes and bowed his head, nodding. When he opened his eyes, he was smirking.

"It's so simple that it's almost stupid. They're all about cosmic debris."

"Cosmic debris?"

Alan wagged his head.

"Yes. Every so often, debris from out in space collides with the Earth. When it's been a huge impact, like the one at Chicxulub sixty-five million years ago, or like this Nostradamus one we're dealing with now, almost all life disappears from the face of the planet. But there have been smaller ones over the last five thousand years of recorded human history, and these have caused varying degrees of destruction on Earth: earthquakes, floods, fire raining from the skies, great islands sinking into the ocean, the so-called Dark Ages. From their struggle to understand these events, which reflect the balance between order and chaos on the cosmic scale, human societies have created their various doomsday myths."

Alan peered into Davis's eyes, trying to discern if he understood.

"In school, you ever remember reading the myth about Phaethon, the son of Helios?"

"Vaguely. Refresh my memory."

"Helios was the sun god. So one day his son, this Phaethon, he yokes his father's chariot—the chariot that carried the sun across the sky each day—and because he is unable to drive it along the course taken by his father, he crashes the fireball into Earth and burns the planet."

Alan flipped through a thick, black notebook and found an entry before continuing.

"In telling the story, Ovid says, '*the Earth caught fire, starting with the highest parts. With all its moisture dried up, it split and cracked in gaping fissures. The meadows turned ashy grey; trees, leaves and all, were consumed in a general blaze, and the withered crops provided fuel for their own destruction. But these are trifles to complain of, compared with the rest. Great cities perished, their walls burned to the ground, and whole nations with all their different communities were reduced to ashes.*' Sound familiar? Like I lifted a page from Dr. Smock's *Cosmic Impact Projections*, doesn't it? And there's plenty more where that came from."

Davis nodded in amazement.

"And where would I find—"

Alan handed him the heavy notebook.

"Here, take it. It's all right there. I'm leaving in a few days, and where I'm going, I won't need it. I'm already a part of it."

There was a hint of suspicion in the female voice that broke in from behind the men.

"Let me guess—a discussion about doomsday myths, right?"

Dr. Isabel Benoit wore an oversized white lab jacket and glasses. Her hair was pulled back as she stood with her arms crossed, speaking to Alan.

"You're thirty minutes late for your final physical exam and cold sleep prep. If you have any plans of surviving the journey, Dr. Chan, I suggest you get on down there now."

Alan stood, extending a hand to his lunch partner.

"Well Davis, looks like this is it. Today is my final day of life. For all intents and purposes, tomorrow I'll be in Tartarus. I look forward to the day you join me. I'm sure our first encounter there will be enlightening, if nothing else."

With Alan gone, Davis invited Isabel to sit with him for a cup of tea.

"I think there's something unsettling about him. I just don't trust him. Why'd you choose *him*?"

"He's the alpha male, the best genetic male specimen available on Earth today. Even going back to Eden or Lucy, whichever you prefer, there probably haven't been many like him. He's genetically resistant to just about every disease known to medicine, and beyond that, his immune system is virtually impenetrable. I was floored when the computer projected that, based on his health and metabolism, he could potentially live one hundred and fifty years or more."

Davis's face appeared even more concerned.

"So he's one of your breeders?"

"Like I said—he's my alpha male. Through the first five generations, almost thirty-five percent of the human population will be related to Alan Chan."

Isabel's face brightened as she glanced at the six-foot-eleven-inches, muscular, intimidating man coming toward the table. Smiling, she removed her glasses.

"And this is my gamma male."

She extended her hand as he approached.

"I'm glad you decided to come, Magnum."

She turned to Davis as both stood, tilting their heads back to look into Magnum's eyes.

"Davis Franklin, I'd like you to meet Magnum Barnes. Magnum, I'm certain you know Davis Franklin by reputation."

Magnum's eyes widened.

"I sure do. It's an honor, Mr. Franklin."

Davis was unnerved by the man's sheer size and the power of the hand clamped around his own.

"It's Davis. Just call me Davis. Magnum, is it?"

"It's Magnum, but most people just call me Bubba."

Isabel checked her watch.

"I was just headed over to the Med Lab, where I'm sure Dr. Hernandez is having fits about her missing gamma male. I'll walk you on over."

After Isabel and Bubba were gone, Davis sat and flicked Alan Chan's notebook open to a random page.

The Priest of Sais, a city in the Nile Delta which was a central point of contact with Greece, to Solon, Greek statesman: "There have been and will be many and diverse destructions of mankind, of which the greatest are by fire and water, and lesser ones by countless other means. For in truth, the story that is told in your country as well as ours—how once upon a time Phaethon, Son of Helios, yoked his father's chariot, and because he was unable to drive it along the course taken by his father, burnt up all that was upon the Earth, and himself perished by a thunderbolt. That story, as it is told, has the fashion of a legend. But the truth of it lies in the occurrence of a shifting of the bodies in the heavens, which move around the Earth, and a destruction of the things on the Earth by fierce fire, which recurs at long intervals."

It was as if Alan Chan had given him the book for a covert purpose. Perhaps somewhere in Alan's cryptic notebook would be the crucial proof that would either identify him as this "Misanthrope" character or the evidence that would exonerate him. Although Davis had never been one to believe in the supernatural, he had suspicions about Misanthrope from the beginning.

This person knew things that no ordinary person should have known. He or she usually knew computer protocols and access codes on the same day Davis created them. It was unnatural. It defied logical probability. Even the ever-changing computer-generated random codes were not totally secure beyond ninety minutes, limiting Davis's sessions accessing Calypso to forty-five minutes or less.

And Isabel Benoit's disclosure about Alan's genetic resistance to almost every human disease and his potential for living one hundred and fifty years! Unreal! Much to his surprise and against his scientific method of thinking, he was beginning to become a believer. Something supernatural was happening right under his nose.

He had never believed in God and had not read the Bible, but he had heard the word, *antichrist*, though he never understood its exact meaning. He understood it meant something bad, and more specifically, something bad for humankind.

Thus he wondered: Far from being merely this "Misanthrope" character, was Alan Chan trying to make himself this great destroyer he seemed to idolize? Was he trying to make himself, or was he in fact, Loki or Chaos personified? Was Alan Chan the great Antichrist, whatever that meant?

He was distracted from his thoughts and the notebook when he noticed who had just sat at the table across the aisle. Smoldering, he stood and walked over.

"Asia—I think you need to excuse us."

Asia began a protest, but after gauging Davis's expression, she bowed her head and slipped out of the booth. Davis's voice was angry as he spoke to the younger man still seated.

"I heard just today Dr. Benoit made you the delta male, Adam, and I realize you're leaving tomorrow. But you're playing a dangerous game here if you think you're going to have your last night with my wife."

Adam Smock raised a hand in protest.

"It's not what you think. We we're just—"

"It doesn't matter. You should just realize that Life Ark up there will be running on *computers*, and you should also realize that I created the operating system, the protocols and all the access codes for those computers. Your father has the codes, but I left myself a few backdoors. So I have the ability to cut the power to your cryopod and let you rot up there in space."

Adam stood, stuttering.

"It's not what you think. I'm sorry. I promise. I won't say another word to her. I'll stay away from her."

"I'm not saying you have to spend your last night alone, but my wife is definitely *off* the menu, you understand?"

"Yes, completely!"

Davis turned, anxious to leave.

"As long as we're clear on that."

He took his time as he walked toward the door. The bluff had worked, *but why* hadn't *he left himself backdoor access to Life Ark's individual cryopod controls?* All access had been turned over to Don Smock and his engineers in January.

In order to deny Misanthrope access to Lazarus, the supercomputer was endowed with a sixteen-tier series of complex anti-hacking programs that even the Lazarus system itself could not breach.

Somehow, Davis would have to find a way to either crack the impenetrable security system of the Lazarus supercomputer in his lifetime or convince Don Smock that unless the cryopod containing alpha male Alan Chan on Life Ark could be shut down or placed on extended stasis, the entire Lazarus Project and the future existence of humans on Earth might be at risk.

Chapter 14

The emaciated man reached toward the girl who brought in the juices, grasping her hand in desperation.

"If I go, and I never get the chance—thank you, young lady, for taking such good care of me."

She bowed her head.

"You don't have to thank me. I like taking care of you. It makes me feel better about everything for some reason."

Too weak to sit up, Rabbi Blum strained to breathe as he spoke.

"Is it because you're pregnant?"

She sighed.

"No, it's not that."

"Is it because the babies aren't Dexter's?"

She looked up, surprised.

"How did you know?"

"I've lived a few years, young lady. Besides that, Dexter was always very honest with me. Maybe because I wasn't his father."

"Does the Reverend know?"

He patted her hand.

"Jonah's a busy man. Besides, the thought of having a part of Dexter in this house probably makes them *both* feel better. It's given Aaliyah new life."

Brenda smiled, embarrassed.

"You really think so?"

"I *know* so. But sometime, before the babies are born, you've got to tell them. I might not be around, but you owe that to them and you owe it to Dexter's honor."

"But I can't—"

David Blum raised his hand, cutting her off.

"I'll give you my word I won't tell the Reverend I know, but only if you make a vow to me before God that you'll tell them before the babies are born that they're not Dexter's. No two ways about it. Will you make a promise before God?"

She stared at the Rabbi in silence before nodding, accepting the onus of the vow.

"Thank you, Rabbi. Yes, I promise I'll tell them the truth before the babies are born."

****

"You nervous?"

"Not really, but what's that you're putting on me?"

"It's a super-oxygenated, nutrient-enriched gel developed in the last two months specifically for this project. Under slight pressure, it'll circulate between you and the computer-controlled cryosuit you'll be wearing. Respiration will take place through your skin for the most part—in almost the same way it works with frogs and salamanders. Computers will feed you intravenously through an interface with the suit, and wastes will be passed through separate lines."

Layla looked over at the cryosuit on the table behind the doctor. Hours earlier, her body had been completely shaved. Her head was devoid of hair, her eyebrows were missing and all her body hair had been removed, though she was still pretty.

Over the last two weeks, she had undergone an unexpected transition. It started on the day of her funeral when she began to let Layla go, when she made a conscious decision to let Layla die.

As Layla departed, the Matrix began to assume her honored place as the mother of the next human population. She began to understand the importance of her role, the significance of her destiny. The Matrix had taken on the regal air of a goddess.

"Will I be the first one to be frozen?"

"You won't actually be frozen. You'll just be very cold. Your metabolism will be lowered to one-tenth of one percent your normal rate, so you'll actually age during the process. You'll just age very slowly. Three, maybe four months over four hundred years."

Layla reflected on the assiduous cryogenics research she had undertaken and asked the questions.

"And the cellular damage?"

Dr. Hernandez lifted the empty cup from the table.

"The solution we've had you drinking, we call that final process 'drinking the Soma.' It'll reduce the freezing temperature for all the water in your body. That way we'll be able to get you very cold and yet cause minimal cellular damage. Most of it your body will repair in the two-month-long recovery and repair period prior to revival. Believe me, this process is an incredible breakthrough. Think of the cryosuit as a high tech placenta. We'll essentially be returning you to the womb and suspending you there for four hundred years. A year ago, the thought of it was impossible, but necessity—it's the mother of invention."

"And the glycerol-based injection into my spinal fluid?"

"We do that after you're asleep."

Layla reached out with her hand and touched Helen's distended stomach.

"Does it move?"

Helen laughed.

"Only all the time!"

"Can I feel it?"

The Matrix touched Helen's swollen stomach and smiled. Her eyes filled with tears as she moaned aloud.

"I *felt* her. She responded to me. But, but she'll never know me."

She looked up toward Helen.

"What will you tell her about her mother?"

Helen's eyes were beginning to swell with tears as she stroked the Matrix's cheek.

"I don't know *what* I'm going to tell her, but I promise you this: I've carried her for you, and so I'm going to *love* her for you, with all the love I have inside me."

Layla sniffed.

"I brought a crate of little girl's clothes down here for her so she'll have new things as she grows. And I have a journal and videotape for her. All of it should have been delivered to your room this afternoon. I'd like you to give her the journal when she turns eighteen. Will you do that for me?"

Helen smiled.

"Of course."

Layla was crying.

"Thank you. Thank you for everything you're doing for me. But, but there's one more thing."

"What's that?"

"My husband, Reggie, or the man I was married to—he's a good man. He needs, he needs his *family*."

Helen squinted in confusion.

"I don't understand."

"If you like him, I want you to *be* with him. I want the three of you to be a family."

****

Over time, the tide had turned. It was a combination of nightly bombing, daytime raids and counterintelligence, but after fifteen days of a concentrated campaign by the U.S. military, the California Militia's strength in the state began to show signs of erosion.

The Army's response to the bombing of the Presidio golf course clubhouse was swift and severe, beginning with the execution of five guards and four other enlisted men accused of the seditious act. Soon after, U.S. soldiers canvassed neighborhoods in San Francisco, Oakland, Berkeley, San Jose, Sacramento and Stockton, arresting thousands of men and women accused of either being Cal Mil or being supporters of the California secessionist movement.

Many of these were executed after military tribunals heard specific charges and handed down death sentences. According to some estimates, at least fifteen hundred and perhaps as many as twenty-five hundred men and women were executed as a result of the tribunals. Many thousands more were killed during fighting in the cities and in rural areas of the northern state.

Over a period of three days, the California Aqueduct, a marvelously engineered concrete structure designed to carry precious water from the Mediterranean climate of northern California to the dry southern state was gradually reduced to a trickle. The reservoirs, lakes and rivers, located outside the metropolitan areas of southern California, and thus at safe distances from Cal Mil strongholds, fell under U.S. Army control. Only after huge populations began to panic about water shortages did the Army go into the cities with individual public rations. Extra rations were promised to those who could provide information that would lead to the arrest of Cal Mil leaders.

To accelerate Cal Mil's decline, the federal government attacked its financial base, beginning with the revenues the California Militia received from the state's renters. Under a special order from President Whitmore, the United States Army was authorized to collect rents in California. All monies were to be turned over to the Internal Revenue Service, who would issue checks to landlords after a 62% tax was taken. Many disgruntled landlords complained that they probably wouldn't see any real money from rents until July, when it would be too late to enjoy it. Yet for many others, late money from the federal government was better than none at all from the California Militia.

The shortfall made no difference to thousands of fiercely loyal and protective men and women who swore unwavering allegiance to the California Militia, but for the majority of Cal Mil fighters, no pay meant finding another quick source of cash and supporting Cal Mil in a tacit spirit. Two weeks after the initial invasion by the U.S. military, the California Militia's presence in northern and central California was virtually non-existent, as many loyal fighters fled to strongholds in the southern state where, ironically, there was still money.

Cloistered in the basements of financial district skyscrapers and in the population centers of Los Angeles and Long Beach, the uniformed California Militia prepared to make a stand against the United States Army, while a rumored twenty-two thousand other fighters, invisible in a sea of thirteen million residents, stood ready to carry the real battle.

Eight thousand soldiers from the United States military were stationed in two camps just south of the San Gabriel Mountains, while five thousand more landed and set up a base on Orange County's north coast. During the night, the Army and Navy released their elite forces, many in civilian clothing, into the Los Angeles area. Their mission was to search out and assassinate Cal Mil leaders and to destroy Cal Mil command centers. Notwithstanding, Special Forces commanders had specific orders regarding former California Governor Creighton Dobbins: He was to be taken alive for public execution.

****

He peered through the narrow opening at the door's edge.

"Franklin? It's me. I came because I didn't want you to get the wrong idea about me. Can I talk to you?"

The door swung open.

"Thanks. Just so you know, I have no idea where your wife is tonight, and I was figuring if you couldn't find her, you might think she was somewhere with me. I haven't seen her."

His unexpected guest inside, Davis shut the door.

"Neither have I. I've been looking for her. She's got my daughter, Blake, and she's been out of touch since three this afternoon."

Adam scanned the room. He had heard rumors about the technological wonders of Davis's personal residence, and yet so far nothing seemed extraordinary.

"Does she disappear like this often?"

"Sometimes, when she's on a vodka binge."

"She doesn't drink vodka anymore. Only wine."

Davis sat at the computer on the other side of the room and began typing.

"Really?"

"Yeah, it's just wine now. What are you doing?"

"Accessing the camera in her room."

Adam approached the computer.

"What? You *spy* on her?"

Davis spoke without looking up.

"All the cameras in the Crypt, whether they're off or on, have an access override I can control from here. I've never used it before, but here goes."

He typed a series of commands and stared at the monitor. Prompted to do so, he typed another series of commands. The screen instantly dissolved to a wide shot inside Asia's room. The title at the bottom of the display read, *Asia Franklin's residence, main camera*.

The primary living space was empty, though the television was on, but Asia always left the television on when she went out. A few keystrokes later, Davis and Adam were looking at her bed as the camera panned her room; both were empty. Davis smiled and sighed with relief. Blake's room was also empty. He closed the override program and sat back.

"It's a good thing you're here. I would have thought she was with you for sure."

"Would you have cared?"

"Of *course* I would."

Adam took a seat in a chair next to the computer.

"What is it with you, Franklin? You take the cake for no appreciation! If being here is any indication, you're the best in the world at what you do. You have a smart, beautiful daughter and an incredible wife who loves you in spite of the way you treat her. Everyone down here knows you treat her like shit—they all talk about it. They say you're in love with a computer program. Calypso? *National Enquirer* stuff."

Davis ignored the invitation to converse about his private life, but Adam continued.

"Do you love her? Asia—not the computer program."

Davis stared at the screen.

"Yes."

"So what are you *waiting* for? When are you going to show her that? You going to hold off till it's too late? I mean, I know you do important work here for the government, but what could possibly be more important than someone you love—especially if that person loves you as much as I know Asia does.

Davis bowed his head.

"And how do you know so much about how Asia feels?"

Adam wagged his head and shrugged.

"All right. I *did* make a play for her. I gave it my best shot. She was drunk, even. But she turned me down cold. You're the only person she wants. You're everything to her, Franklin, and the sad part about it is you don't deserve her."

Davis started to respond, but he stopped himself. Instead, he listened as Adam went on.

"Over six billion people on this planet will be dead in three and a half months—dead, but you're one of the lucky ones. You get to live, and more than that, you get to live with an incredible, fine-ass wife who's endured your utter stupidity for eight years and has always been there for you. All she wants is for you to pay some attention to her. She doesn't want *all* your precious time—just a little attention every once in a while, and you're too lame to even give her that! I used to admire you, Franklin, but now... Now I feel sorry for you. You're not half as brilliant as they say you are."

Adam had one more point to make before he was through.

"You complain about her drinking, but have you thought for once about how miserable you've made her? She's married to a *freak* who prefers a cybernetic fantasy he's created to a flesh and blood woman! You're *lucky* I'm leaving tomorrow. If I thought for once I had a chance with Asia, I'd stay. So wake up, Franklin—one of these days, she's going to find someone who's going to love her, and when she does, it'll be too late for you. You're the base Indian who threw away a pearl richer than all the tribe."

Thirty minutes later, both men were more at ease with each other. Adam announced his concerns about the cold sleep process Dr. Hernandez was using for Life Ark. Because Davis had written and tested all the programming and programming sequences for the cryosuits, cryopods and the Ark itself, he assured Adam that the project, through the return to Earth, was at least technically sound.

Adam despised Alan Chan, and he thought Magnum Barnes was a "scary guy, probably with some dark secret in his past." Magnum had been Dr. Benoit's choice for beta male from the beginning, but he had indicated, until late January, that he wasn't interested in being part of the project. Don Smock warned Isabel that Barnes might have a hidden military agenda and urged her to be careful where he was concerned. Thus Barnes became the gamma male.

The man who Isabel moved up to beta male was a huge, swarthy, muscular giant from an isolated tribe in the Jordan River basin. Dr. Benoit went there personally to recruit him for Life Ark. The locals called him Rephaim, referring to a tribe of giants, or *"men of great stature, whose fingers and toes were four and twenty, six on each hand, and six on each foot,"* who had inhabited the region long ago. Goliath, the Gittite of biblical lore, was said to be descended from the Rephaim. The giant called himself Ittai.

To Dr. Benoit's extreme fascination, tests performed on the giant revealed the latent genetic code for six fingers on each hand and six toes on each foot. He was seven-foot-nine-inches tall and powerfully built, though at thirty-five years old, he was more than ten years older than most of the other selectees. He spoke no English.

Dr. Philip Chenkovich, the fifth male selectee, was not designated as a breeder. He was a physicist-chemist-engineer-genius professor from MIT. According to Isabel, he was genetically flawed, though she did not elaborate on his inherent deficiencies. He was forty-five, the oldest on Life Ark, and he would be responsible for re-establishing and reshaping the technology of the new world. Despite his science background, he was a devout Christian.

Adam sat back, stretching.

"So what do you think about Dr. Isabel Benoit?"

Davis turned toward Adam.

"She's definitely a professional, maybe a little too Machiavellian for my sensibilities, but I guess you need someone like her in that position."

"I think she's totally hot."

Davis laughed.

"She's kind of pretty, but I wouldn't exactly call her hot. Glasses, baggy, frumpy clothes? And you call that hot?"

"I know women like that. They use that frumpy gimmick to throw you off. But she's a freak behind doors, a freak and I know it! I've met enough of them in my lifetime. I know em when I see em."

Davis shrugged.

"Maybe she is, but I just don't see it."

Adam stood.

"I got an idea. That override access thing you do with the cameras? Access Isabel's room."

"No, no, that would be an invasion. I couldn't do that. That would be wrong.

"Come on Franklin, you just invaded Asia's privacy without worrying about it. Besides, you've heard the rumors about Isabel. Maybe Asia is really over at *her* place when she disappears like you say she does. Come on!"

After Davis typed the command five minutes later, the screen dissolved to a wide shot of a seeming orgy. *Dr. Isabel Benoit's residence, main camera.*

Adam stared at the screen.

"Looks like a party and I wasn't invited."

Three women were washing a squealing suckling pig in a shallow tub.

"I recognize that woman! She's a surrogate. And that other one there—she called herself Misty. She doesn't speak English. Can you move the camera to the right?"

Intent on glimpsing Asia, Davis manipulated the camera direction controls. Adam called out.

"Stop! There's Chan. Waitaminute! Back up. I think you went past her. Go back. Yeah, right there."

The nude woman before the group of fifteen was draped in the sheer silken white robes of a High Priestess. There was a coiled golden serpent on her right arm and gold bracelets on her left wrist. Her breasts were exposed. Her headdress held a ruby diadem at her forehead, and her face was painted in a way that exaggerated her exotic eyes. Two other women stood behind her, mimicking her movements; they were also dressed like priestesses, though less elaborately.

"Didn't I tell you she was a freak?"

She held a golden vessel in her hands, filled with a sacramental communion of some kind. She raised it to her lips and drank. Then she uttered unintelligible words toward the sky and passed the vessel to one of the other priestesses, who repeated the ritual.

Adam's mouth fell agape in sudden realization.

"I know what this is. I read about it when I was nineteen. It's a goddess cult ceremony. They're speaking ancient Greek. That drink is called the kykeon. The whole ceremony deals with Demeter, the goddess of fertility, whose daughter Persephone is kidnapped by the infernal god, Hades. She looks for her daughter and can't find her. Then she finds out Zeus approved the abduction in advance."

Davis manipulated the camera to scan the faces of the other women in the room. So far, he hadn't spotted Asia. Adam continued.

"Demeter gets all pissed off, goes to a place called Eleusis and establishes her cult there. Because she's the goddess of fertility, she refuses to make the seeds sprout in the dark earth, and everyone starts suffering. There's a great famine on earth, and men don't even have gifts or sacrifices for the gods. So finally Zeus orders Hades to send the girl back up to be with her mother, though Hades contrives a way to have her one-third of each year. This whole ceremony is about the reunion between Demeter and Persephone and the blessings for participants in the goddess cult."

Adam closed his eyes, reading the words from a page in his memory.

"*Happy is he among men upon Earth who has seen these mysteries... Right blessed is he among men on Earth whom they freely love.*"

Content that Asia was not in the room, Davis was ready to turn off the camera until Alan Chan, in the robes of a High Priest, raised his hands to the sky. In each he held a relic, symbols of fertility sacred to Demeter and Persephone, and seeing these, all the women in the room began to prostrate themselves and utter phrases of praise and respect to the goddesses.

Davis cut the feed.

"What does all that mean?"

"I just told you."

Davis wagged his head, a sense of worry carving wrinkles around his eyes.

"I wasn't asking that. I meant what does all that mean for *Life Ark*? I wonder if your *father* knows about this."

"Wouldn't matter now. Launch is in fifty-eight hours. He wouldn't stop it. We'll all be in cryopods in the next twenty-four hours."

Adam shrugged and stood.

"Guess I'll have to see what it means when I wake up on the other side. I'll let you know. I'm late. I've got to go."

Davis stood.

"Do me a favor."

"What's that?"

"Alan Chan—if he wakes up on the other side, keep an eye on him. I think he could be a very dangerous person. I don't have time to explain everything now, but I'll try to send it to you. Between now and the time I die, I'm going to try to override Lazarus protocols to put him in permanent stasis until I find out what he's up to. If I'm not successful, you might take care of things on your end. You might have to kill him before he manages to destroy you all."

Chapter 15

He was already badly injured by the time Army Rangers kicked in the door and identified him crouching in a corner of the room. The early morning blast from the shoulder-launched missiles came as a surprise to the men inside the hidden fortress in the basement of a huge building in Los Angeles's financial district. The perimeter security and warning systems had apparently failed sometime during the night. Acting on a tip from an inside, high-level Cal Mil officer, the U.S. Army had sustained heavy losses in the prior day to stake a position within striking distance by nightfall.

During three days of intense fighting, the U.S. Army had lost more than five thousand soldiers in Los Angeles in battles against the California Militia and anti-government groups; most were victims of guerilla warfare and surprise attacks by small groups dressed in civilian clothing. Perhaps as many California citizens were killed as well, though there was no way to tell how many were Cal Mil soldiers. Three hundred fifty child casualties had resulted from U.S. Army attacks on buildings and other targets. If attitudes about the federal government hadn't been clearly polarized before, the attack on Los Angeles consolidated the hate and resentment many southern Californians felt for Whitmore and government policy in the state. Some influential Californians were vocal about their anger with the actions of U.S. military.

"Over the past three days, I have seen so many innocent women and children killed, crippled and maimed," lamented one prominent state senator, "that I fret when I consider what atrocities the U.S. Army committed in Afghanistan, Iraq and Sudan. If they can treat innocent Americans like this, what in God's name did they do to innocent people in those other countries?"

"Stand up and turn your crippled ass around, motha fucka! Don't think just because they got a price on your head I won't fuck your ass up!"

Shivering, crouching in the corner, California Militia leader Creighton Dobbin stood, his back still turned toward the arrogant Army Ranger.

"Now turn your ass around! Turn it around now!"

Dobbins turned. His whole face and his left shoulder were bloody. On the left side, his jaw was broken and his ear was missing.

An eighteen-inch-long portion of an exploded hot water pipe protruded from his upper chest. His eyes were full of hate and resolution as he raised his right fist.

"What's that?"

He spotted the wire.

"It's a detonation device!"

The Ranger's eyes followed the wire to the end of the room and then over to a cache of explosives.

"It's a bomb! Everybody get the fuck out!"

He aimed and shot at the wire along the wall to sever it, but he missed. By this time, a few of his partners were scrambling toward the door, but it was too late for them. It was too late for the thirty or more U.S. Special Forces agents and other Army personnel already in the building. Dobbins widened his eyes, grinning.

"Let's all go ta Hell!"

The fireball was huge. The explosion rocked downtown Los Angeles for six blocks in every direction from the blast's epicenter. Fire trucks were dispatched, and firemen doused the violent flames with thousands of gallons of precious southern California water, but the fire burned all night and was expected to smolder under collapsed debris from the building for at least a week. One thing was for sure: Far from being used by the government to symbolize the defeat of the California Militia, Creighton Dobbins had disappeared without a trace. For all Californians and the world knew, he was still in hiding, he was still alive and leading the militia from some undiscovered crypt.

****

"...Eight, seven, six, five, four, three, two, one... and we have launch."

The super-sized shuttle vibrated, seeming on the verge of shaking apart, as it streaked upward in the early morning Florida sky, propelled toward escape velocity by two huge rockets suspended on either side of its fuselage. The forty-four humans aboard in forty-four individual cryopods had been preserved in an artificial state of suspended animation where they would sleep four hundred years before returning to Earth.

Engineers on the project estimated the shuttle had to be launched by April 1, though Dr. Isabel Benoit had been instrumental in deciding the actual launch day of March 22. For three and a half months, NASA engineers would work sedulously to manipulate the shuttle into an energy efficient and safe orbit around Earth. From Earth, the engineers would initiate various computer programs aboard the shuttle to enable the vessel to avoid or to destroy incoming cosmic debris, to reassume the original default orbit pattern and to record and monitor events on Earth as they would unfold in August and beyond.

After fifty years, the shuttle would approach and attach itself to the completely reprogrammed International Space Station, where it would stay for the duration of cosmic winter. After conditions on Earth improved to the point that the reintroduction of humans would be feasible, the computers would initiate a "revitalize and repair" command on the cryopod computer system.

Two days before the launch, the forty-four cryopods arrived via C-130 transport at Cape Canaveral in the early morning and were transferred directly to technician-filled shuttle bays. For more than forty hours, engineers scampered about performing tests and analyses to make sure cryopods and cryopod computers were functioning within prescribed specifications.

Dr. Benoit was the last of the Life Ark selectees to undergo the process that would induce cold sleep. She smiled proudly as Dr. Hernandez stroked her bald head. Even her eyebrows had been shaved, giving Isabel a strangely "alien" look. The translucent, stretch-to-fit cryo suit, with dark lenses inserted to cover and protect the eyes, would make her look eerily similar to the aliens depicted in Hollywood movies.

Isabel sat up and kissed Helen on the mouth.

"And now, Doctor, the fate of the human race, the fate of life on Earth is in your hands."

Helen laughed.

"The Refugium, maybe, but I'll leave the heavy stuff to you, Smock and Davis Franklin."

She hesitated, her face becoming serious.

"So, you mean to tell me you *really* married him?"

"Yes."

"Now you know I'm not into that stuff, but from what I've read, I thought the marriage was purely ceremonial."

Isabel smiled.

"Not this time. This time it was the real thing in more ways than you might imagine."

"So what do I call you?"

"Isabel."

Helen nodded.

"Good, because I don't think I could ever call you anything else. In a hundred years, I could never think of you as Mrs. Alan Chan."

Chapter 16

"Mr. President, with all due respect, the time has come when we *all* must think about where we'll be on August 7th. You appointed me to this position because you said you trusted my instincts, and those instincts are telling me that you have to make that choice now... for the good of the country. It's already April, for God's sake!"

Joseph Whitmore sat at his desk, his head bowed, his eyes closed, his palms pressed together. Uneasy, Jett glanced toward General Draco at his left and continued.

"It's either Cheyenne Mountain or the Crypt. They're both in Colorado. Only, one holds your continued command, and the other your dear daughter. One will house five hundred people for five to ten years, the other one hundred people for up to one hundred years. Cosmic winter will last at least three hundred years, so of course, no one alive now will ever see the end of it."

The President opened his eyes and raised his head.

"I don't have a choice."

"What was that?"

"I said I don't have a choice. The American people elected me to lead this country in times of prosperity and in times of tribulation. It's not my fault or theirs that the tribulation has come, but now, with confidence in government as low as can be, they need me more than ever. If I gave up command now, I would do the American people immeasurable harm."

Jett reached across the desk toward his old friend.

"Joe—you're the fuckin president of the United States. You *have* to be protected, you have to go to one safe keep or the other."

"Why, Jett? When Nostradamus hits, what will I be the president of? There'll be no United States—just hundreds of millions of dead people. The only thing that matters right now is the four months we've all got left and what we make of them. I'm not going to any panic room. I'll be right here, speaking to the American people when it hits."

Uncomfortable with Whitmore's apparent resolve, Jett appealed to protocol.

"Let's be reasonable, Joe. Drake'll tell you. Your own security and the security of America are at risk here. With the collapse of the Mexican government in January, there's no telling who or how many terrorists and other operatives have entered the country from the southern borders. What we know is some of them are already here. And I don't have to remind you that al-Qaida is still out there. They're right here under our noses as a matter of fact. If they manage to kill you, or worse, kidnap you, what do you think'll happen to America and the American people you love so much?"

The President looked over at the General.

"What do you think, Drake?"

General Lucas Draco swallowed, cleared his throat and spoke.

"Mr. President, while I seldom agree with Mr. Turner's assessments and recommendations, I have to grant that any public or exposed leadership role you might contemplate puts you at risk, and worse, it puts the security of America at risk. I recommend Cheyenne Mountain. Protocols are already in place there for you to maintain command through August 7th and beyond."

Whitmore stood.

"I am the president of the United States and I'm not hiding from *anyone*. Any terrorists out there—they're your concern. You find them and take care of them if you have to. But the people of America are my concern. Their destiny is mine. If they're going to die on August 7th, then so am I. I will not run away. I will not desert them."

Jett shrugged, standing to confront the President.

"It sounds like a speech, Joe. You're good at making speeches, but let's get real here. This isn't some Hollywood movie where the president nobly sacrifices his life to stay with the people. The captain going down with the ship. What the fuck! I mean it's really happening! In three months all this'll be gone, everything above earth burned to a crisp. You can either be dead, or you can be at Cheyenne Mountain working to make sure that something survives."

Jett turned, speaking with his back to Whitmore.

"And you have a daughter. You could go to the Crypt and stay there. Isn't that what Oprah and all the love brigade are preaching lately: In the end, all that matters is the people you love and the people who love you? Love is all there is? All that's real?"

He turned and clutched Joe's shoulder.

"No one'll blame you if you go to be with your daughter. We can even set up a staged assassination so the people won't think you ran out on them. You *can* be dead for all they know. We can—"

Whitmore raised a hand.

"Stop."

He closed his eyes, massaging them through eyelids with his fingertips. After a minute, he sat, took a deep breath and spoke to Jett and Draco.

"Jean was right. She thought it all out. I didn't understand it at the time of her suicide, but it's just hitting me. There is so much we can enjoy right now. If we spend all our time and energy worrying about the future and about the fact that we'll eventually die, we'll never get to enjoy the here and now. We'll never see the sunrises, smell the first rains of spring. I'd never feel the summer sun on my skin, enjoy the song of a mockingbird, or *crickets* for God's sake. I'd miss it all."

He smiled, thinking of Jean.

"I'd rather spend three full, experience-filled months on Earth than a hundred years of existence in a dark hole in the ground. And just to say I'm alive? No, I won't go to either place. For once I want to live in the present. I'll live and die between now and August 7th."

He stopped.

"Why don't *you* go to Cheyenne Mountain, Jett? I'll make sure they save you a spot. They'll need someone down there with your unique abilities."

Jett turned away, mouthing the word "fuck."

"No, that's okay. If you're not going, then neither am I. Someone's got to stay up here and look out for ya."

****

Brenda's stomach was distended, owing to the fact she carried twin boys. Her stomach protruded forward and outward at both sides, though she hadn't gained weight in her legs, arms, neck and face. She struggled to walk in the morning, especially down and up the stairs leading to the bedroom she occupied in the Williams' home.

Yet by midday, she saw the stairs as a challenge and forced herself to exercise by completing ten staircase cycles per day. The excuse for the majority of her journeys up the twenty-two steps involved aid and comfort to her ailing friend and confidante, Rabbi David Blum. On April 9, however, that particular mission of nurturing and love came to an abrupt end.

The dinner table was set in formal order. The head of the table was reserved for Jonah, while there were two places at his right and two at his left. At his immediate right sat Aaliyah smiling, tears in her eyes, and Brenda sat at his left. Next to Brenda, a place had been set for Dexter, just as a place had been set for him since the day he disappeared. It represented the hope of seeing him again. Next to Aaliyah, a place had been set for Rabbi David Blum, Jonah's dear friend and brother in faith.

Even before the dinner prayer, Jonah bowed his head and spoke in a low tone.

"I would like to take this occasion to honor a man who, over the last few months, honored this house with his deep knowledge and discernment about spiritual things, through his teaching and his example, through his humor and his great faith in God."

Aaliyah was quick to concur.

"Amen!"

Brenda repeated the endorsement with even greater passion. Jonah paused, smiling, and continued.

"This has been a trying year for all of us. A great tribulation has fallen upon us. As we draw each breath, we cannot escape the thought that with each second, God's judgment draws nearer and nearer. Our faith is truly being tested."

He looked toward the empty place where Dexter used to sit.

"And it is this faith that allows us to endure the challenges and the great loss we feel. We might never understand exactly why God allows unfortunate things to happen to good people, but our faith gives us the hope that he'll work it all out for us. It gives us the hope that we'll see our loved ones again."

He took a deep breath and sighed.

"When I first met David Blum, I didn't think much of him. I knew he was a Jew and I knew he was a rabbi. That was ten years ago. After we talked a few times, he told me I should think about converting because he said I'd make a good Jew. I told him he'd make a good Christian."

Jonah smiled.

"I guess what we saw and appreciated about each other early on was the fact that, while our religions made us very different and while our respective traditions and lifestyles were different, our underlying faith in God united us in no ordinary way. United by faith, we grew to love each other over many years. I have met no Christian to whom I've felt a greater bond, and I believe he told me more than once he felt closer to me than he felt to any Jew."

He wiped a tear from his eye with a napkin.

"Naturally, our open friendship presented problems for both of us—from our respective congregations and from the Christian and Jewish communities at large. That didn't matter to us. It was their problem, not ours. Religion divided them, but our faith in God and our love for God united us. So we both became outcasts of sorts. We were Jonathan and David."

He paused.

"Last August, when we all heard about the asteroid, David and I realized we had it right all along. In this last year, during the next three months, religion, with all its divisions, arguments and grudges, will become entirely irrelevant. All that will matter will be our faith. It is our faith that will unite us or divide us in the end. Where will we place our faith? In God? Or elsewhere. It's the only question that matters."

He nodded.

"It mattered to David. When Dr. Levin told him he had inoperable cancer that would kill him, David had to choose whether he would put his faith in the miracles of modern medicine to save his life or if he should trust in God. He chose to trust God. The doctors called it a foolish gamble, but David was convinced the Lord would sustain him."

The tears from his wife's eyes filled him with great regret.

"Of course he took measures to help heal his body. He filled himself with fresh fruits and grain, blessings from God. He rinsed himself internally and externally with fresh spring water. He prayed constantly day and night. All that being done, he left it to God."

He stopped as a stomach growled to his right, while embarrassed, he moved toward his conclusion.

"As I watched his physical body waste away, I came to admire David all the more. Even as he agonized in his bed, he rose from the clutches of his affliction on several occasions to give me comfort and encouragement, as I know he did for both of you."

"Amens" from both women at the table.

"And so I'd like to take this moment to honor David for his faith and his example. I only hope I can demonstrate a faith like his as I face the tests ahead of me in the last days."

Unable to withhold comment any longer, Jonah's houseguest cut in.

"The cancer I survived, but I'll *starve* ta death for sure if you keep this up. Let's say we eat already."

David Blum had survived. His body wasted away through January and February, but by mid-March, oncologists performing tests were amazed to find that the cancer in his body was in remission. In fact, by April 2, and after additional tests and retesting, Dr. Levin declared the cancer was gone and that David's body was recovering.

The doctor called it a miracle of God. On April 9, David Blum told Brenda to find Aaliyah's *Jane Fonda Workout* tape if she needed exercise. He said he could get his own fruit and juice.

He was still underweight. At one hundred and twenty pounds, he had lost almost eighty pounds since December. Thus with no fat reserves, he was hungry all the time. He became dizzy if he didn't eat at regular two-hour intervals. Doctors said some of the weight would return, but it would be a slow process.

David was much more animated after the meal. He laughed and joked with Brenda about names for the twins, "maybe Leroy and Roscoe." He explained to Aaliyah why Lynda's cherry pie was superior to the peach cobbler on his plate. He joked that Jonah was blessed to be in the company of two wonderful women he didn't deserve, "women who certainly deserved much better." As he sipped green tea, he began with his own announcement.

"I was gonna let you all be surprised, but I talked to Lynda on Tuesday. Since her father died last month, she finally convinced her mother, Claire, to come back ta Los Angeles with her and Stephen, but first she had ta prove that California was still part of the United States. They'll all be here next week."

Aaliyah hugged him at once.

"Oh David! That is such *wonderful* news!"

Jonah smiled.

"Congratulations, David! I know what it must mean to you."

"Thank you. I thought I'd never see em again. The mother-in-law, I was kinda *hoping* not to see again."

As Jonah's eyes moved from David to the empty seat Dexter used to occupy, his countenance fell. He was happy for David, but for some reason David's good fortune and joy made him feel his loss more profoundly. Jonah's faith was solid, but for a first time, he worried that he might never see his son again.

Chapter 17

"Yeah, but you're workin. You have a reason for bein here. And Asia there? She's Davis Franklin's wife. Susan's the President's daughter. Dexter there's her husband. I've asked around ever since I got here last week. Everyone has a reason for bein down here, everyone but *me*."

JR wrinkled his brow as he thought, trying to discern an answer for the large man seated at his bar.

"One more time, exactly how *did* you end up down here?"

Asia and Susan listened as the man began explaining the story again.

"I'm in rehabilitation for that accident I told you about? So I go to see my doctor, Dr. Jacoby in Jersey City. So I'm sittin in his office and I feel myself gettin real sleepy. Then I wake up and I'm down here, and they're tellin me congratulations, tellin me I was chosen to survive the asteroid."

He shrugged.

"And next thing ya know, they're cuttin my shit, ya know—that vasectomy thing they do on every man comin down here. I told em my shit wasn't workin, but they cut it anyway."

He cringed at the memory.

"Anyway, someone told me you know alotta the secrets of this place, so I came in here."

Susan looked up from the notes she was writing.

"So you say your wife was Layla Reed, the famous athlete? And she was killed in a car crash in February?"

Reggie nodded.

"Yeah."

"Just an ordinary accident? No special circumstances?"

"Not as far as I know. Just a freak accident one day when she was drivin home."

Susan nodded, still writing.

"Freak accident, yeah. And did you see the body?"

"I went down to the hospital to identify her, and it was her. They slid a drawer out and she was on it. It was her."

Asia cut in.

"And she was definitely in the casket at the funeral?"

"Of course she was, I think."

He stopped.

"I mean I'm *sure* she was. It was a closed casket deal."

JR leaned close.

"That's funny. Why the closed casket? When you saw her at the morgue, was she all bloody and bruised up."

"No. Come ta think of it, she looked normal. When I saw a little blood on her forehead, I couldn't look anymore. I'm squeamish."

"Did you see any injuries?"

Reggie squinted, staring back to that time and place.

"No. No, just the blood. She wasn't torn up or nothin."

He panned the faces around him, the questioning expressions and the inquiring eyes unsatisfied thus far.

"I never thought about why it was a closed casket. I just figured it was what she wanted. Why? What are you all thinkin?"

Susan closed her notebook and sighed.

"Well, first of all, we think you're on the right track. All of us are down here for a reason, even you. But we don't know what yours is yet. I thought from the beginning there was something more to this whole government Crypt project. It's not about giving us a few extra years. Believe me, they're never on the level about anything."

Asia took over.

"None of us have been anywhere beyond Levels One and Two, but I've heard there are at least five. There's something else going on down here, and we're thinking maybe your wife has something to do with it."

Reggie was baffled.

"So you think *Layla* might be down here somewhere, alive?"

Asia answered.

"Possibly. Susan and I have been doing some research and investigation over the past few weeks, but so far we haven't gotten very far. JR's worried he might get thrown out if he gets involved, but you? Obviously someone needs to have you down here. So you want to help us?"

JR reached over and grabbed Reggie's left shoulder.

"You'll wanna think long and hard before agreeing to somethin like that. You don't even know the *reason* you're down here yet. They're leadin ya on."

Reggie gulped the last of his cognac.

"Of course I'll help if it means I might see Layla again."

He grabbed Asia's hand.

"Do you really think she's down here? Alive?"

Asia set the half-full wine glass on the bar.

"*Allegory of the Cave.* Anything's possible. And you don't have to help us if you think we're leading you on. You can spend the rest of your life down here in ignorant bliss if you want to, or you can pursue the truth, which comes at a price. The choice is yours."

****

By April 15, the California secession was officially declared dead by presiding Governor Steffes. There was still discontent in the southern state, but two visits by President Whitmore and beefed up protection at the southern border convinced many that California's interests were best served united with the other states of America.

All over America, people feared eleventh-hour attacks by foreign terrorist groups, and California was no exception. In the end, when citizens were forced to consider who could better protect the people of California from foreign enemies, they chose the already-mobilized American Armed Forces over the shadowy and mortally wounded California Militia.

The victory in California was a major coup for Whitmore for two reasons. First, it demonstrated to the world the lengths America would go in order to achieve its desired ends, and then it effectively put an end to populist secessionist ambitions of other states, namely Washington, Texas and Florida.

On April 17, the Army announced the beginning of Operation West Wing, wherein the entire state was placed on highest security alert status. Acting on intelligence gathered since January, the Army began its initially controversial process of arrest and execution. Officials admitted that mistakes would be made. West Coast Commander General Irving Cross acknowledged that a few innocent citizens would probably be unjustly executed,

"But in the balance hang millions of Californian lives. Experience has shown that all it takes is one man with a belt clip fulla grenades to exact tremendous carnage. So if you look like a possible terrorist or if ya were born over there, be careful what you do. If you've associated with any terrorist or received any communication from any of them—even a son or brother—now's the time to come clean. Turn them in and save your own life because we *will* be coming after you."

Three days after the U.S. Army's Operation West Wing began, the Middle Eastern, Latino and Jewish communities of southern California appealed to Whitmore for intervention. Leaders complained that rogue and undisciplined Army death squads, ignorant and lethally armed, were invading their communities and were killing hundreds of innocent men, women and teenagers. The arrests and executions, protested Antonio Garcia, a former state senator and the chair of an emergency "Brown" coalition, were based solely on a man's appearance and his ability to speak English.

"If ya have brown skin and dark, straight or wavy hair, they suspect you're a terrorist. That's strike one. Then if ya can't speak English too well, they think you're a terrorist. There's strike two. An last, if you weren't born here or ya can't prove you're an American citizen, you might as well kiss your ass goodbye, cuz they're gonna kill ya for sure."

President Whitmore, ignoring the urgent protests of top advisors, arrived in Los Angeles on April 22. True, a public appearance was risky, and interference with Army operations was politically unwise, but he insisted on making one last trip.

Air Force One landed on a secure runway at Fort Irwin in the Mojave Desert at ten a.m. There, Whitmore met for two hours with General Cross and the entire West Coast command. Careful not to undermine the objectives of West Coast operations, Whitmore urged the generals to reassess current policies regulating execution of suspected terrorists.

Then Whitmore met in Los Angeles with "Brown" coalition leaders, assuring them that, while the Army would continue to seek and destroy enemies of the state, commanders would be more sensitive to the concerns of the multi-racial, multi-cultural communities in the southern state.

The President overnighted at Fort Irwin. His dinner guest was a friend he had grown very close to during the last year. In fact, over the past few months, they talked as friends once a week. While they usually got together for a meal when he was in southern California, both were certain it would be their last together.

"You look weary."

"I *am* weary. I'm tired, Jonah. I'm tired of it all, but what do you do?"

"You could resign. You could let someone else take over."

Whitmore sighed.

"And so could you."

It was an old discussion, but the conclusion was always the same. For both men, family and personal interests were outranked by a profound dedication to the public good. One man considered himself a servant of the people and the other a servant of God.

"Truth be told, the main thing keeping me where I am is the fear of who they'll put in place after me and what they plan on doing. They're out there waiting, Jonah, and I don't know how long they'll let me stay where I am."

"Who are they? Do you know who they are?"

Joe raised a half-full brandy bottle.

"You mind?"

"Go right ahead."

Joe continued as he filled the highball glass.

"I don't know who they are, but they're out there, lurking in the shadows, hiding in dark corners, lying just beyond the realm of perception."

"Demons?"

"I don't know what they are."

He raised the glass and hissed as he sipped.

"Lately I've been thinking about Robert E. Lee. I couldn't fathom it last summer, but maybe he was right. Maybe there's more to this Nostradamus threat and a secret government agenda than any of us could have ever imagined."

He gulped from the glass again.

"I know they're out there, and I know they have a serious agenda. And I'm thinking it's an agenda that doesn't *include* me."

Perhaps it was the spirit in the room at that moment, but Jonah reflected on his own shrinking sphere of influence and the likelihood of his eventual ouster.

It was no accident that over the last two months, his broadcasts were canceled in fifty-two of the fifty-seven markets where they had once flourished; it was no accident the flow of donations Greater Faith received had slowed to a strangled trickle after the newspapers and the broadcast news ran unsubstantiated stories involving fiscal improprieties by the church; and it was no accident that Greater Faith was denounced by ecumenical societies as an apostate church.

Like Joe Whitmore, Jonah could palpably feel unseen forces working against him as August 7 drew nearer. Bowing his head, he reflected on a scripture that was on his mind of late.

For wide is the gate, and broad is the way, that leadeth to destruction, and many there be which go in thereat: Because straight is the gate, and narrow is the way, which leadeth unto life, and few there be that find it.

"Any news about your daughter?"

Joe hesitated, on the verge of telling everything.

"Nothing. Any word on your son?"

"No, except that he's supposedly going to be the father of twin boys."

Whitmore was more than casually interested.

"Supposedly? And I suppose the mother is Brenda Brown?"

Jonah nodded.

"At one time I disliked her, but she lives with us now. It's funny how things have changed in this last year. She's become a member of our family—she's like the daughter I never had."

"Really? And do you think the babies are your son's?"

"*I* don't think so."

After five minutes of silence, Jonah spoke with apprehension.

"You know, it's hard to let my guard down with people, but I can with you. If anyone, *you* must understand. I never admitted it, even to myself, but I've been thinking Dexter is... Well, I've been thinking he's *dead*. Otherwise, I know he would have found some way to let us know he was all right. We've had our differences at times, but he was responsible like that. I've heard nothing from him since he disappeared at the end of December, so I have to assume he's dead. I die a little each day at the thought of it."

He rubbed the tears from his eyes.

"The only thing that keeps his mother sane is the hope he's still alive out there somewhere."

Joe clutched Jonah's hand.

"He *is* alive out there somewhere. I know it. Don't ever give up your faith in that."

As both men stood, Jonah clutched Joe tightly.

"I needed to hear that, Joe. You lost your family, and I lost part of mine. I'm your brother, Joe. Liyah's your sister. We're your family now."

Joe clenched his teeth and batted back tears as he realized he would probably never see this "brother" again.

"Of course we're family. And don't worry about Dexter. I'm sure wherever he is, he'll get in touch with you and let you know he's alive and well. In fact, I know he will."

****

"Library, access encyclopedia, entry: doomsday, spelling d-o-o-m-s-d-a-y, read."

After ten to fifteen seconds, Calypso's voice responded pleasantly.

*"**Doomsday,** central point of early Christian, Jewish, and Islamic eschatology, sometimes called the Day of the Lord. References to it throughout the Bible are numerous. The Christian belief in the Last Judgment asserts that this world will end, the dead will be raised up in the general resurrection, and God, or his agent, will gloriously come to judge the living and the dead. The sinners shall be cast into hell, and the righteous shall live in heaven. These concepts are also common themes in early Jewish apocalyptic speculation. No generally accepted Christian teaching pronounces when Judgment Day shall occur, but many individuals have prophesied its date. Doomsday believers are called chiliasts, millenarians, or, specifically, Adventists."*

Programmed to read encyclopedic entries in 30-second passages, Calypso moved to the next command.

"Continue?"

Davis watched the entry text being printed.

"Quit. Entry: antichrist, spelling a-n-t-i-c-h-r-i-s-t."

This time, the response was immediate.

*"**Antichrist,** from the Greek 'antichristos', meaning 'adversary of Christ,' it is the name of the demon who is supposed to precede the Second Coming of Christ, as mentioned in Revelation 13 (also referred to as "the second Beast"). The Antichrist is also mentioned in the Bible in the First and Second Epistles of John, where the term is applied to anyone who in the "last time" denies that Jesus is the Christ, that is to say, the Anointed One."*

Calypso paused for five seconds.

"Continue?"

"Quit, exit encyclopedia."

Davis removed the entries from the printer bin, stacked them on the desk's corner and resumed reading from Dr. Alan Chan's black notebook. In the weeks following the Life Ark launch, the notebook, or the cryptic message to him contained therein, had become Davis's obsession. At one point, he wondered if the notebook itself was a set-up, a deception disguising a final effort to breach Calypso's elaborate security protocols.

The Life Ark launch was touted as a better-than-expected success by engineers at the Crypt's NASA Life Ark Project Command Center and a satellite station of United States Space Command located in a restricted area on Level Three. The cryopods were functioning within expected specifications, and the shuttle had settled into a safe deep-space orbit around Earth. According to data sent back and interpreted by the Lazarus computer, there were zero casualties so far. Earlier in the day, Davis had tried unsuccessfully to access the cryopod controls, but he was denied. Lazarus reported the attempted breach to the Crypt's computer security administrator, Davis himself.

While Alan Chan was his primary suspect in the Misanthrope mystery, Davis did consider other antagonists and possibilities. He speculated about the dual involvement of Chan and Isabel Benoit, especially after hearing the cryptic comments she made about Chan in Dubya's. And he became even more suspicious after watching Chan participate in the bizarre ceremony in Benoit's room.

If they were both involved, then shutting down Chan's pod would not be enough. And yet if Davis shut down Isabel Benoit's pod, the Life Ark project would die, and with it all hope for humans surviving the effects of Nostradamus. Misanthrope, whoever or whatever it was, would win.

If Isabel Benoit *was* involved, Davis was facing a lose-lose scenario: destroying her would doom humankind and not destroying her would also doom humans. With growing clarity, he began to see Isabel could be the key; she had refashioned herself as this Demeter, this mother goddess with remarkable power over fertility. If Isabel alone was Misanthrope, she already possessed the power to accomplish her aims. His paranoia grew.

But who had chosen her for the Life Ark project and why? Davis wondered about Don Smock early on. In fact, Don Smock was Davis's primary suspect before Alan Chan arrived. From the beginning, Smock knew about Calypso and, like Misanthrope, he had specific knowledge about her that defied reason. Smock also made ambivalent and incriminating statements from time to time, toying with Davis in the same way Misanthrope toyed with him in the emails and the note. More than once, Smock had likened the Lazarus Project to the Tower of Babel, a God-defying project, "whose top may reach unto heaven."

After investigation, Davis discovered Dr. Don Smock was a brilliant geologist and scientist who, like his son Adam, possessed a static memory—ninety percent visual recall, seventy-nine percent audio, seventy sensory and sixty-one olfactory and palate. Davis also learned of Don Smock's extreme fascination with computers, software programs and, more specifically, with Calypso. Davis was certain that the relative proximity to Calypso he brought, perhaps more than his own ability, caused Smock to choose him for the Lazarus Project.

If Misanthrope wanted to ensure the destruction of all humans, there could be no better station from which to accomplish that goal. As director of the Lazarus Project, Smock could change computer commands to sink Life Ark and ruin the Crypt. Yet if Don Smock was Misanthrope, there was at least the possibility of overriding all his access codes, rewriting commands and saving the project.

If Davis found proof to determine that Smock was Misanthrope, he would first have to figure a way to reprogram the entire Lazarus operating system and eliminate Smock's access or kill him in order to guarantee computer programs on Life Ark and in the Crypt would run as planned. Of course by killing Smock, he would probably get himself killed, but he had already determined that he was willing to sacrifice his own life to save the world.

And still there was the possible dual involvement of Don Smock and Isabel Benoit, with Misanthrope being a composite of two persons. Still more worrisome—perhaps Misanthrope was composed of three persons: Smock, Benoit and Chan working together. With each day that passed, Davis grew more frustrated, obsessed and uneasy.

It was April 29. *Only one hundred days until August 7!* He spent hours each day poring over Alan Chan's black notebook, hoping to understand and solve Chan's Cosmic Riddle. Overwhelmed by rife suspicions, he slept less and less each night, and his paranoia began to fuel itself on his resulting fatigue. He felt his very sanity slipping. Orderly and intellectual though she was, Calypso could not help him solve the riddle. In desperation, Davis turned to the one person in the world he knew who would understand his angst, the one person who could restore the balance he needed.

"Help me, Asia. I need you. I can't go on without you."

****

The succinct knocking, three staccato taps on the ancient wooden door, startled Jett Turner from the unplanned nap. Anxious and nervous, he hadn't had a good night's sleep since January. Since January, he knew it was coming, but he had no choice; he wasn't making the decisions.

Days before Easter—the last Easter the world would ever celebrate—he watched George Stevens' *The Greatest Story Ever Told*, with Max Von Sydow as Jesus Christ. As always, he was disappointed with the movie, and yet he felt a great sadness that he would never see it again.

Then, on Easter Sunday, he watched Andrew Lloyd Webber's and Tim Rice's *Jesus Christ Superstar*, with Carl Anderson II as Judas Iscariot. He had seen the movie at least a dozen times before, but he never truly understood it until that night. He completely sympathized with the anguished and put-upon Judas. Would-be martyrs left practical men with little choice.

"Good evening, Sir. Are you Jettson Turner?"

"Yeah."

"Got ID?"

Jett reached into his inside breast pocket, flicked the black leather case open and returned it to its place. Then he took the package, signed the mini computer screen and closed the door in the young man's face. He hesitated before pulling the tab to unseal the small parcel.

"Fuck!"

When he pried the lid open, a small cellular phone fell into his hand. Within seconds, it began ringing. He answered.

"Five, seventeen, thirty-one, seven, three, forty-three, eleven, one."

Pen at the ready, he copied the response from the person on the other end, and then he copied a phone number. Terminating the connection, he sighed with regret. He bowed his head, and then he dialed the phone number he had just written down. When he heard the click completing the new connection, he began reading the numbers he had copied moments before.

"Twenty-nine, five, nineteen, forty-one, seventy-nine."

A short beep indicated he had spoken the numbers correctly and slowly enough. Seconds later, a voice came online. He listened for a moment and answered.

"I talked to him, I pleaded with him, but he's determined to stay in Washington."

He paused again, listening.

"No, no, I don't think that'll be necessary. I think if I put it to him like that, he'll definitely see things your way."

He closed his eyes, listening.

"No, you won't have to. Give me a week. If I can't convince him in a week, then I guess you'll have ta do whatever you think you need ta do."

Chapter 18

April was a trickle, but May was a torrent. April was a shadow, but May was a shape. April was spirit, but May was blood. By the beginning of the month, the glorious cherubs of light and warmth had spread out over the valley and plains of the Midwestern states, driving the vengeful demon of cold back up the mountain and into hiding once more.

With the warmth and light came U.S. Special Forces, while deep in the mountain with the demon lay the heart and soul of the New Republic. The demon took its time, knowing that in a very short while it would prevail.

The advance of the U.S. Special Forces was not swift, nor was it without substantial loss of life on both sides. The ground assault began in late April when the snow began to melt, though the Air Force had flown strategic bombing sorties throughout the winter. Detailed satellite imaging allowed the U.S. military to detect unnatural concentrations of carbon dioxide and methane gases, which resulted from the respiration and waste of the thousands within the mountains, and to approximate the locations of the cave entrances. Based on that data, B-52s dropped over one hundred and seven bombs in the middle Rocky Mountains between January 6 and April 30.

The bombs were designed to send mortally concussive shockwaves through the cave complexes. Aware of U.S. cave-busting tactics, New Republic engineers created a series of dead-end passages and tunneled into the mountain from the sidewalls of these passages. Heavy baffled steel blast doors were installed flush with the sidewalls to minimize the stress on the protected openings.

In most cases, the shockwave traveled through the tunnel, impacted the dead end and rebounded back through the tunnel and out into the atmosphere. On February 26, one of the blast doors blew because lock-bolts had not been properly pumped into place. The seventy-two New Republic soldiers living in the natural cavern on the other side of the failed door were killed instantly.

New Republic engineers spent the winter pushing farther into the mountains and working to disguise perceptible signs of human habitation, while New Republic Special Forces spent chilly nights laying mines and booby-trapping areas leading to the approaches of the mountain caves.

In the meantime, Robert Lee and strategists were looking to an end game. By February, they realized the California secession was unlikely to succeed, diminishing hopes that Washington, Texas and Florida would also defect.

Robert Lee surmised that without the distraction of secession from disparate regions of the country and without the distraction of terrorist threats from within and without the country's borders, the U.S. Army would come after the New Republic army in full force.

Through a still-intact transportable radio station, he and lieutenants contacted agents on the outside and launched "Operation Distraction," where through a series of sustained attacks on military and political targets, teams of revolutionaries could create enough mayhem to hold key divisions of the U.S. Army and Air Force in place while the New Republic army, under the cover of weather and darkness, disappeared deeper into the central Rockies.

Captain Clyde, Shoshone elder and shaman, would lead the army into the treacherous and impassable mountains. No one in the world knew the terrain, hidden trails and the availability of resources better.

"In the path that the demon walks, we will follow. We will eat the scraps he leaves behind and pitch our tents in his spent camp."

Once the army had dispersed into the mountains, New Republic officers would set up a hidden headquarters, a loose command structure and a system for communications. Soldiers would dig in and forage for food and provisions.

In late July, the order would go out and the reunited army would assemble at a strategic location on August 5. There, Lee and other leaders would detail the New Republic's plan for survival and defense on post August 7 Earth.

Lee, Clyde and top advisors set out after the demon amid a nighttime blizzard in early March, leaving a plan for an organized exodus of the remaining troops from the cave complexes in the Absaroka Ridge. Clyde's Shoshone apprentices would lead successive groups of soldiers into the perilous mountains, following a series of cryptic signs posted by their master. Half the New Republic's Special Forces personnel would stay to defend the caves until the majority of the army had escaped.

From the beginning of May, U.S. Air Force bombing increased precipitously, setting up the expected ground invasion up the mountain. Despite the demoralizing impact of hundreds of tons of bombs exploding all over the ridge, New Republic Special Forces held their positions. A half dozen former Navy SEALs and Army Rangers were even brave enough to venture out in order to re-employ traps and mines after the most devastating raids. It was, in fact, this practice of re-employing mines and traps that accounted for more than seventy-five percent of U.S. military casualties in the early assaults.

The first casualties of the U.S. offensive, however, occurred miles away from the cave complexes of the Absaroka Ridge. On April 27, smoke from an open campfire led U.S. Special Forces to the foothills of the Salt River Range, less than twenty miles away from the craters and debris that had once been New Lexington. U.S. Special Forces crept up on the camp and observed fifteen young men eating a meal together at a long, wobbly, unfinished pine table. After determining that at least some of the bones in the refuse area were human, U.S. soldiers swept in with guns drawn. The team leader was aghast.

"What in God's name are you guys doing up here? You're *eating* people?"

The longhaired, unkempt teenager who responded slurred to the point of unintelligibility. His eyes were so puffy that his dilated pupils could barely be seen. Many of the boys were high.

"Man, we're so glad ya came. We're *starvin* up here!"

He extended a hand.

"My name's Danny. Ma dad was a Marine. Name was Buck Schaeffer. Purple Heart in Afghanistan. Maybe ya heard of im?"

The soldier waved a hand before his face to interrupt the stench of Danny's fetid breath.

"Back off!"

He recognized the odor.

"What have you kids been smokin up here?"

Another soldier called from the cave entrance.

"Killer Green Bud. Must have two kilos of it. They also got a shitload of guns in there."

Another teenager with raised hands approached the soldiers.

"We got guns, but we got no ammo. We got the KGB, but we got no food. Can you guys spare a few rounds of ammo for us so we can hunt? Got some bighorn sheep farther up the mountain."

The soldier slammed the boy in the forehead with the butt of his rifle, shouting as the cursing, bloodied and disoriented kid scrambled on his knees back toward the table.

"What the fuck do you think this is, huh? You think this is a fuckin *rescue* mission?"

Another soldier broke in, addressing Danny.

"Where are your folks, Son? Where're your families?"

"They're all dead. We're all that's left. There was bout two hundred twenty of us up here in January after they blew up New Lex, but we didn't have no food. Wasn't long for the grown-ups all turned on each other and killed themselves and a buncha the kids. But we're the survivors. We didn't ask for any of this. We're just ready to get outa here."

The team leader answered in an ominous tone.

"Fraid it's not that kinda mission, Kid. We're not here ta rescue you."

"Then what're ya *here* for?"

No answer coming from the leader, Danny looked to the other soldiers.

"We don't have a watch or calendar up here. Is it August already? What month is it? What *day* is it?"

The leader leveled his rifle at Danny's face.

"For the whole lot of ya, it's August 7th today. This is a search and destroy mission. Just do what we tell ya ta do, and we'll *all* be better off. It'll be quick and painless."

****

No sooner had she sat down to eat did she feel that irritating sensation again! The swollen feet, she could stand. The discomfort in bed, she tolerated. She had even grown accustomed to the constipation, shortness of breath and fatigue, but she would never be comfortable with the chronic demand to urinate.

On some days, she would have to go three of four times an hour all day long. It eventually got to the point that she hated the physical trip to the bathroom as much as she did the wiping. The constant wiping caused tenderness, irritation and inflammation *down there*, but it was worth the trouble. In three months she would have a healthy little baby girl. Her prayers had been answered. Through divine providence and the miracle of science, she would actually have the family she had sacrificed for her career.

When she returned from the restroom, Dubya's had gotten busy. Two of her lab technicians were eating at the bar, and there were three people she didn't recognize at a table on her left. At a larger table in the middle of the restaurant, she recognized several of the patrons. There was Susan Whitmore, the President's daughter, and her new husband, Dexter. Asia Franklin was at the table, along with her young daughter. JR, the guy who normally tended bar at Dubya's, was also there. And finally, Reggie Reed was seated there, his back to her.

Reggie Reed was the father of the baby Helen carried, though she had never met him. She eavesdropped and watched him as she nibbled on her grilled chicken sandwich. He was a little loud and obnoxious for her tastes, but she found some of his antics amusing, especially at times when he teased the little girl at the table. She watched him for twenty minutes, reflecting on Layla's last request. He was handsome, strong and funny. She thought he might be an adequate enough prospect for a husband and father.

Smiling to herself, she finished her lunch, collected her reading material and headed toward the door, only to be stopped by a booming voice that called out after her.

"Hey you! Waitaminute! Aren't you pregnant?"

She knew his voice. She didn't even have to turn, but she did.

"Now that would be a very rude thing to say if it turned out I *wasn't*."

He bowed his head, embarrassed.

"I'm sorry. You're right. But *are* you pregnant?"

"Six months."

"How'd *that* happen?"

She shrugged.

"You mean you don't *know* how it happens?"

Reggie stood on wobbly legs.

"No, I mean all the men down here have been cut, or so I thought."

He looked to the other men for support.

"I mean, right JR?"

JR nodded.

"Yeah Reggie, but some of the government people get ta go up top and come back down on business. They won't be stayin, so they don't get cut."

Reggie turned back toward the woman and took a few steps closer. He whispered.

"Hey look, I'm sorry. I didn't mean to put ya on the spot. It just struck me as odd, that's all. I haven't seen ya down here before. My name's Reggie."

She grasped his extended hand, speaking softly.

"Good to meet you, Reggie. I'm Helen."

Chapter 19

The pressure-sensitive tripwire had been set in January when there was less cover. It had endured fifty-eight inches of snowfall, shockwaves from dozens of bombs exploded nearby and a good part of the spring thaw without incident. Patrick Eisner, the engineer who set it, had been America's top munitions expert before he defected over to the New Republic, legendary because his traps were exceptionally creative, ambitious and lethal.

Two pairs of Air Force F-18 fighter jets streaked through frigid black skies over narrow and tortuous Coyote Pass, leading up into the mountains. In the distance, pilots could see the smoke trailing up from a recently bombed cave entrance.

Flying slightly above and behind the ascending jets was the Air Force's B-1 bomber, loaded with two of the Pentagon's latest weapons. The B-83, known as the Robust Nuclear Earth Penetrator, was a hydrogen bomb designed to slam into the earth at high speed and then explode underground. Developed by Lawrence Livermore Laboratories, it was two million times more powerful than the bunker buster bombs the Air Force had used against the Taliban and al-Qaida in Afghanistan.

Employing sonar and infrared imaging, the U.S. Army possessed the ability to look inside the mountains in order to identify tunnels, caverns and groups of soldiers. Military commanders knew exactly where the enemy was hiding. They could see twelve hundred or more soldiers living in a tight complex of tunnels and caves one hundred feet underground. Penetrating the mountain in order to get to them had presented the greatest challenge since January, but hopes were riding high on the efficacy of the B-83 and another cave-buster, known as the B-61.

The sun was outlining the horizon in shimmering gold when the B-1 and its escorts reached the target. As anticipated, there was some initial flak from ground-based anti-aircraft weapons. Two surface-to-air missiles were fired as the array passed, but they were jammed immediately and their launch sites were targeted. The B-1 released the bomb two miles before it flew over the target, and then it veered upward, disappearing in the clouds.

The U.S. soldiers and Special Forces inching forward on Coyote Pass felt the seeming earthquake caused by the B-83 explosion underground. Some rocked back and forth to steady their footing and some clung to each other, while others fell to their stomachs.

Coyote Pass, a narrow, winding trail leading up into the central Rockies, was an ancient, direct, though unreliable way into the mountains. Shoshone Indians and ancestors had been using the pass for more than ten thousand years in moderate winters. During severe winters, like the one just passed, the trail was completely covered with snow. An experienced guide might have wondered why it was so accessible that morning, but the young Indian who led the Army on the mission into the mountains was arrogant and unfamiliar with the old and genuine arts. Emboldened by the ease and speed with which he ascended, he urged the soldiers into the open jaws of the ready trap.

For the United States military, it was a practical gamble. Getting troops up the mountain meant either dropping them in or scaling the mountain. The problem with dropping fighters in involved the six to ten dozen former U.S. Army snipers on the ground. If troops were dropped from high altitudes, they would be cut apart by sniper's bullets as they descended. Dropping men from lower altitudes involved a great risk to aircraft, as the New Republic had trained specialists to fire surface-to-air missiles from shoulder-held rocket launchers with great efficiency.

Scaling the mountain also involved a degree of risk, but military strategists believed such a risk could be mitigated if not completely eliminated by heavy bombing in the hours prior to the surreptitious attack. Three thousand soldiers had waited at the base of the mountain for orders to begin the raid. Only after the B-1 reached Wyoming airspace did the Army begin to ascend Coyote Pass. In a little over three hours, the biggest offensive of America's war against the New Republic was set to begin.

The genius of Eisner's trap involved getting the U.S. Army strung out along the tortuous pass. During the summer, he and his engineers had secretly constructed a tree and rock dam a half-mile up the mountain. The construct had a gravel and rock base and was designed to trap snow along six miles above the pass. When it was filled, the gravity dam was barely noticeable in the landscape, its heel under thirty feet of snow, ice and rocks, its toe covered with a twenty-four-inch layer of powder snow.

The tripwire was attached to the underside of a huge boulder that blocked the end of the pass. This strategic obstruction was too large for any single human to clear. It was too steep and pointed for an army to go over, and it stretched from the cliff edge to the wall, making it impossible to go around. Blasting it entailed the risk of an avalanche. It caused a delay, with soldiers stopped, stacking up behind the boulder, like a line of ants reacting to an irregularity or blockage in the trail. The commander made the only decision he could make. Rather than marching the Army back down the pass, he decided to clear the boulder by prying it up and pushing it off the cliff edge.

The action of lifting the boulder set off a series of charges along the foundation of the rock, wood and snow barrier, allowing the compressive stress from the upside of the mountain to destroy the dam and cause the eruption of a tsunami-like wave of water, rock, ice and snow. The twenty-eight hundred soldiers on the path heard the explosions and watched in anguish, frozen helpless in the face of the immeasurable, almost cosmic force confronting them. Seconds later, it was as if the twenty-eight hundred soldiers and Coyote Pass never existed. The slate, with all its history, with all its Shoshone mythology, with the soldiers and their individual hopes, dreams, memories and more recently, their collective sense of abject horror, had been wiped clean. The demon had reclaimed the mountain.

****

Pregnancy was a global phenomenon. As the countdown of the last one hundred days continued, it became increasingly clear that individuals were making conscious choices about how they would spend their final months, weeks, days and hours. During September and October, millions of women and girls earth-wide decided they wanted to experience pregnancy and childbirth for a first or last time before the end came.

In the United States alone, an estimated thirty million pregnancies were underway, with thousands of babies being born each day that passed. The mothers' ages ranged from eleven years old to fifty-five years old, and in one extreme case, fifty-seven years old. Government officials on the federal and state levels and many prominent women from pro-life and pro-choice groups alike criticized the new and expectant mothers, calling them "extremely selfish for bringing babies into the world knowing full well they'll be dead in three months." The overwhelming response to the criticism was the reflection that every baby ever born has faced the same ultimate end. *A couple months or a couple days of life are better than no life at all!*

Scientists and sociologists explained that the increased pregnancy phenomenon was a natural reaction to the impending cataclysm. They called it Cataclysmic Preservation Syndrome, or CPS. According to science, human beings, like many animals researchers had observed, were instinctually inclined to breed prolifically in periods just prior to imminent natural disasters. The obvious rationale for such a behavior involved increasing the chances of a species surviving the disaster. Studies showed that generations born and reared *during* the challenging circumstances resulting from profound environmental changes had proven better equipped to adapt and survive.

The sexual activity that accompanied this innate drive to breed was no less astonishing. Sex had become the national compulsion. All convention and moral rectitude cast aside, men and women of all ages went at it with shameless abandon. The "quickie" became an established greeting between friends. Most of the still-existing workplaces had rooms set aside where employees could go to relieve stress by engaging in "chat room orgies," nonstop sexual encounters based on the Internet chat room model, with guests freely entering, exiting and moving in between rooms. Couples traded partners and loaned out their young teenagers, bartering for entrance and position in the most salacious weekend sex fests.

Many of the pregnancies were the result of unprotected sex. The use of condoms became absurd to men, while women abandoned the pill and other protective measures. The age of consent was lowered de facto to ten years of age. The penis became an idol of worship in America and the world over. Women openly wore large phalluses on chains around their necks for immediate self-gratification. As the days counted down, men and women became more frantic and desperate in their sexual urges. Few adults or young people spent nights alone or without having sex with at least one other person.

In the minority, however, were the voices that called for restraint and warned that lives of lechery and depravity would lead to certain destruction.

Among those was the Reverend Jonah Williams, whose television ministry had seen better days.

"And God spared not the old world, but saved Noah the eighth person, a preacher of righteousness, bringing the flood upon the world of the ungodly; and turning the cities of Sodom and Gomorrah into ashes condemned them with an overthrow, making them an example unto those that after should live ungodly; and delivered Lot, vexed with the filthy conversion of the wicked... The Lord knoweth how to deliver the godly out of temptations, and to reserve the unjust unto the day of judgment to be punished."

Following the media's lead, the American public developed a fixation on events of the last month, the last day, the last hour and the last minute. The question was constantly before the people. Much of the programming and the new shows on still-existing networks involved going out into America to find answers to the questions: How will you spend your last month? Your last week? Your last day? Your last hour? Your last minute? Your last few seconds?

Overall, the questions seemed to sober America. Americans certainly hadn't abandoned their sexual promiscuity, their alcohol and drug abuse, their profligacy, their shallowness and their egocentrism, but the questions forced individuals to at least consider the real meaning in life and death, the real meaning of existence. As Nostradamus drew nearer, individuals were forced to think about what gave their lives meaning. The answers were telling.

Although the majority revealed they wanted to spend their last minutes *in flagrante dilicto,* or in the act of sexual intercourse, almost twenty-five percent of persons surveyed had other ideas. A woman from Nebraska echoed a fairly common desire.

"I suppose when it happens, God willing, I'll have my eyes closed and I'll be huggin ma babies. I'll be clingin ta every one of em. And we'll be prayin and askin God ta remember us, ta save us. We'll be recitin Matthew 26:39."

Over the months, Matthew 26:39 had replaced John 3:16 as the world's most publicly displayed scripture. The words were spoken by Jesus himself when faced with his imminent betrayal and death.

"O my Father, if it be possible, let this cup pass from me: nevertheless not as I will, but as thou wilt."

Despite the mass exodus from the churches between November and March, by April many prodigal Christians began to return to the fold, Jews to the synagogues, Moslems to the mosques and Hindus to the temples. During May, even Jonah's Greater Faith Church began to show signs of recovery. Although the majority still put their trust in the mainstream Christian churches who preached the asteroid's impact would mark the coming of Christ and the Rapture, a surprising number believed that by their faith, prayers, righteousness and supplications to God, the world could be delivered from destruction.

The world and the people in it were deeply divided. On the one side were *love, joy, peace, longsuffering, gentleness, goodness, faith, meekness and temperance,* while on the other were *adultery, fornication, uncleanness, lasciviousness, idolatry, witchcraft, hatred, variance, emulations, wrath, strife, seditions, heresies, envyings, murders, drunkenness and revelries.* Religious affiliation was irrelevant. People identified themselves by their works. As August 7 grew nearer, it became increasingly clear that as all eyes turned toward the heavens, each person on Earth would be forced to take a stand. Each person would be forced to choose a side.

Chapter 20

"Dubonnet, chilled, stem, twist."

Impatient, she tapped on the glass while she waited and snatched the drink from the dispenser when it opened.

"Anyone else want a drink, you all know the rules."

It was the first time she had entertained guests in her quarters, but she felt familiar with everyone in the room. Not feeling especially gracious that night, she had initialized the "party bartender" program hours earlier.

She plopped down on the living room couch.

"So as you know, I had dinner with Davis last night. And while I'm sitting there, I'm thinking: *He doesn't have you here for you. He wants something, and it sure ain't sex. So what is it?*"

Reggie answered from his seat in an armchair.

"He's a flesh'n blood man and it's slim pickins down here. He wanted sex, right?"

"Wrong. He started asking me about *literature*! He starts with these mythology questions, and then he asks me about the Bible. He seemed... he seemed desperate."

Susan leaned forward from her place beside Dexter.

"Isn't he more the scientific type? Why would he invite you out after all this time to ask you about literature? What did he ask?"

"He asked what I knew about doomsday myths. He wanted to know about the Antichrist. He had some kind of black book he wanted me to look at."

JR called his question from the dispenser as he waited for his beer and another drink for Asia.

"So where is this book?"

"He wouldn't let me have it. He just wanted me to *look* at it."

Susan dragged her fingers through her hair, shaking her head.

"It doesn't make sense. There's something really strange going on down here. I mean, for the government to spend as much money as they must have spent on this place—especially when they already had Cheyenne Mountain."

Reggie interrupted.

"Cheyenne Mountain?"

"It's a huge military complex they built in the 1960s. It's inside a mountain here in Colorado, beneath two thousand feet of solid granite. They run NORAD and SPACECOM out of there. Cost somewhere around one hundred forty-two million dollars to build and twenty-three a year to operate. But I've heard the Crypt is bigger."

"So they have people living in Cheyenne Mountain already?"

"About eleven hundred people work there. It's a military defense facility, built to withstand a direct nuclear blast. One of its main functions is to preserve the chain of command during a nuclear attack or global nuclear war. It's where I figure my *father* will be on August 7th."

She paused, thinking to herself, and continued.

"But if Nostradamus is going to destroy all life on Earth, what good is a chain of command? Everyone'll be dead."

Dexter, reticent by nature, couldn't help continuing the implication.

"Unless the government's been lying to everyone about the asteroid all along. Maybe it's not as big as they've told us it is, or maybe it'll be a glancing blow like some of the scientists are saying. Maybe everyone *won't* be dead."

Asia raised her hands to halt the growing speculation.

"No. No, let's not start going down the Lee and Krebbs road. There *is* an asteroid out there. Astronomers have documented that. The government couldn't make it up."

Dexter wasn't through.

"But maybe it's smaller than they've made us believe it is. Maybe it won't even hit us. I don't know about you, but I don't believe everything the government puts out there. Their agenda's different from ours."

There was an uneasy silence before Reggie spoke.

"Let's get back to the point. If Cheyenne Mountain's function is military, and this Crypt is supposedly bigger, then what's this place for?"

JR answered.

"It's got something to do with science. Look at all the scientists, engineers and doctors they've got down here. And what about all those women who were here with Dr. Benoit? Did they go back up, or are they still down here somewhere?"

Reggie tapped his friend.

"Isn't that the group you said you thought Layla could have been with?"

JR hesitated before answering.

"I didn't actually see her, but I've heard there were more than a few black women with Benoit."

Susan stood, walked to the front of the room and turned to face the group.

"Will you all just hold on for a second? Now, the reason we're here is to come up with a plan of action, and hopefully whatever truth we're able to get at will provide answers to all our questions."

She had their attention.

"What we have to figure out is how we get at that truth. Asia, you're probably our best bet. You're married to the man who has some of the answers and who's probably got access to all the others. We need to find a way for you to reconcile with Davis."

Asia gulped the last of her drink and laughed.

"Really? Well maybe you know something I don't, Miss Nineteen. I've tried for months and I'm fresh out of ideas."

"Is he jealous?"

"Tried it with Adam Smock. Davis threatened him and he never talked to me again."

Susan shrugged and continued.

"Well, try it with someone Davis can't intimidate, maybe someone who might intimidate *him*."

"Someone like who?"

Susan hesitated and smiled.

"Reggie! Start dating *Reggie*! Davis'll go bonkers. He'll have to do something."

Asia looked over at Reggie and wagged her head.

"Davis would see right through it. Why would anyone date Reggie? His *equipment* doesn't work!"

He objected right away.

"It works now! It does—now it works."

JR sided with Susan.

"I think it's a great idea. Davis'll have to get off the fence. He's a born control freak. It'll drive him nuts. Tell im you'll help im out with whatever he needs, but tell im you're ready to either reconcile or move on."

Susan nodded, agreeing.

"Reggie, is it something you think you can pull off?"

"Datin her?"

"Making Davis jealous."

He smiled.

"I can do it. I'll be so convincing none of you'll know I'm actin."

Susan paused in contemplation.

"Good. In the meantime, I'll go after Don Smock. I'm going to test the limits of his patience, and then I'm going try'n get down to some of those other levels to see what's going on."

JR spoke to Dexter in a whisper.

"Rein in your wife."

Then he spoke to Susan.

"Listen Girl—I don't think you realize the danger you're courtin. You might be the President's daughter, but they're not gonna let you run around down here and ruin their entire multi-billion dollar project. Upset Smock, and he can make you disappear. I've *seen* it."

Susan considered his words and spoke aloud, trying to reassure herself.

"My father still *is* the president, and he knows I'm here. Smock wouldn't dare do anything to hurt me."

She crossed her arms, took a deep breath, went back to the couch and resumed her place beside her husband.

"One way or another, I'm going to find a way to get down there, and when I do, we're all going to find out what this Crypt is about."

When the phone rang, the room fell silent. Asia located the receiver and started to answer it, but she stopped. Turning, she reached over and handed the phone to Reggie.

"Hello?"

Attitude contorted his face. His voice boomed.

"What do ya mean 'who am I?' Who the fuck are *you*?"

A brief silence as he listened.

"Well, she's busy. She's... in the shower. Is there a message I can take?"

Reggie listened for a few seconds, removed the phone from his ear and turned it off.

"He says to turn on the TV. Says it's big."

No one in the room was prepared for the immediate images or text on the screen when the set came on, especially Susan. The picture was jerky, obviously the product of a panicked video photographer using a hand-held camera, but the text was clear:

BREAKING NEWS: PRESIDENT WHITMORE KILLED IN SUICIDE BOMBING ATTACK

Everyone in the room sat in horrific silence as the high-pitched British voice detailed the story.

"As is typical in these attacks, no one immediately knew the identity of the young woman who detonated the bomb, and so far, no terrorist group has taken credit for the bombing. Apparently, she managed to slip in among a group of young people who were to be included in the President's evening prayer. Many of these young people were survivors of the Echo Valley poisoning of last November. We have no details about how many of those young people were killed or injured. Early on, there was speculation that Robert Lee and the New Republic might be responsible, but as details have unfolded, and they're unfolding fairly rapidly here, a distinctly different suspicion is being offered by some top government officials.

"Just minutes ago, National Security Advisor Jettson Turner indicated he has reason to believe the government of Iran is responsible, though the Iranian president has emphatically denied having any involvement and has publicly condemned the bombing. Turner further indicated that, within a matter of days, he will be able to provide credible evidence that will link Iran to the assassination.

"If Iran is found responsible, one can only imagine that U.S. retaliation will be swift and formidable. But once again, President Joseph Whitmore is confirmed dead at the scene of what government officials are calling a suicide murder-assassination here in Washington. Back to you, Leon."

Chapter 21

"Why are you cryin, baby?"

Tears streaming down her agony-contorted face, she dropped her head and fell onto the table, sobbing.

"I'm sorry. I'm so sorry."

Aaliyah slid her chair over and began rubbing Brenda's back, consoling her.

"You're emotional. It's natural. I remember when I was pregnant, I cried every day for a month."

She continued weeping.

"No, you... you don't understand. That's not it."

Jonah's gentle voice urged the confession.

"Well then, what *is* it? Why are you crying?"

He offered a handkerchief to his wife, who gave it to Brenda.

"We love you. Nothing will change that. Now sit up and talk to us."

Brenda raised her head and wiped her face. She looked from Aaliyah's compassionate face to Jonah's steady, comforting expression. The tears began flowing again as she spoke.

"It's just that, you two have been so nice to me. You've taken me in and you've treated me like a daughter."

She wiped her eyes again.

"You've made me know what it feels like to be cared about. I never felt that way with my parents. They never wanted me, not even when I was little. Then, when I was on TV, they tried to make it seem like they cared, but they didn't."

The hurt in her eyes became anger.

"They couldn't wait to kick me out when I got pregnant—said I betrayed them, said I embarrassed them, but I didn't betray them. They let *me* down. They were my parents. They were supposed to love me, but they never did. They've never even called here to see how I'm doing."

Brenda shivered in her seat at the cleared dinner table, at last resolved to tell her story.

"I never betrayed them, but I've betrayed you."

Aaliyah's voice was tender.

"You've betrayed us? How?"

Brenda looked into Aaliyah's eyes.

"I lied to you. I told you these babies were Dexter's when I know they aren't."

She bowed her head and continued.

"Dexter and I never had sex. *I've* never had sex."

Aaliyah and Jonah exchanged a confused glance before Aaliyah began.

"Well, you're pregnant, and unless you want us to believe there's been some kind of Immaculate Conception going on, you had to have had sex."

"No, I was raped. My friend Joyce and I were *both* raped. It happened the night before they let us go. Earl Krebbs' guard raped us in his tent. That's where I saw the metal box with the poison. He would have *killed* us like the others if we didn't let him."

Her eyes were glazed over, fixed on the horrible scene being replayed in the distance.

"I should have let him kill me. Whatever he did to us, it wasn't sex. It was sickening. I watched him kill all those other kids, and I was afraid to die. I'm sorry."

Brenda looked to Jonah's face.

"It was my fault. Dexter and I planned on running away so we could get married, but he changed his mind. He stayed because he had parents he loved who cared about him, but I had nothing. So I got mad, and I went without him. It was a huge mistake."

She closed her eyes and bowed her head, trying to contain her emotion. After a moment, she looked up.

"When I came back, I felt different. I no longer felt like the clean, innocent girl he loved. I felt dirty, but like it or not, I had become a woman. Everything Dexter and I had, the ideal little world we dreamed about, died when I was raped. His name was Bubba Barnes, and he murdered a little girl the night he forced himself on me."

She reached out and grasped Aaliyah's hand in both of hers.

"The day I realized I was pregnant, I wanted to kill myself. My friend Joyce took one of those pink pills when she got back home. Her mother never knew what happened. I was going to take one too—I even had one, but I knew God wanted me to testify about the New Republic before the church and the world. And after that, I realized that while I could choose to take my own life, I had no right to take the life of any other person. I had no right to take the lives of these babies."

With one hand, she stroked her swollen abdomen.

"But my parents kept insisting I have an abortion. I was desperate, and so I came to you with a lie. I knew you were vulnerable, and I knew with Dexter missing, you'd accept me—even if you didn't completely believe my story. I'm so sorry."

Aaliyah put her arm around the crying girl, patting her back.

"It's okay, Baby. I know it's been hard on you—"

"Do you want me to leave?"

Aaliyah reacted with a degree of surprise.

"No! Is that what you thought? That we'd put you out? Is that why it took so long for you to admit it to us?"

Brenda looked up, pleading.

"You mean you *knew* all this time?"

Jonah answered.

"Yes, we knew, but that doesn't change anything. We know Dexter loved you, and since you've been with us, we understand why. You're a wonderful young lady, and we're glad to have you here."

"How?"

"How'd we know? Let's just say we've got a few years of age and experience on you. We knew the babies weren't Dexter's the day you came, but that didn't matter. You and your babies are part of our family now."

Aaliyah continued the endorsement.

"You and Dexter wanted to be married, but we wouldn't let you. If we had, maybe we'd all be together right now. The Lord has his own reasons and his own timetable for doing things. We just have to be patient. We can only hope and pray that one day soon, Dexter will come back to us... and to you and your babies."

Brenda smiled feebly, crying for joy.

"Amen."

****

Television sets all over the world were once again tuned to *The Titus Coffee Show*, the cable news program scheduled to precede the greatly anticipated swearing in ceremony. It had been a topsy-turvy week in June. President Joseph Whitmore was assassinated in Washington on Tuesday evening. Upon confirmation of Whitmore's death, Vice President Jack Bray was sworn in as president. However, on Thursday morning, President Bray convened an emergency joint session of Congress and indicated he would resign his office on Friday afternoon.

Rumors swirled in Washington on Thursday evening as insiders, analysts and professional prognosticators speculated about Bray's surprise resignation announcement and its significance to America and the world. Insiders suggested he was too old and didn't have the stomach or the heart for the job. Bray had undergone angioplasty surgery a little more than a year earlier.

Several analysts hinted that Bray had been pressured to resign by National Security Advisor Jettson Turner, along with other key Whitmore Cabinet members who wanted a more hawkish leader at the helm during June and July. Turner denied any involvement in Bray's decision and warned media leaders against fostering rumors that would poison the public. Political prognosticators predicted U.S. nuclear missile attacks on Iraq and Iran and on Chinese positions in North Korea.

In the wake of Whitmore's assassination and Bray's pending resignation, the American people began to consider who would lead the nation to the end of the conclusion. And so the world began to focus on Rep. Chuck Bentsen of Arizona, the man who was set to replace Bray as president of the United States.

Titus Coffee's guests were former National Security Advisor Ophelia Riego, former U.S. Vice President Norman Hertzberg and Jettson Turner, speaking in his capacity as National Security Advisor to President Jack Bray.

Titus began the discussion after a two-minute lead story depicting the turmoil of the past week and its international impact,.

"We've heard story after story this week about chain of command. There have been fantastic conspiracy theories, wild conjecture and, quite frankly, a good deal of misinformation. So before we get started here, would any one of you like to set the record straight about chain of command once and for all?"

Former Vice President Norman Hertzberg was quick to respond.

"It's actually not very complicated, Titus. In the case of removal of the president from office by death or impeachment, he is succeeded, in turn, by the vice president, the speaker of the House of Representatives, the president pro tempore of the Senate and the Cabinet officers in order of the creation of their departments."

Titus interpreted for his television audience.

"Which means when Whitmore was assassinated, command went to Bray, his vice president, who in effect has turned it down. So now command goes to Speaker of the House Chuck Bentsen, who by many accounts is a shadowy, pro-military figure who literally seemed to come out of nowhere when he became speaker just last month."

Jett was quick to defend the future president.

"Now we have to be fair here, Titus. Chuck Bentsen is a true American hero: decorated Marine, RECON unit He was special operations in Iran, Lebanon, Iraq—wounded in action in Iraq—Congressional Medal of Honor. You couldn't find a better man than Chuck Bentsen to lead America during these times of challenge and crisis."

Titus rebutted.

"But isn't that *it*, Jett? Many people in America think you did just that, and by you, I'm not suggesting you alone, but you, the National Security Council and some secret shady government agency. Many Americans believe you set this whole thing up after the assassination, that you handpicked Bentsen months ago because he was a company man who would carry your 'America versus the World' agenda without questioning orders. Then you pressured Bray to resign and there you have it—Jett Turner's running the show."

Not one given to even the slightest smile, Jett's laugh played counterfeit.

"That's absurd, but you and I both know something like that would not be impossible. It's not surprising that the conspiracy theory mill is running overtime lately. People are afraid and concerned, and rightly so. The American people have shown themselves very strong and courageous since August, and we have every reason to believe they'll adjust to the new leadership and support President Bentsen through the end of the conclusion."

Titus turned.

"Ophelia Riego, you once held the Cabinet position Jett Turner occupies now. Do you buy his contention that it would be impossible for the National Security Council to maneuver affairs in Washington in order to essentially call all the shots from here on?"

Ophelia, seated in a San Francisco studio, cocked her head as she listened to the question coming to her via an earphone.

"Titus, I simply don't believe your question and many of the questions we've heard lately are on the minds of the American people. I believe most of the questions and conspiracy theories are media driven, and that's unfortunate. Like Jett explained, people are afraid. As we move into July, we'll all be facing our deaths, our certain destruction, and there's nothing any of us can do about it. We can only hope we'll have a strong, steady government in place to provide leadership, comfort and a sense of security. I'll think we'll have that in Chuck Bentsen."

Sensing solidarity among his guests, Titus shifted to another subject.

"When considering conspiracy theories, one that's gotten a lot of attention lately is the Glancing Blow-Trilateral Commission-New World Order conjecture, wherein several prominent scientists and a group of former U.S. government officials contend the government knows that, owing to the curvature of the Earth and the shape of the asteroid, Nostradamus will deliver more of a glancing blow than a direct impact. They say the resultant damage will be significantly less than what the government has predicted."

Titus studied his guest's blank faces.

"Don't pretend you haven't heard it. They suggest billions might die, but possibly ten to twenty percent of Earth's population will survive. In the middle of it all is the supposed Trilateral Commission plan to create a single world government, a New World Order, if you will. Comments?"

After a noticeable silence, former Vice President Hertzberg responded with reluctance.

"I agree with Ophelia Riego, though she and I are *usually* on opposite sides. I don't think any of these outlandish theories are on the minds of the American people. I think they're purely media driven. There's no question that there's an eight-mile-wide chunk of metal on its way here. We can see it on *Nostradamus Watch* twenty-four hours a day. And we all know the one that killed all the dinosaurs was only six miles wide. It doesn't take a genius or a scientist to understand the degree of destruction we're facing. The American people know what they're up against, and they've shown tremendous character so far. I think they realize Chuck Bentsen has got some tough decisions to make, and I can only hope they continue to show their courage by supporting those decisions."

Since January, Titus Coffee and other news commentators had found it difficult to schedule high-profile government guests on their shows. Appearance requests were often answered with long lists of demands and conditions that compromised the integrity of the subject matter and the discussion. As a result, Titus had spent the last few months interviewing disaffected government insiders, outcast scientists and conspiracy theorists. On occasion, he got a juicy interview with Joe Whitmore or Jett Turner, but the majority of his guests were outsiders.

Prior to taping, Titus had been given a list of questions that had been approved by Turner, Hertzberg and Riego. Not surprisingly, all the questions were set-ups so that each guest could heartily endorse Chuck Bentsen's pending presidency. Rebellious by nature, Titus tried to steer the discussion in other directions, but none of his guests budged or strayed far from the script. As Titus sat there, he realized he had been played. He realized he had been set up by the government to lend a sense of objectivity and legitimacy to the Bentsen presidency. The questions he asked did not matter; in each answer was an endorsement.

He seethed in his seat, unwilling to continue the sham. For him, it was a defining moment. He could have sat silently while his three guests continued to perpetrate a con job on the American people, or he could have simply excused himself from the show, but he did neither. Instead he risked his reputation, his job and his life to speak the truth he believed. Turning toward his camera, he cued the director and scowled.

"All three of my guests today are liars. They're here to make you all believe Bentsen could be a *legitimate* president of the United States when he's nothing more than a pawn for Turner. You want to know who's running America? You're looking at him—Jett Turner, and he's a conniving, mean-spirited an dangerous man. But he's totally in charge. The only way America is going to avoid bloodguilt and disaster in the last days is to reject Turner, Bentsen and anyone associated with either of them. We need a leader who's from the people. The government is *not* to be trusted!"

His shocking statement finished, Titus rose and walked off the set, leaving his guests bewildered and fuming. He was in his dressing room for less than a minute before a hulking man in a suit and dark glasses came in, pinned him to the wall and slapped handcuffs tightly around his wrists.

"What am I being arrested for? I need to call my lawyer!"

The agent only slammed Titus' face into the wall. Titus' nose felt broken as the warm blood rushed over his lips, dripped from his chin and spattered on the floor. He groaned from the pain.

"I have a right to know. What am I being arrested for?"

The agent jerked Titus around and slammed the back of his head into the wall.

"High treason. It's a capital offense during martial law. You've sealed your fate, you idiot. You'll be tried, convicted and dead within the hour."

Chapter 22

Applying gentle pressure, he dragged his thumbs up the *latissimus dorsi* muscles on either side of her spine and stopped, using his thumb and fingertips to massage her *trapezius* on both sides. Tall, lean and muscular, he stood next to the bed, wearing only shorts, while she was nude. He took up a canister from the table, poured the vanilla-scented oil in one hand and rubbed his palms together to warm the oil before smoothing it onto her back. She moaned with pleasure, speaking.

"Did I tell you today that I love you?"

He leaned over her body and kissed the back of her neck.

"Only a few times. I love *you.*"

Abruptly, she turned over and threw back the sheet, inviting him into the bed.

"Prove it!"

Thirty minutes later, they still lay there, holding each other. His hand and gentle fingers stroked her cheek.

"Are you okay?"

"I'm fine. I told you I'm fine."

"Are you going to watch the funeral on TV?"

She sat up, turning away.

"No."

He tried to turn her face toward his, but she resisted. Sighing, he began.

"I know this is a rough time for you, and I know you don't want to accept it, but the whole ceremony thing is to honor him, to *honor* your father."

She crossed her arms.

"Fine, they can honor him in their way if they want to. I'll honor him in mine. He's not dead. I know it."

He leaned over and peered into his wife's distraught young face, worried.

"Okay, maybe he's *not* dead. But if that's the case, they did a convincing job with that tape. The explosion, the blood, his face—they all looked real."

"I don't want to talk about it."

After a long lull, he spoke.

"Okay, we don't have to talk about it, but there's something else we really do *need* to talk about."

"What's that?"

"You and Asia Franklin and your plans to figure out the real purpose of the Crypt. Before, you had your father and his clout as president behind you, but now, even if he isn't really dead, the world thinks he is, so you're on your own."

She rolled her eyes at Dexter, mimicking the way she had seen Aaliyah roll hers at Jonah.

"So?"

"So it's dangerous, and I don't want anything to happen to you. Let Asia pursue it if she wants to, but I don't want you involved in it. I don't want to lose you."

Susan pulled her knees to her chest, resting her chin between them.

"You really don't *get* it, do you, Dexter?"

"Get what?"

"Do you have any idea about *why* Asia and I want to know the truth about the Crypt? About everything the government's got going on down here?"

He thought for a moment, and then he shrugged.

"No. I can't say I do."

"Let me put it this way: Which existence would you choose? Fifty years of living in ignorance, frightened by the cost of getting at the truth, even when you know it's sitting right under your feet? Or a life that's possibly shorter, but a life that has meaning because there's probing, reason and discovery?"

He nodded in silence, letting her continue.

"I didn't ask to be down here. I wasn't worried about dying from the moment I found out about the asteroid. I'd rather be with your father and mother, in the church praising God when and if it hits. But I'm not going to live the rest of my life down here in ignorance, in a sort of darkness. There's more going on around us than what we see, and our lives mean nothing unless we struggle to get at it. I can only wish that you as my husband will be with me in that struggle."

Dexter leaned over and kissed Susan on the forehead.

"Now how could I possibly argue with that? Of *course* I'm beside you. So I guess now it's you, Asia... and me?"

"And Davis."

"Davis?"

She smiled, nodding.

"Asia says he doesn't trust what's going on down here either, and he knows a lot more about this project than *we* do. This sounds a little over the top, but according to Asia, the four of us and Blake might be the last and best hope for the survival of the human race.

****

Complying, he placed his right hand on the Bible.

"I, Charles Ashcroft Bentsen, do solemnly swear that I will support and defend the Constitution of the United States against all enemies, foreign and domestic; that I will bear true faith and allegiance to the Constitution of the United States; that I take this obligation freely, without any mental reservation or purpose of evasion; and that I will well and faithfully discharge the duties upon which I am about to enter."

The oath taken, former Marine Colonel Chuck Bentsen became president of the United States. Half the members in the special joint session of Congress rose to their feet and applauded, while others sat in their seats, still stunned by the sheer speed in which he had gone from virtual obscurity to unmatched prominence as the leader of Earth's greatest superpower. Time and circumstance had made him the most powerful man the world had ever known.

Remaining at the dais, President Bentsen opened a notebook and leaned toward the microphones.

"My fellow Americans, I assume this office during a time of grave urgency and concern. We are a strong and powerful nation, but we are a nation in great turmoil. Less than a week ago, the enemies of America managed to penetrate our highest security and assassinate the greatest symbol of America, our president, Joseph Whitmore. In many foreign countries, our enemies have spent the last year watching and waiting, seeking to exploit any moment of weakness or apathy in order to kill and punish Americans.

"Within our own borders, a substantial army of traitors and deserters from our military ranks still threatens national security from hidden positions in the middle Rocky Mountains. Even in our great cities, order has given way to chaos. On streets and in neighborhoods of Los Angeles, the Army is still at war with Creighton Dobbins and his California Militia. Several times in the last month, the curfews of New

York City have failed, leading to a massacre in the street last Thursday."

When he raised his left arm in gesture, all those watching him for the first time realized that three fingers of his hand were missing.

"Not unlike Abraham Lincoln, I take up the reins of office looking over a discouraging, dangerous and savage landscape. When Lincoln assumed office, southern states were seceding daily, and he was forced to make several difficult and controversial decisions. He ordered a blockade, he suspended habeas corpus, he called the state militias and spent money far beyond the legal limits of his office. Difficult and sometimes controversial decisions, but he saved America."

Some in the audience applauded, though the room returned to its uncomfortable silence.

"And that's why I'm asking for your patient indulgence in our last fifty days of life on this Earth. Many of you won't understand why I'll be doing some of the things I'll be forced to do, and some of those things won't be exactly nice, and that's where I'll need you to trust me. The enemies of America have sworn to make our very last days a living hell. As we bravely face our deaths on August 7th, they want us to sting with the pain of the punishment and persecution they plan to exact on us during our final days. As your president, I assure you that will not happen."

More applause.

"One of these enemies is the president of Iran, and another is the current leader of Iraq. Our CIA has provided us with irrefutable proof that the government of Iran is planning several attacks on U.S. domestic targets during the first week of August. In at least one of these attacks, there is a manifest concern that Iranian and Iraqi terrorists are planning to make use of low-grade nuclear weapons."

Not an eloquent speaker by any means, Bentsen was clearly reading from a prepared script. In several phrases, he stressed the wrong word. In others, his inflection was off.

"We also have proof of the Iraqi president's involvement in the assassination of President Whitmore. And that is why I will come before Congress again tomorrow to seek a formal declaration of war against the nations of Iran and Iraq. As president, I will use all the power, technology and weapons at my disposal to provide for the security of America and Americans all the way through the end of the conclusion. God Bless America! God Bless Americans!"

Chapter 23

"So, tell me the truth—do you still *see* him?"

She glanced up into his large brown eyes and smiled, pensively. "Yes."

"You in love with him?"

She placed her fork on the front edge of the plate and sat back, resigned.

"Yes, I think I am."

Helen Hernandez was born in East Los Angeles to a schoolteacher father and a dentist mother. It was the fourth marriage for her father, Don Julio, who was twenty-five years older than her mother, Vanessa. Don Julio had a total of fourteen children from previous marriages and other liaisons. Helen was Vanessa's only child.

Helen was bright little girl, and her mother noticed it early on. Vanessa wanted to enroll her daughter in a private school, but Don Julio was opposed to *wastin family money just so Helen could go out and be around a buncha white-ass kids.*

When Helen was six, Don Julio was shot to death in a mistaken raid of the family house by the LAPD SWAT team. Vanessa suffered a bullet wound in her shoulder and little Helen was severely traumatized. Nonetheless, the one hundred and fifty thousand dollar wrongful death settlement from the city was ample enough to ensure Helen's tuition through private grade schools; Mount Vernon College in Washington, D.C., where she earned Bachelor of Science and master's degrees in electrical engineering; and UCLA Medical School.

While at Mount Vernon, Helen became involved in the Women in Science and Technology Program. During postgraduate studies, she worked on the program's Human Genome Project, where she met and fell in love with Isabel Benoit. Thus when Isabel was selected to head a two-year human gene research project at UCLA, Helen applied to the medical school. At UCLA, Helen became involved in a cold sleep project and decided to pursue a career in medical cryogenics.

Despite the fact that Helen and Isabel were working in two disparate disciplines, they had remained close all along, spending weekends and vacations together when they could get away from work. So when Isabel was named director of the Life Ark Project, it was no surprise that she chose Helen to administer the Refugium.

Helen didn't typically date men, though for a first time, it seemed there was a little chemistry going on. She had felt stomach flutters while she waited for Reggie to come over for dinner on their first date. Her body tingled when he touched her hand and stroked her face that night. She even felt sexual excitement when he rubbed her back after dinner. It had never happened before. Not with a man. Perhaps it had something to do with the pregnancy.

"When they lock all the doors to this place in August, will he be down here or up there?"

She smiled, waiting for the server to clear the table, before answering.

"He'll be down here... with me."

Reggie didn't try to disguise his disappointment. Frustrated, he wagged his head.

"So what's *this* about? Why are you doin this to me?"

"What?"

"Playin with me. Playin with my emotions. I thought cuz he wasn't cut he couldn't be down here! You let me think you were gonna be available, when all along, you knew he was comin. You let me think you had feelings for me."

She reached over and grabbed his hand.

"But I *do* have feelings for you."

On their second date, Reggie and Helen went on a picnic with Dexter and Susan. The picnic area was a portion of a recently opened relaxation and wellness facility designed by Davis, called Franklin Park. Once inside the large room on the east end of Level Two, visitors could actually forget they were in the Crypt under thousands of feet of granite. Rather, it resembled a sunny, outdoor park in every detail.

The sky overhead was blue, though on some days, cirrus or cumulus clouds dominated the heavens. Fresh, soft **grass grew** underfoot, the shrubbery and small fruit trees were fragrantly real and a digital sun mimicked the actual sun in its trek across the skies, according to the season.

Finches darted from tree to tree, while graceful swallowtail and monarch butterflies danced in the garden, poising on flowers and leaves. Sunsets in the park were breathtaking. Breezes blew in the afternoon, and the temperature dropped off precipitously in the evening. The moon rose and set in the nighttime sky, as did the constellations. It was a wonderful escape from the routine of life in the Crypt. In every way, it seemed like a return to the surface.

Helen and Reggie's first kiss happened just after sunset on a late June evening, and oddly enough, Helen initiated it. She surprised herself by falling in love with Reggie. She thought about him constantly and doted on him, like a high school girl going steady for the first time.

There was a rational part of her mind that attributed her feelings and behavior to hormonal factors brought about by the pregnancy. Millions of years of evolution had probably predisposed pregnant women to develop deep physical and emotional bonds to men, who served as protectors, thereby increasing unborn children's chances for survival. Notwithstanding, science aside, she had fallen in love with Reggie, and it felt real.

Sometimes Helen thought of Isabel. She thought of all the wonderful times and conversations they had shared. But Isabel was gone, just like Layla was gone. It was useless to dwell on the past or worry about the future when there was so much living to do in the present.

Her eyes swelled with tears as she looked up into his anxious eyes.

"You're not understanding, Reggie. The man I'm in love with, the man I want to spend the rest of my life with, the father of my baby—do you want to know who he is?"

"Yes! I wanna see him, I wanna face him. I wanna tell him he doesn't deserve you. What kinda man is he anyway? You're pregnant! And where is he?"

She stroked his huge hand, took it and placed it on her belly.

"He's right here, Reggie. He's you. I'm in love with *you*. I want to spend the rest of my life with *you*."

She nodded.

"And yes, Reggie, it's you. *You* are the father of this baby."

****

Jett ran his fingers through his short, black hair and sighed as he lit another cigarette. His face seemed more tired and old. The man who sat across the desk from him studied his demeanor, concerned.

"You okay, Jett?"

Jett blew smoke.

"I'm fine. You know I'm doing what I have to do. I don't have a choice in the matter. It's not me, it's protocol."

The man nodded.

"I understand, but that doesn't make you feel any better about it, does it?"

During June, Jett Turner's Pentagon office had become the U.S. government's de facto seat of power. President Bentsen occupied the White House, led the military and rallied the nation, but it was obvious to government insiders and operators that Jett Turner and his National Security Council were calling the shots.

He dialed his secretary's extension, leaned forward and answered his visitor.

"I feel nothing. I got a job to do, that's all."

His eyes flashed before he responded to the voice on the line.

"Talk to Draco. Find out if anything's come in from those Predator missions we're flyin over the Rockies. Tell him we gotta find those bastards, today!"

Under President Bentsen's orders, the government had completed bombing all U.S. prisons earlier in the month, eliminating thousands of convicted felons and the need for guards and staff. Thousands more perished in jails around the country due to food poisoning and outbreaks of disease, freeing sheriff's officers for duty on the streets. It was enough to make death penalty opponents lament, "Our prisons and jails are empty, but our cemeteries are full!"

Elsewhere in America, F-16s patrolled areas outside government-controlled metropolitan areas, targeting and bombing camps, buildings, shelters and gatherings of people. Never before had government aggression against U.S. citizens been so fierce.

Jett hung up the phone, smiled and eased back in his chair. As he lit another cigarette, his eyes studied the man across the desk.

"My wife and son?"

"Arrived at the Crypt yesterday. Your wife is settled in. Your son is still in the infirmary recovering from required procedures."

Jett nodded.

"Thank you, Don. So, how *is* Dr. Benoit's Life Ark project?"

"So far, everything's gone as expected. The shuttle is in a safe orbit up there, and all the selectees survived the cold sleep induction process as well as the launch."

"And Magnum Barnes is *aboard* the Ark?"

Don Smock eyed Jett with suspicion before answering.

"He's Isabel Benoit's gamma male... against my admonition. I already *know* what Barnes is. My concern is that he's on a mission, with orders from you. Dr. Benoit says he's on the level, but I'm still investigating. If he comes up questionable, Jett, I swear I'll shut his pod down."

He stared into Jett's eyes as he continued.

"I mean it. I'll save the energy. You and I have been friends for almost two decades, so we can be straight with each other. I don't particularly like what you're doing up here. You might be in control of the government, but the Lazarus Project doesn't fall under your jurisdiction. I've got congressionally guaranteed autonomy. I don't take orders from you."

Jett laughed as he mashed the cigarette.

"Of course you don't, Don. Not for the Lazarus Project. But there is another way I'm sure you're going to help your government, and it has nothing at all to do with your precious project."

"Really? And how's that?"

"I need the locations, specifications, and engineering plans for every shelter, fortress and bunker ever built by your company, New Millennium Construction."

He opened a folder and withdrew a legal paper.

"Now, before you say you won't release the information or start to criticize my methods, I have to tell you I've gone through great pains to assure this executive order will stand."

Jett shoved the document across the desk toward Don, who lifted it and read. After studying the pages for over two minutes, Don raised his face and angry eyes.

"Why?"

"Classified, but you're supposed to be the genius around here. Figure it out."

Smock shook his head.

"Not even *you* could be that wicked."

"I'd rather call it expedient, or Machiavellian, whatever. My job here is to make sure that if anyone or anything survives your cosmic winter, it'll be American. But it's just like you to judge me when the pre-emptive measures I'm taking are actually assuring the success of your project."

Jett raised his hands in frustration and continued.

"I mean, what difference does it make if we take em out? Your company engineered all its shelters to fail in twenty years anyway! What did you care about people's lives when you did that? You knew they were all gonna die."

"Exactly! So if they're going to die, why would the government need to take the shelters out, as you put it? What difference should it make?"

Jett lit yet another cigarette.

"We're not takin any chances, that's all."

Smock stared at the document again, thinking. Hesitating, he began.

"Unless there's something more sinister going on here. Maybe Helen Engstrom was *right*. Maybe you guys really *did* find a way to manipulate telemetric data on a global scale—you've no doubt got hackers who can do that. Maybe it serves your purposes to exaggerate the asteroid's impact on the Earth."

Jett interrupted.

"Helen Engstrom was a brilliant scientist, but sometimes even brilliant people, under stress or dangerous influences, do very foolish things. Fortunately for her, she wised up and disappeared from the scene on her own. Has she contacted you recently?"

"No."

"Good. If I were you, I'd focus on the task at hand. Questioning and criticizing the government, rehashing and helping perpetuate these conspiracy theories, will do nothing but create problems for you and jeopardize your project. You want a new, improved human population on Earth in four hundred and fifty years? Do your job."

Jett checked his watch, his demeanor indicating that the impromptu appointment had run overtime. He spoke without looking up as he jotted a note to himself.

"In the meantime, the information I requested on the locations of the shelters your company built—I'll expect it in this office by nine tomorrow morning."

Jett looked up as Smock reached the door.

"And Don—"

Smock stopped and turned.

"Yes?"

"If you hear from Helen Engstrom, let me know. She's gonna surface sooner or later, and when she does, it'll be my job to make sure she disappears... for good this time."

Chapter 24

"So if we weren't down here, and you had to choose how you'd spend your last moments, what would you *really* do?"

Davis considered the question before responding.

"A year ago, I would have said, 'I'd be in control somehow, at the top of my game,' but my thinking's changed since then."

"Oh really? How so?"

"When the real impact of what's going to happen on August 7th finally sunk in on me, with ninety-five percent of all life on Earth wiped out in a week, I realized I was stupid to think I could control anything."

He gazed straight ahead.

"I've never been one to believe in God—you know that. But over the past few months, I've felt like I've been drawn to something. It's something huge, something more than I can begin to describe. A presence maybe? It feels like a presence, but sentient, and I'm connected to it. You think I'm crazy, don't you?"

Asia sat up in the bed, pulling up the sheets and tucking them under her arms. Her sweaty shoulders glistened in the light.

"Not at all. Go on."

He bowed his head and continued.

"I don't know. Maybe I *am* crazy. Maybe it's the work. But when I look out at the world and the universe now, I feel a connection. Before, I felt connected to nothing—not especially to you, and not to Blake. That's why I was so aloof and insensitive. But now I *want* to be close to you. I'm just glad I didn't wait until it was too late to come to my senses."

She studied his face, amazed.

"You don't sound crazy. Definitely out of character, but not crazy."

"There's something else."

He hesitated, reluctant to begin, and spoke.

"I've been having dreams. I don't remember any of them, but I just know they're related to this whole thing—Life Ark and what I'm doing here. And in them there is a distinct presence with me. There's something I have to do. I don't know what it is, but I think I'll know when the time comes."

Asia sighed.

"And I would imagine Alan Chan, Isabel Benoit and the Smocks are all tied in somewhere?"

She looked over at Davis, who nodded. Reaching across his naked torso, she took Alan Chan's black book from the nightstand next to the bed, sat back, opened it and read aloud.

"*I will ascend into heaven. I will exalt my throne above the stars of God. I will ascend above the heights of the clouds. I will be like the most High.*"

She stroked the black leather cover.

"This book's one big, clever, interconnected, chaotic riddle. You know that?"

"I know. The question is: Is there an answer to it?"

"I think so, but it's going to take all of us working on it—you, me, Susan, Dexter, Reggie and maybe even Blake when she gets older. We have time, but we're all going to have to work on it together."

She put the book down on the bed and turned toward her husband.

"Which brings me to my next question: Are you ever going to fill me in on secrets *you* know about this place? You ever going to tell me what's on the other levels? Why they made the Crypt in the first place? What happened to Dr. Benoit and all the women with her?"

She suddenly remembered.

"And what about the thirty-nine women and five men I read about in your classified notebook? If I'm going to be of any help to you, you have to open up to me, Davis. You can say you've changed. You can say you want to share everything with me. You've talked the talk. Now walk the walk. Now's the time to either put up or shut up."

Her eyes, filled with tears, pleaded her case.

"If you're really going to be committed to me, Davis, there'll be no more locked doors or security codes, there'll be no more ignoring me or putting me off, no more resentment for the chaos you say I bring to your life. We'll have to be open with each other about everything."

He turned toward her, tears swelling in his own eyes.

"You're right, Asia. I swear to you that from this day on I'll share *everything* with you: my life, my love, my hopes, my fears..."

He stopped.

"I love you, Asia. It was the wedding, Dexter and Susan's. But when I saw you standing there, tears in your eyes, and while I listened to the wonderful words Joe read about love and marriage, I fell in love with you all over again. I'm sorry for being so horrible to you. I'll never take you for granted again."

Davis and Asia embraced, trembling, holding each other for a while. Yet, the bloom of renewed love and passion faded for Asia because she still wasn't satisfied. A lingering, unsettling matter remained to be resolved, and for Asia it was personal.

"What about Calypso?"

"Calypso's gone. She's gone forever."

Her eyes searched his for signs of insincerity.

"Gone just like that? You were obsessed with her. I don't believe you."

He crossed his arms and nodded.

"It's true. As of 12:01 a.m. last Friday, I abandoned all Calypso's programming so I could find you again."

She kissed his cheek.

"Thank you, Davis. I'm proud of you. But I'm married to you. I understand you well enough to know you didn't scrap or erase all her programming. Where is she really?"

Davis smiled.

"Asleep in the ocean. I initially took her off-line in February to keep Misanthrope from getting to her, but I engineered a way to retain limited access. And I downloaded some of her sub-routines into a secret database here. Over the past few months, I've been eliminating Calypso-based programs from my operating system. I created another, less powerful, less intrusive program to run the house. So Asia, I'd like to introduce you to our home computer valet. His name is Sven."

He spoke the command.

"Please introduce yourself, Sven."

The effeminate male voice that responded had an unmistakable Swedish accent.

"Hello Asia, Velcome home. I am here to serve your every need. Your vish is my command."

Asia looked to her husband.

"No, that's not gonna work. You had this sexy, slinky Calypso bitch flirting with you and doing her best to shut me out. So then what do you give me? Some gay guy!"

"I thought he sounded like Arnold. He doesn't sound like Arnold?"

He spoke toward the ceiling.

"Sven repeat: I'll be back."

"I'll be back."

Asia wagged her head.

"No. That voice would drive me nuts."

"It's either Sven or Aunt Bea."

She smiled.

"Aunt Bea it is. Just as long as I don't have to hear the name Calypso ever again."

Chapter 25

The cavernous Refugium on Level Six dark, and the remaining space on the level was also dark, except for the tiny corner on the west end where Dr. Helen Hernandez had her office. She and colleagues had spent nine months gathering and preserving samples, the most impressive among those being the twenty-four newly weaned whale calves collected from various cetacean species.

The Refugium was divided taxonomically, with twenty-five percent of its area dedicated to preserving Monera, Plantae, Protista, and Fungi and with over seventy percent specifically set aside for the perpetuation of Animalia. Although Mammalia made up less than .006 percent of the animal kingdom, over fifty-five percent of the entire space available in the Refugium was used for mammal preservation.

Dr. Hernandez, from her lab in the Crypt, coordinated species collection with teams of scientists, biologists and cryobiologists at laboratories stationed on every continent and with seventeen teams at sea. Very little of the actual cryopreservation process was accomplished on Level Six. Rather, nearly all the creatures flown in were already in cold sleep stasis. Helen and Crypt biologists spent most of their time inserting specimens into customized, computer-controlled cryochambers and monitoring initial life signs.

The cetaceans were fully installed by early January, while fish collection was completed by the month's end. The arthropods proved the most difficult to collect and preserve, especially insects in imago form. Entomologists concluded that for many arthropod species, preserved larval specimens stood the best chance for survival over four hundred years of cold sleep.

Monera, Protista and Fungi were completed in February and Plantae was installed by March 10. With the completion of Mammalia on April 17, Animalia preservation was concluded and the Refugium collection process was pronounced a success.

On May 1, the Lazarus computer locked the Refugium and began to execute a series of programs that would preserve all life forms of Earth in stasis for more than six hundred years if necessary.

With the monumental task of preserving specimens of Earth's flora and fauna done, most of the scientists, biologists and cryobiologists had returned to complete their lives on the surface.

Only Dr. Hernandez, one molecular biologist, a zoologist, a botanist and an ecologist remained.

In May, the five began reviewing and rewriting the plans for the reintroduction of species into re-created ecosystems in a new world. Naturally, species would be reintroduced along the order of food chains, from bottom to top. Predators would be reintroduced only after prey species had reproduced healthy, growing populations that could withstand predation.

After the reintroduction plan was finalized on June 7, Helen, at eight months pregnant, began to perform the last of her duties as director of the Refugium. According to the plan, five scientists would be placed in cold sleep stasis in a chamber outside the Refugium on Level Six, and the five would administer the reintroduction of life to Earth after cosmic winter.

All were volunteers, aware of the risks involved. Thus the molecular biologist, the zoologist, the botanist and the ecologist were installed on June 20, taking up four of the five spaces available, but the fifth chamber was not empty. Many months earlier, there had been another person who had insisted, rather than volunteered, on occupying that fifth cryochamber.

———————————

Dr. Hernandez was at her computer when he arrived. He stood in the doorway, glancing up toward the ceiling.

"So it's all done?"

Helen nodded.

"We can't afford to be arrogant, but we've done it. Even if the Ark doesn't survive, we should be able to restore life to Earth from here. Prokaryotic and eukaryotic—we know life will survive this thing. We've exceeded all our expectations."

In the silence that followed, she squinted toward Smock.

"But you didn't come all the way down here to look at the locked doors of the Refugium, did you?"

Smock entered, hands in his pant pockets. Approaching Helen, he sat and crossed his arms.

"It's what I've always admired about you—your 'cut to the chase' attitude about things."

"I wasn't always like this. It's just that when we've been told we've only got one year and the clock's ticking, I've come to realize the futility of small talk. What's going on?"

Smock took a deep breath and sighed. He stroked his chin and nodded, acknowledging his hard wrought decision to himself before beginning.

"I had a meeting with Jettson Turner last month, and ever since that meeting, I've had these nagging doubts about some of the things Helen was claiming in the end."

"You mean Dr. Engstrom?"

"Yes. I told her flat out back then I didn't believe her. I thought it was impossible, but now I'm not so sure."

Helen removed her glasses, leaning forward.

"Are you saying now you believe the United States government or someone else hacked into worldwide data systems? Are you saying they introduced a superprogram that's overwriting and distorting telemetric data about Nostradamus on the global scale?"

"Maybe because it's July, maybe I'm going crazy like everyone else, but I don't know what to believe anymore."

"Believe me, I understand. So why are you *here*?"

Smock handed her a directive.

"I know this changes my twice-altered plans, but I want you to bring Helen Engstrom out of cold sleep. Can you do that for me?"

Helen shrugged.

"It's an involved process. Takes a minimum of forty-five days, but I can do it."

Smock tapped his temple with his right index finger.

"I'm old, but it's still static. The minimum's thirty-three days. You wrote it yourself in a report dated March 15, page eleven, third paragraph down. Are you saying now your report was in error?"

"No, I'm not saying that. It can be *done* in thirty-three days, but I would personally recommend slowing it to forty-five at the utter minimum."

"I appreciate your recommendation, but it's my call."

He stood, turning his body toward the door.

"It's July 2nd now—so we're figuring on having her back on August 4th. That's cutting it close, but yes, I'd like you to bring her out of it. Put in the command now."

Helen hesitated and began typing on her computer keyboard to access cryogenic restoration protocols. Abruptly, she stopped typing, looking up.

"Of course you know Dr. Engstrom was put under last October, at a time before we had fine-tuned the cold sleep initiation process. On the computer she seems fine, but there *is* the possibility of some side effects, possibly some brain damage, especially if we rush the process. A longer recovery of fifty to sixty days in her case would minimize the risks involved, but as you already know, thirty-three is the absolute minimum."

Smock nodded, assessing the potential danger to his colleague.

"Thirty-three days. If she comes through it all intact, great— she can finish the work she started. She can help us connect the dots, make a difference here. If she's brain damaged, then we all lose. I know Helen. I happen to think she would prefer it this way. Wake her up."

****

"For as the lightning comes out of the eastern horizon and shines to the western, so shall be the coming of the Son of man."

The flock had returned. Beginning on June 18, when the fifty-day countdown began, the prodigal had begun to swell churches worldwide. More than that, desperate people began to focus on the message, and that brought thousands back to Jonah's church.

It brought more than seven million television viewers who saw Reverend Jonah Williams as God's last prophet on Earth. Jonah ignored the sweet words of praise poured out by his followers at every public appearance, opting instead to call himself "the humblest of God's servants."

"But directly after the distress of those days the sun will turn dark and the moon will not give its radiance, and the stars will fall from the sky, and the powers of the heavens will be shaken; and then will the token of the Son of man appear in the sky."

He paused.

"And this is from the Byington Bible, and it says, '*then will the token of the Son of man appear in the sky.*' Now we have to remember that this token of the Son of man that will appear in the sky happens *after* the sun turns dark and *after* the moon gives off no light. So it's logical to reason that, if that token or sign of the Son of man appears for us *after* the sun and moon turn dark, then we, the faithful, have to be around to *see* that token. And to see that sign we can't be dead. Look to your faith, Brothers and Sisters, *for if ye have faith as a grain of mustard seed, ye shall say unto this mountain, Remove hence to yonder place; and it shall remove and nothing shall be impossible unto you.* Look to your faith, Brothers and Sisters, for the Lord God has heard our earnest prayers and supplications."

The congregation responded with shouts of agreement and praise to God. Jonah raised a hand to quiet the crowd before resuming his sermon.

"The world's leading scientists have predicted a horrible cosmic winter after the asteroid's supposed impact. They've painted a dreary, scary, hopeless picture for us. They predict an era of total darkness that no human on Earth will survive, a time when the sun and moon no longer dominate the sky. The sun and moon, they've told us, will grow dark."

Aaliyah sat in her usual seat, nodding, amening and encouraging her husband. Brenda Brown sat next to Aaliyah, holding her hand as both listened.

"These same scientists tell us we're all going to die, but what does Jesus tell us? Does he say, *'the sun and the moon shall grow dark and ye shall all die'*?"

The congregation answered, "No!"

"No, he didn't say that. Jesus said, *'the sun shall be darkened, the moon shall not give her light, the powers of the heavens shall be shaken.'* Jesus specifically says that *after* these things happen, *'then shall appear the sign of the Son of man in heaven.'* He says, *'then shall the tribes of the earth mourn,'* and then *'they shall see the Son of man coming in the clouds of heaven with power and great glory.'*"

In the Crypt beneath two thousand feet of solid granite, Dexter and Susan sat cuddled on a couch in front of the television. They had been able to watch Jonah's sermons on cable since national coverage resumed in late May. In fact, Dexter and Susan had encouraged so many others in the Crypt to listen to Jonah's message that all activity ground to a halt whenever he was on. Nearly all the televisions in Level One residences were on as Jonah's message resonated within even the most remote and hidden places of Earth.

"August 7th will be a defining day for all of us, Brothers and Sisters. For where will you be on that day? And what will you be doing? Will you be in the house of the Lord, filled with the Holy Spirit? Or will you be in some dark, dungy place, filled with corruption, carrying out your fleshly, bestial inclinations right up to the last moment? If that won't define who you are, Brothers and Sisters, I don't know what will."

He paused for effect.

"Will you soberly hold your children, your parents, your brothers and sisters, your friends and fellow believers as you share your faith in the Lord and your love for each other? Or will you be high on alcohol or drugs, engaging in mindless, meaningless sexual intercourse, clutching and groping blindly, or letting yourself be groped and used by some drunken and ungodly person you hardly know? Is that how you ultimately want to define yourself, your life, your very existence?"

The audience in the church was silent as the import of the questions bled from their minds into their hearts.

"August 7th will be the day to choose. You'll have to choose who you are. You'll choose in what and in whom you believe. Your faith will be put to the test. You alone will have to decide whether you will serve God the spirit or your own flesh. Will you place your faith in the Lord Jesus, our Savior? Or will you become as senseless, frightened beasts, groping about in darkness, where there shall be weeping and gnashing of teeth?"

Even Jettson Turner was watching Jonah on television, though for a very different reason. Jett was interested in the Reverend's growing influence and his interpretation of upcoming events. Curious about how he himself fit in apocalyptic Bible prophecy, Jett taped all Jonah's sermons and analyzed them in the days that ensued. This particular discussion was especially fascinating to Jett, who smoked a cigarette as he stared, smiling.

"And yet after August 7th, after the skies have grown dark, will you raise your eyes to the heavens? Will you continually and faithfully search for the sign Jesus promised we would see? Will you exercise faith in him, that you might not perish, but have everlasting life?"

A loud man's voice called out from the audience.

"*I* will, Brother Jonah!"

His affirmation was followed by shouts from many in the congregation who began declaring their faith with great exultation. Jonah waited for the din to die down before resuming.

"Two thousand years ago these things were prophesied. In thirty days they will come to pass. As we enter this *great tribulation, such as was not since the beginning of the world to this time, no, nor ever shall be*, as we enter this trial, let us pray that when our master returns, we will have lived such lives that he will happily pronounce, '*Well done, good and faithful servant; thou hast been faithful over a few things, I will make thee ruler over many things; enter into the joy of thy lord.*' Amen."

Jonah's 'amen' was echoed throughout the building.

"I know where I'll be on August 7th. I'll be right here in the church with many of you. With the government's help, we've made arrangements to have the August 7th sermon broadcast live for anyone out there who wants to join us in worship that day. So whether you are here or at home, whether you're in your church, in your favorite place on Earth, beside the people you love, in your child's room, in your parents' home, on a mountain ledge overlooking creation or on a quiet sunny beach, just remember that the true church lies within you, and no matter who you are or where you are, God is always with you. He resides in you and in all creation."

Many in the audience bowed their heads as Jonah's sermon began to take on a prayerful tone.

"On August 7th, as we face the challenges of that day and of the days beyond, let us trust in the Lord with all our hearts, and lean not on our own understanding. Let us make the Lord our strength and our shield, for salvation belongeth unto the Lord. He said his sign or token will appear in the heavens after the sun and moon grow dark. He told us when he cometh with clouds, every eye shall see him. So let us abandon our earthly, corporal ways and our fleshly fears. Let us raise our eyes to the heavens. Let us demonstrate by our thoughts and deeds that we believe in him. Let us pray for our salvation and seek him out, that we may be blameless in the day of our Lord, Jesus Christ. O our Father, if it be possible, let this cup pass from us: nevertheless not as we will, but as thou wilt. Amen."

Chapter 26

In most areas of the venerable city, the seven hundred mile-per-hour wind arrived before the sound of the explosion and the blast's shock wave. More than a million people were dead before anyone knew what had taken place. The forty-megaton bomb was detonated 17,500 feet over the city in order to maximize damage. After the wind, there came a huge concussive shockwave that leveled homes and buildings within a 7.5-mile radius from the epicenter of the explosion. Some of the strongest buildings, those made of reinforced, poured concrete, still stood, barely. In a city of over five million, three million were dead in the first thirty seconds.

Since being founded in A.D. 762, it had been one of the greatest cities ever to flourish in the cradle of civilization. During the 8th and 9th centuries, it was at the height of its commercial prosperity. The city was a bustling metropolis that left Europe standing cold. It held a university where women taught, as well as men, and public lectures on history and philosophy were delivered to as many as four thousand people at a time.

Farther away from ground zero, in a city twenty-three miles away, a father cringing behind a concrete embankment watched his two young sons disintegrate in a surreal wave of thermal radiation. In an instant, the buildings and houses in his city had quickly collapsed like a stack of cards, with many exploding into flames. Looking toward the sky, he fancied he saw a colossal angel of destruction standing in the middle of the plain, his head reaching up to the clouds and his fiery sword drawn.

Ironically it was on July 17, in the land between two rivers, the Dijla and Furat, on the plain of the Fertile Crescent, the birthplace of civilization, that the greatest destructive force ever engineered by man was unleashed upon the Earth. In the end, man had, through fear and arrogance, unconscionably destroyed his birthplace, the roots of his existence and the very seeds of hope for his continued presence on Earth. The Great Tribulation had come early.

In Iraq's national capital, five million were dead. In cities up to one hundred miles away, the carnage was unimaginable with early estimates projecting fifteen million dead and many more to come as the effect of nuclear radiation began to take its toll. Radiation levels were considered lethal at even two hundred miles from ground zero.

Radioactive contamination would cause death for most within that radius in two to fourteen days. The contamination was certain to cause major health problems and deaths in neighboring nations on all sides, sparking angry protest from leaders, while from the populaces there were calls for immediate retaliation.

A second forty-megaton bomb fell on Tehran, the capital of Iran and Tehran province, killing an estimated three million persons and sending the nation into panic and desperation. Fighters took out all military and domestic airports in the country, the main hubs for the railways and the major roads.

On the eastern seaboard, Americans awoke to the announcement of America's controversial military action on the early morning news. And yet, despite the degree to which the public had been desensitized by shock over the previous eleven months, the overwhelming response was one of anger and alarm.

The attacks did not bode well with America's traditional allies either. The British prime minister publicly condemned President Bentsen's action as "the working of an insane lunatic bent on the destruction of the world."

"Here we are at the end of the conclusion, and in one bloody day he's brought us to the brink of World War III!"

Other world leaders condemned Bentsen as "the most notorious mass murderer in the history of Earth—exceeding even Hitler in his racist cruelty." The Pope, from the Vatican in Rome, warned the world of Bentsen's resemblance to the modern antichrist. Bentsen's only supporter was the prime minister of Israel, who praised the bombing for its pre-emptive benefits.

The legislative and judicial branches of the American government, moving to distance themselves from the President, at once took up the process of impeachment, prosecution and apology, fully aware that the world and humans were on the brink of global war and destruction, regardless of the asteroid threat.

Nonetheless, President Bentsen was not without his cadre of loyal and powerful supporters in Washington. By noon, Jettson Turner and his public relations team were spinning the story to Bentsen's credit and advantage. Turner cited "a credible and looming domestic threat" with its roots in Baghdad and Tehran. He said America, its military and all its citizens and allies should be on the highest alert through August 7. The FBI, according to Turner, had been tracking groups of al-Qaida operatives in New York, Pennsylvania and Maryland. The mission for all three cells involved detonating a nuclear weapon on U.S. soil in a large, densely populated American city.

"President Bentsen has vowed to do everything in his power to make sure that doesn't happen, and what he did early this morning will go a long way toward preventing such an attack. One thing's for sure: You can't have Baghdad or Tehran-sponsored terrorism if there's no Baghdad or Tehran, and I think we can safely say those cities no longer exist."

By eight p.m. in Washington, Turner's media spokespersons had been so effective at establishing justification that even the senators who were most critical of the unauthorized military strike decided to refrain from expressing disapproval until after President Bentsen's address to the American people. Thus at eight p.m., the President sat before an emergency joint session of Congress, listening as Jett Turner whispered last-minute advice into his ear. After a brief introduction by the House Speaker pro Tem, the President stood.

"My fellow Americans, certainly by now you are aware of events unfolding in distant quarters of the world. Last night, American bombers dropped individual twenty-five-megaton nuclear bombs on Baghdad, Tehran, Pyongyang and areas in the American Rocky Mountains. I come before you today to encourage you not to panic and to assure you the attacks in all instances were completely justified. In the case of Iraq, where we actually dropped two bombs, our action was retaliatory.

"On July 15th, I received the CIA's conclusions from the investigation of President Whitmore's assassination. From that report I learned Baghdad was directly responsible for putting the assassin and other suicide bombers in place last month. Baghdad's expressed objective was to kill our president, and for that Baghdad and all the people of Iraq have paid the price today. The report also linked Tehran to the assassination plot. Today Iraq, Iran and their people have paid for their involvement in the plot. As I have said many times before, the U.S. will make no distinction between terrorists themselves and those who lend them assistance in any form."

Bentsen glanced toward Jett Turner, who nodded in approval. His eyes panned his quiet, concerned, somber and unblinking audience. The animosity from congressional members, especially the senators, was palpable. Drawing a deep breath, the President found his place in the script.

"Pyongyang in Korea suffered by the same logic and the same U.S. policy. Recently, CIA agents foiled an al-Qaida attempt to smuggle three low-grade nuclear bombs into our country from the Canadian border. Aggressive interrogation and intensive investigation has convinced us that the bombs were produced at an underground facility near Pyongyang. It has been one month since China, its government imploding, withdrew its forces from Korea, and since that time, we have seen terrorist activity in Korea grow to alarming proportions. By taking out Pyongyang and most of Korea, we have eliminated an increasingly persistent menace to our security and to the security of the world at large."

He looked toward the small group of anxious reporters seated in the front of the congressional chamber.

"I'll take two questions, and then I'll have to go."

The tall female news anchor in the front began speaking immediately.

"Mr. President, in your statement you gave a rationale for nuking Iraq, Iran and Korea, but you said earlier U.S. attacks also included areas of America's Rocky Mountains. My question is: How could you possibly justify nuking Robert E. Lee and the New Republic when they're obviously no longer a threat to our national security? How could you or Jettson Turner justify using nuclear weapons against a harmless, isolated group of Americans on American soil with all the contamination risks that brings?"

Bentsen paused before beginning a response.

"Perhaps I need to clarify things here. While I did say a few Rocky Mountain locations had been bombed, I did not indicate that nuclear weapons were used in those specific attacks. In fact, the dozen or so bombs we dropped in the Rockies were all conventional weapons. No nukes were used in those..."

The persistent reporter interrupted with her follow-up question.

"But why bomb the New Republic in the first place? How could they possibly still be a threat to national security?"

"Next question?"

A balding reporter on the left cleared his throat and called out.

"Mr. President, will you or your administration, at any time, be able to provide proof or validation of your claims that Iran was responsible for Whitmore's assassination? And proof of Iraq's involvement?"

Bentsen nodded.

"That proof will be provided over the course of the next few weeks. But of course, you all must realize that certain elements of the investigation by their very nature might compromise national security. Those details will have to be omitted. This August 5th jihad chatter is no joke. You'll have your picture, but it might not be a complete picture. I know it's asking a lot, but you'll just have to trust us on this one."

Bentsen spotted a familiar face.

"Sam?"

"Mr. President, in the course of a single day, you've just destroyed two and a half, maybe three, countries and wiped literally millions in villages, towns and cities from the face of the Earth— something unprecedented in world history. Arab and Asian nations are ready to go to war. Britain and NATO allies seem to have turned against America. Aren't you the least bit concerned that your actions today pose as great a threat to man's continued existence on Earth as Nostradamus ever has?"

Bentsen glared at the news correspondent.

"This is the end game, Sam. *The end of the conclusion.* Either good will prevail or the entire Earth will be overwhelmed by evil. There's not a lot of time, but we all must choose a side. I regret the millions of lives that were lost today, but I don't regret giving an order that saved possibly billions more on August 5th. I stand proud as an American on the side of good. If other nations want to stand beside Americans and fight evil to the end, we welcome them and call them friends. If not, the evil side has already overtaken them. As evidenced by this morning's events, God has given us the power to overcome evil in the world, and I vow to use that power to fight and win the last, decisive battle between the forces of good and evil, before Judgment Day."

He smiled toward the cameras.

"That'll be all. Thank you. And God bless the United States of America!"

****

"When they asked me to do it last August, I was a little leery, especially of Smock, and I didn't particularly trust the government. But then when they laid out the plan and I watched them execute, I was just amazed at the degree of organization, sophistication and the amount of detail they had invested. Technically, it should all work— Life Ark, the Refugium, the return to Earth and the reintroduction and resurgence of life. If Nostradamus was destined to destroy humans on the planet, Smock and his scientists have found a way around it."

Davis sipped from a glass of rich and aged, sepia-colored Syrah. Directly across from him at the dinner table sat Asia, and next to her was little Blake. On his left and right were Dexter and Susan, respectively. The remainder of Blake's devil's food birthday cake was still on the table.

"Since the beginning, Smock's likened this project to a modern-day Tower of Babel. He's seen the conflict as one that pits man's ingenuity and technology against the potential will of God. Until just this week, I thought Smock could have been Misanthrope, but now I think he's on our side. He's just as desperate as we are to know the truth."

Dexter pushed his dessert plate toward the table's center.

"So what did he say to you? What did he ask you?"

"More than that, it's what he did. He gave me source codes for entry into the Pentagon computer system. He took great risks in order to get them. It's just an in. It'll be up to me to go in unnoticed and to find out if the government is on the level, and if not, to find out what they're up to."

Susan was standing as she stacked the dessert plates near the table's edge. The forks were stacked separately six inches away from the china.

"Housekeeping, dessert plates and silverware, clear."

She moved her chair closer to Davis before sitting, allowing access for a robot that immediately moved toward the table in order to perform the task.

Susan turned toward Davis as she reached for her wine glass.

"So what does Smock think they're up to?"

Davis sighed, shrugging.

"Well, turns out he thinks there might be something to Dr. Engstrom's theory about the government manipulating telemetric data. He thinks the government might have distorted the data from the beginning in order to exaggerate the size of Nostradamus and maybe its trajectory."

Susan persisted.

"And why would they do that?"

"Who knows? But if we find out the data *is* being manipulated, we'll know the most powerful people in the world, whoever they are, have a secret agenda and the Lazarus Project is just a cover to fool the insiders. That would mean Life Ark, the Refugium, Smock and the rest of us down here are expendable, and worse, that we've already been expended."

Davis paused to let the idea ferment in the minds and hearts of the others seated at the table.

"Smock's greatest fear is that the Lazarus Project might be nothing more than a government test, a government exercise to assess man's chances for survival in the event of a *real* asteroid impact situation. If it's a test, they're probably sitting out there somewhere, studying us, analyzing our behavior and our ability to cope down here. They could study us until we die and glean whatever they need to glean to improve their plan."

He paused again and sipped from the wineglass.

"What really worries me is that no one, not even Smock, has access to the outside world anymore. And only a few powerful people in the government know we're down here. Because they're linked to Lazarus, they're controlling the information we receive about what's happening on the surface. So if the asteroid is significantly smaller than they've told us, or if it doesn't hit at all, we might never know it down here. We could live the rest of our lives like lab animals in a sort of elaborate government test."

Asia interrupted.

"Is there any way to *independently* establish what's happening up there?"

"One way, and Smock's already asked me about it."

"What is it? Tell us."

Davis took a deep breath and blew it out, his eyes fixing on his suspicious, impossible-to-fool wife.

"It's also the only way to get inside the Pentagon computers to find out if the government's on the level. Smock has asked me to access Calypso in order to hack into government agency computers. She can get in and out unnoticed. She could determine if they've used some kind of undetectable overwriting program to distort telemetry coming in from Nostradamus. Calypso and her programming might be our only hope."

Asia called out her order.

"Bartender, double Grey Goose, chilled, up."

She stood.

"Calypso. Well, wouldn't you know it! I don't know about the rest of you, but somehow, I feel better already."

Chapter 27

He was alone again. In his career with the government, he had spent countless hours, days and evenings by himself, but he had never really felt *alone*, not until recently. Even a month earlier, he had reveled in moments of solitude; he had eagerly anticipated the quiet and stillness, which was his special time for reflection and deep thought.

In college, he had read a short story called *The Man of the Crowd*. He had forgotten who the author was but he remembered the gist of the story. It was about a tortured, secretive man who went from crowded scene to crowded scene in London because he feared solitude. Perhaps it was Poe.

Eventually, the reader understood. The man had a horrible secret that he was keeping to himself, a secret he would carry to his grave. He remained in the crowd because his guilt would not let him face himself or any other person. The author had quoted from Shakespeare's Julius Caesar in lines that lamented the evil that men do lives beyond them while their good deeds are often interred with their bones.

In moments of solitude, Jett felt guilty about the role he had assumed in the end game. The launch codes and sequences had already been preprogrammed and could not easily be aborted. On the morning of August 14, sixty-five percent of the U.S. nuclear missile arsenal would be spent launching over-the-top attacks against targets in the United States, Great Britain, Canada, France, Germany, Italy, Russia, Japan, China, Australia, Turkey, Greece, Nigeria, South Africa, Brazil, Argentina and every other foreign government or entity that had paid Don Smock's New Millennium Construction Company to design underground shelters for protection from thermonuclear war and cosmic debris. Jett knew the plan was evil, though he had convinced himself it was the only way.

The knock at the door was sudden and unexpected.

"Good evening, Sir. Are you Jettson Turner?"

"Yeah."

"Package for you."

Jett hesitated.

"Don't you want my ID?"

"Oh, that's right. I'll need to see your ID."

Jett reached into his inside breast pocket, flicked the black leather case open and returned it to its place. Then he took the package, signed the mini computer screen and closed the door in the young man's face. He hesitated before pulling the tab to unseal the small parcel, mumbling to himself.

"Well, *this* is irregular."

When he pried the lid open, a small cellular phone fell into his hand. Within seconds, it began ringing. He answered.

"Three, seventeen, seventy-one, seven, five, forty-three, eleven, one."

Pen at the ready, he copied the response from the person on the other end, and then he copied a phone number. Terminating the connection, he sighed with regret.

He regretted that he had been so cold to his wife over the years, regretted that he had never gotten to know his son. Just then, he remembered his son's surprise announcement, but then it really wasn't much of a surprise. Jett had a special knack for reading people. He saw it coming years earlier. But that didn't change his reaction to the announcement. He never spoke to the boy again.

Jett bowed his head, and then he dialed the phone number he had just written down. When he heard the click completing the new connection, he began reading the numbers he had copied moments before.

"Twenty-nine, thirteen, nineteen, forty-seven, seventy-nine."

A short beep indicated he had spoken the numbers correct, and distinctly enough. Seconds later, a voice came online. He listened for a moment and answered.

"Yeah. Drake?"

He paused, listening.

"Why? What's going on?"

The voice on the other end was loud enough to be heard three feet away.

"Answer the door, Jett. Answer it now."

"Drake?"

In the moment that the line went dead, there was an abrupt knock on the door.

"Fuck!"

Tossing the phone onto the counter, Jett walked over to the door, unlocked it and pulled it open.

"No!"

"Checkmate, mother fucker."

Four muffled shots, all at center mass. Jett just stood there for a moment in sheer shock. Still looking at the space where his assailants had stood, his left hand fumbled on his chest, his fingers searching. He intuitively found and began fingering one of the hot, oozing holes through his right breast. His mouth opened as he tried to turn and call 911 for help, but he realized his body felt paralyzed. He could not move.

He knew he would die in that place. He raised his eyes toward the heavens, acknowledging his audience in the same way an actor does at the final curtain call. Never one to smile or laugh, Jett managed a twisted grin and mocking gurgle before his spirit's departure wiped his face blank. He fell to the floor, lifeless, his eyes wide open.

****

The knock at the door was sudden and unexpected. Davis rose and approached the door, speaking through it.

"Who is it?"

"It's *us*, Fool! Open the damn door!"

Davis unlatched the safety chain and yanked the door open.

"You brought the baby?"

"Yeah."

Susan, Asia and Blake mobbed Helen Hernandez, who carried a gurgling bundle in her arms as she stepped through the doorway. The vodka had slowed Asia's reflexes, so it was Susan who ended up running off with the two-week-old baby.

Davis extended his right hand toward the huge man whose eyes followed Susan over to the couch where she sat with the child.

"Congratulations, Reggie! I mean, this is great! Here you thought you were alone, and now you have a daughter down here. Your daughter is now have the youngest person in the Crypt."

Reggie beamed as he continued to monitor what Susan was doing with the child.

"Yeah, thanks."

"And then there's Helen. It seems you have a nice little family going on down here."

Reggie watched Helen exit into the bedroom with Asia and Blake before responding.

"Helen's somethin else."

He leaned toward Davis, speaking.

"So do you think Layla will ever come back?"

"Not in our lifetimes. They'll be up there for four hundred to five hundred years. I know it sounds harsh, but whatever you and Layla had—it's over. This is your life now, so count your blessings. You've got a beautiful little daughter, a wonderful woman and you're down here where you'll all be safe."

When the women returned, Helen was carrying a stack of little girl's clothing as she and Asia discussed the joys and pains of breastfeeding. Susan brought the crying baby to Helen, interjecting a comment of her own, though on an unrelated matter.

"The real challenge is going to be having clothes for her as she grows. The boutiques won't have little girls' stuff, and last I heard, I don't think they brought any designers down here."

Helen laughed.

"Let's just say I did a lot of shopping before they shut the doors. She'll have clothes as she grows, but I also got her a sewing machine. If she doesn't like what I got, she can make her own."

Blake tugged at Helen's sleeve.

"Dr. Helen, can I hold baby Gala?"

"Sure you can, but let Susan help you. Sit on the couch there."

The three women and Blake retired to the living room with the baby while Davis and Reggie spoke to each other in the hallway.

Dexter hadn't moved since dinner. He remained motionless at the kitchen table, his eyes fixed straight ahead in a detached gaze. He heard the women's muted laughter in the other room, the baby's cries, the men's hushed voices and George Benson's *The Greatest Love of All* in the background, but he was lost in a world of memory.

He was thinking of his father's voice. Closing his eyes, he recalled the unmistakable pride on his father's face after eighth grade graduation. Dexter knew he had pleased his father that day. Dexter was the class speaker, and he and Jonah had worked on his oration together. The speech was called "Life's Most Important Moments."

He thought of his mother's face and the girlish way she sometimes looked at his dad. Sometimes she seemed more like a big sister than a mother, but she had always been there for him. He had never thought of her as pretty before, but she really was a beautiful woman. He remembered how she smelled when she got in the car for church. He thought about how many diets she attempted and about the time she and his dad were almost killed in a car accident.

It was the first time he had ever dared to imagine what life would be like without them. He was twelve years old. For two weeks after the incident, he cried himself to sleep at night in fear of losing his parents. Then he became a teenager and learned to resent them. He resented them for being parents, he disliked what they stood for and he begrudged their interference in his life.

They were always there with the unsolicited advice, the repetitive lectures and the self-righteous judgments. He hated it! But now... now he missed it, and them. Now he missed the parents he had taken for granted over the last few years. "Life's most important moments"—now they had meaning to him.

His parents probably thought he was dead because he had been gone so long without contacting them. How his mother's heart must be aching! How his father must have pleaded with God for an answer to why he had lost yet a second son! Dexter was dead to his parents, dead to the world. He wished to reach across the great chasm to comfort them, to let them know that he was in a better place.

"*There* you are, Dex! With the baby and all, I had no idea you were still sitting in here. You ready to rejoin the world of the living?"

Susan's kiss awakened him. He looked up at her and smiled, remembering his wife and life's precious moments still ahead.

"What were you thinking about, Dexter?"

"The *present*, the *now*. I was just realizing we have to enjoy the people we love and every moment we have with them. The past is gone and the future's not guaranteed. We have to live and enjoy the present."

She stared at him for a moment and then she eyed the empty goblet at his right.

"Told ya you shouldn't have had that second glass. Come on."

In the living room, Helen was discussing the slow revival of Dr. Engstrom and her role in Smock's quest for the truth. Lazarus had been gradually restoring and repairing Dr. Engstrom's body since early July. According to the program Helen chose, the doctor would be conscious within two weeks.

Once she was awake, Don Smock hoped to work with her and Davis in order to independently determine the actual size of Nostradamus. Once the size and mass could be revised, Smock would rework his impact analysis. In the meantime, Davis and Smock would attempt to hack into the Pentagon computer to determine the government's ultimate objective.

"And that's where Calypso comes in. I still don't trust Smock. He wants me to access her through a secret link he had constructed, but I've got my own line. I'll only access her if I absolutely have to."

Helen looked up from her breastfeeding.

"Speaking of Smock. He told me today that sometime after Engstrom is revived—and that would also be sometime after the crash on August 7th—he said that after an analysis of the damage to Earth, he wants me to put *him* under. He wants to be put in cold stasis in her empty cryopod. He's programmed Lazarus to wake him up one full year before it begins to revive the forty-four volunteers on Life Ark. Seems he doesn't trust one of the volunteers—that Barnes character."

Davis left the room for a moment to answer the phone. When he returned, his face seemed flushed.

"Speak of the Devil. That was Smock. He said I should turn on the television. Said it was something huge."

Chapter 28

From the moment he assumed office, the senators had made their disapproval plain. Members from both parties unanimously warned that Bentsen and Turner would ruin America and bring about global Armageddon. Utilizing overrides of presidential vetoes, they had passed emergency measures to reduce Bentsen's power and to limit his access to weapons of mass destruction.

They put spies in the White House and watched his every move. They solicited the aid of American allies to help keep the President in check. And yet despite all their planning and their efforts to pre-empt an international crisis, Bentsen had nuked three nations and was set to launch "the last, decisive battle between the forces of good and evil before Judgment Day."

The Senate, outraged on the day of the bombing, had met in private to discuss impeachment and other options. Bentsen's speech before the joint congressional session only convinced them to take action. Impeachment was a lengthy and cumbersome process, steeped in tortuous procedure, so in a private session the next day, the Judiciary Committee met to consider a last-ditch emergency option.

Senate President Donovan Scott of Delaware was a severe pragmatist who had been close to President Whitmore and his administration. Scott and Committee Chairman Tony Conti of New Jersey first solicited and discussed solutions submitted by committee members and then they began to detail an elaborate plan of their own.

The Scott-Conti proposal involved compelling Bentsen to come before the full Senate to answer questions about ignored protocols related to the bombing. The Senate invitation would extend to the nine justices of the United States Supreme Court as well. Senate seating assignments would be changed to allow all Judiciary Committee members to be seated at the front of the room, near the President. After hours of careful, thoughtful deliberation, the Scott-Conti plan was approved. Thus the Senate was prepared to do its part.

Fifteen minutes before he went to the Senate, President Chuck Bentsen heard the news of Jett Turner's suicide. One advisor warned him about the senators and encouraged the President to keep his distance.

"Make up any excuse, but don't go anywhere near that Senate chamber today."

But Bentsen was more the good soldier than the politician. He could not find it within himself to show overt cowardice or contempt for the Senate of the United States of America by lying. He had his orders.

He entered the quiet Senate chamber and walked past senators on his way to the table. A few of the members glared toward him, while the rest just stared straight ahead. Although he did not fear the senators, he felt a certain sense of foreboding. His stomach felt muddy and his intestines roiled as he felt the weight of judgment pressing from all sides, coming from both within and without the room. His legs were weak and beads of sweat rose on his forehead. He sat, closed his eyes to collect his thoughts and looked up.

"Honorable Members of the United States Senate, you called me before you to answer questions about recent decisions I have made and actions I have taken to ensure our national security. When I took my oath of office as president, I swore to do exactly what I have done. I have made America a safer place. You may disagree, but I have a job to do. I owe a duty to the United States of America just as each of you owes a duty to America. Your questions I will answer, but save your judgment. It is not your place to judge me."

Senator Donovan Scott signaled the sergeant and the doors were locked. He looked over to the members of the Judiciary Committee and nodded.

"Who would like to begin with the questions?"

The Utah senator on the committee spoke up.

"Mr. President, are you the *man of lawlessness*?"

Having failed to grasp the biblical reference, Bentsen did not answer. Another senator called out.

"Are you the *son of destruction*? Are you the *second Beast*?"

The President's face signaled confusion. He shrugged and wagged his head.

"I have no idea what you people are talking about."

Yet another senator spoke out.

"Are you *Gog of Magog*?"

Senator Conti had risen. He asked his question as he approached Bentsen.

"Who *exactly* are you, Mr. President?"

"What the hell are you talking about, Senator? And what are you doing?"

Bentsen looked for his personal security detail, but they were absent.

"Guards! Security!"

All the members of the Judiciary Committee had risen behind Senator Conti, who was already upon the President. As the senators closed in, Conti revealed his purpose. From the inside pocket of his jacket, he withdrew a shiny silver dagger with a six-inch blade.

"For World Peace and Safety!"

****

Davis held Asia from behind, resting his chin on her shoulder as they watched the report. Reggie had left his glasses at home, so he knelt next to the set, leaning close to discern the images. Susan's eyes were wide open and her jaw was slack, while Dexter wagged his head in disbelief. Helen held the baby's face to her breast, as if to shield her from the horror on the screen. Blake had fallen asleep.

The news anchor continued.

"For those of you just tuning in, the scene was macabre and bloody on the floor of the U.S. Senate today, where senators from the Judiciary Committee, joined by other senators and at least one associate Supreme Court justice, set on President Bentsen. In shades of Julius Caesar, the senators, armed with daggers, stabbed the struggling president over and over until he eventually succumbed. Three senators required medical treatment for unspecified injuries sustained in the incident. President Bentsen was pronounced dead at the scene."

The mood of the senators outside the chamber was purposeful and somber. Many were huddled around Senator Scott, who answered a few of the reporters' questions. It was apparent that Scott was in charge and that he was prepared to make a statement to the American people.

A burnt umber streak of Bentsen's encrusted blood marked Scott's forehead and the foreheads of many of the other senators. According to one reporter, the senators had dipped their daggers in the President's blood and smeared it on their foreheads to signal their censure for the abominations he had committed against humanity. In a show of solidarity, many of the senators and the Supreme Court justices who were not physically involved in the assassination had marked their foreheads in like manner.

As the coverage of the assassination continued, world leaders responded by endorsing the action of the Senate. The British prime minister went a step further.

"Donovan Scott may very well be the man who altered the ultimate legacy of humans on Earth. The wounds are still raw, bleeding and run very deep, but they are not impossible to redress. We, as humans, must decide now how we will be remembered. We must decide how we will go out. Will our destruction result from an act of God, who may yet show us mercy? Or will we, in our hate, anger and inhumanity, be the agents of our own demise?"

Arab and Asian leaders were less optimistic about how much the assassination would ease world tensions, though several leaders expressed a degree of surprise and satisfaction that the U.S. Senate had the courage to condemn and punish the errant American president.

According to rules of succession, Senate President Donovan Scott was first in line for the presidency. After having been sworn in, Scott, streak of blood still marking his forehead, addressed the American people and the world.

"In eleven days it will be August 7th. As humans on Earth, we have a week and a half before we face three great tests: for one, our faith in God or our belief in some greater plan will be tested, and then our right to life on Earth will be challenged. And yet in the days before August 7th we face another test, perhaps an even greater test, and that is the trial of our collective human character."

President Scott paused for effect, looking toward the cameras.

"Collectively as humans, who are we? *What* are we? Are we capable of forgiveness? Can we forget histories of animosity that stretch back hundreds or thousands of years? Can we transcend the weaknesses of our flesh? Can we lay down our hate, our prejudices and our competitive spirit? Can we come together in peace and safety? Is love important to us? Do we value life? How do we treat our children? Those are the questions that will be decided in the next eleven days. And will the trial of our collective human character affect what will happen on August 7th? Who knows? But if there is a God, and I believe there is, perhaps it should."

Scott bowed his head, nodded and continued.

"As president of the United States of America, I formally apologize to the surviving peoples of Iraq, Iran, Korea and people in other affected countries. Chuck Bentsen's actions were immoral and illegal, and they did not represent the will of the American people. Had we known he was planning to launch a nuclear offensive against non-military targets in those places, we would have acted sooner. Though God is capable of all things, not even he can change what's passed. Eleven days before August 7th, all I can do is apologize and assure the world that America has a safe and steady hand at the helm."

A gifted orator, Scott paused to signal transition.

"But don't get me wrong here. Don't take America's apology as a sign of weakness. America is still the greatest power the world has ever known. We have the ability to take on and take out anyone who challenges us. As President of the United States, my first and foremost duty is to protect and defend my country. I hope we as humans can live the next eleven days in peace and safety. I sincerely hope we do not get snagged in a tangled, inescapable web of violence and death. I pray the violence carried out today is the end punctuation, the final scene in this bloody and barbaric drama, rather than a mere comma or pause."

Senators and justices closing in around him to signal solidarity, Scott extended a hand toward the cameras as he began his conclusion.

"And so, in the spirit of Abraham Lincoln, 'With malice toward none, with charity for all, with firmness in the right, as God gives us to see the right, let us strive on to show the strength of our collective human character in the challenges that lie ahead, to bind up the world's wounds, to care for him who shall have borne the battle, and for his widow and orphan, to do all which may achieve and cherish a just and lasting peace among ourselves and with all nations.'"

****

Though he had struggled with the decision for days, the thought of feeling her again was exciting. He had missed her so much. Things were good with Asia. In fact, his marriage was better than it had ever been. So as he typed the final commands to interface with the awakened Calypso, he felt a wave of guilt, like a man who had just made the conscious decision to cheat on his wife.

Calypso contained the most sophisticated hacking programs in existence. And Don Smock would provide secret access codes to government computers. If information about the Crypt's true mission existed in government agency computers, Calypso would allow Davis to go in, read and access files, copy and get out unnoticed.

With Smock's assistance, Davis and Calypso would be able to access NASA's computers to determine if the government had been distorting telemetric data available to scientists from deep space surveillance devices and systems. Smock specifically asked Davis to attempt to locate and access all data recorded and stored by Dr. Helen Engstrom at the Near-Earth Asteroid Tracking observatory site at the Haleakala Crater from July 7 through July 23 of the previous year.

After spending five hours in the Pentagon computer system, Davis was convinced that the government *had* created superprograms that possessed specific capabilities to manipulate telemetric data on a global scale.

He commented to Smock, who stood peering over his shoulder.

"That's the exact purpose for that system. I can't imagine any other application for the programming. The capability is there."

Hacking into the NASA computer was easy enough, but after Davis had searched for data from Dr. Engstrom's computer recorded between July 7-23 of the previous year, it became obvious that someone had already been there. The data was missing, either erased or removed. If the U.S. government or a secret organization was manipulating global data, then the subterfuge was nearly perfect.

And so despite eleven hours of hacking and researching, neither Don Smock nor Davis Franklin could determine whether or not the government was actually distorting data. That secret remained locked in the head of Dr. Helen Engstrom.

Thus Davis had spent the entire night on Level Four with Calypso. At eight o'clock a.m. he looked at his watch, thinking of Asia. He sighed to himself, realizing she was probably miserable all night. She was probably drunk as well. To his surprise, she was standing in the kitchen fixing breakfast when he arrived home.

"I've decided who I am and where I want to be, Davis. Time for *you* to do the same."

Chapter 29

"Is that it? Can you see it?"

Sixth-grade teacher Elizabeth DeRogatis peered into the eyepiece, adjusting the focus with the knob in her left hand.

"That's it. Who wants to be first to look at it?"

Two years earlier, she had moved to Reasnor, Iowa, less than fifty miles east of Des Moines, to escape a bad relationship and the complexity of life in Pacifica, California. The simple folks of Reasnor, with their snail-paced lifestyle and their religious dependence on the earth and its cycles, moved Elizabeth to find her own spirituality. In Pacifica she was a self-proclaimed atheist, but in Reasnor she had found God. She loved living off the earth and living near the river, but most of all, she enjoyed teaching the children.

Most of the kids in her class came from farms along the Skunk River. They came from working families. Many of their parents had high school diplomas, but few had attended college. The adult community's reaction to the Nostradamus threat was one of uniform skepticism. The community at large had ignored President Whitmore's admonition that all rural communities should relocate to major metropolitan centers. Reasnor folks didn't read the newspapers and refused to watch the news. For the most part, their lives had continued unaffected. Their crops were still in the fields, after all.

The children in Elizabeth's sixth-grade class, however, were another story. Over the school year, the boys and girls had become fascinated with astronomy and the coming of the asteroid. Even after school was out in June, many hurried through chores on the farms in order to return to the school to learn about the sun, moon, planets, stars and asteroids—and they brought fresh, sweet corn for their teacher.

The July 17 nuclear explosions in Iraq, Iran, Korea and Wyoming had dispersed a great cloud of fine dust into the atmosphere, causing the daytime skies to dim significantly. The fine particles in the heavens scattered light, preferentially blue light, causing the moon, almost in its first quarter, to glow a deep red-orange at night. Astrologers called the darkened skies and reddened moon the first of many omens that would be seen in the sky before the end of the world.

On the night of August 1, Elizabeth's students had gotten permission from parents for an overnight stay at the school. According to the television news, on that evening beginning at 11:43 p.m., Midwesterners could train telescopes to twenty-one degrees north of east, thirty-five degrees above the horizon to get a good look at the approaching asteroid.

Ellie May Garner, Elizabeth's pet student, was first to squint through the eyepiece.

"I *see* it! Is that it?"

Elizabeth nodded.

"That's Nostradamus."

"But it isn't comin at us. It isn't movin. It's stayin still. And it's so little!"

The teacher responded as she assisted the next child with the telescope.

"It is moving, Ellie May. It's traveling at sixty thousand miles per hour. It's just the sky's so big we can't tell."

The boy next to Elizabeth looked up from the instrument.

"So we're all gonna die?"

"I don't know, but Nostradamus is definitely coming."

On television screens all over the world, viewers were watching close-ups of Nostradamus captured by the *Helios* space probe, which had been flying alongside the asteroid and sending back visual images since March. With each day that passed, new images and views were presented, leading to interpretation by analysts and mystics.

One popular ecclesiastic known simply as Deborah, Earth's Last Great Prophetess, predicted that on the second day of August, the image of God would appear on the face of the asteroid. Many other interpreters pored over hundreds of views of the asteroid's surface for cosmic signs and answers from God.

Since late July, hastily constructed prayer temples and sacrificial altars sprouted up all over North America and the other continents. Immolation became a nightly ritual, with hundreds of fat, healthy bulls and rams being burned under naked skies as propitiatory sacrifices, that humans and all flesh might regain favor in God's eyes.

Gazing across the fields, the children attending Elizabeth's telescope discovery night could see the flames leaping from an altar in the valley. A few, understanding the significance of the ceremony, bowed their heads and whispered silent prayers to the heavens.

"God won't let it hit us, will he, Miss D?"

Elizabeth couldn't help crying, though she tried to hide her tears from her kids; she was overwhelmed by the children's fear.

"If he truly is a great and merciful God, Billy. If he is a god of love and he is capable of all things, I don't see how he *could* let it hit us."

****

By August 2, the days-to-impact countdown was converted to an hours-to-impact countdown. By 3:33 p.m. in California, clocks showed less than one hundred and twenty hours before Nostradamus would crash into Earth. The ever-present digital clocks hypnotized many people. Some stood staring , unable to experience the present as they watched their lives ticking down to conclusion. Others resented the clocks and protested that the clocks were causing people unnecessary anxiety.

"It's the tenths-of-seconds column on the far right, man. I mean, it's moving so fast. Just looking at it makes me weak in the knees. We don't need to see all that. I don't think we need that much detail, man."

Still others attacked the clocks with sledgehammers and took them out with shotguns. It was as if they had transferred the menace of the asteroid to the clock faces. They hated the clocks, which measured and metered man's doom.

On television, scientists debated about when Nostradamus would be reclassified from "asteroid" to "meteor." The word asteroid came from the Greek *aster*, for star, and is meant to denote a star-like body typically with an orbit between Mars and Jupiter. Even though Nostradamus's trajectory was altered, it had remained within the orbits of Mars and Jupiter, though its skewed elliptical orbit had put it on a collision course with Earth.

The word meteor indicates the luminous phenomenon observed when a solid body, traveling through space, enters Earth's atmosphere. By all accounts, the asteroid Nostradamus would become a meteor at some point. The debate raging among astronomers involved *when*. Many suggested it should be reclassified when it reached Earth's stratosphere, while others believed it should remain an asteroid until the first signs of luminosity resulting from its heated entry into Earth's atmosphere could be measured.

President Scott led the nation in prayer that evening and encouraged American families to stick together and to rely on each other for strength and courage. He shared a recent personal tragedy with his audience, tears in his eyes. Just the day before, his brother had phoned to tell him that the President's wife and two sons were dead, all lost to the pink pill. Apparently they had made a suicide pact, due to be completed on August 1.

Throughout the day, death figures resulting from the pink pill had begun to mount, with an estimated 1.3 million dead since August 1. People all over were exhibiting signs of neurosis, dementia and paranoia. Guardsmen were forced to shoot thousands of mentally troubled, unusually aggressive men and women to protect the general population. Families were encouraged to stay indoors, even during hours when the curfew was lifted.

One guardsman said he had shot twenty-three "loonies" in a single shift that day. He described the situation as "pandemonium."

"And this is just August 2nd. Just wait till bout the 5th or 6th. And the 6th is a full moon! All hell's gonna break loose. We cain't stop it!"

****

To many, it *seemed* like a face. It had two irregularities that could have stood for stern, piercing eyes. There was a line that from certain angles resembled a mouth. Television analysts were even able to trace what appeared to be the outline of a face, complete with a hairline and fleecy hair, in several pictures of the asteroid's irregular surface.

In fact, the last remaining American newspaper published a large, computer-enhanced image of such a likeness on August 3. The image appeared on the front page underneath a bold headline that read, "**The Face of God?**" It was an image that appeared in newspapers all over the world, stirring spirited debate about whether or not the asteroid and the trials ahead for humans were a result of divine providence.

Life in the Crypt was tense for the Franklins and the Williams as Susan and Asia pursued the truth that lay in the lower levels. True to her word, Susan set out to test Don Smock's patience by gaining access to top-secret, military-controlled Level Three.

Even Davis Franklin, with his security clearance and special access, had never been allowed on that level; he was relegated to Level Four and Levels One and Two. Helen Hernandez had access to Level Six and Levels One and Two, but she had never seen what was on Level Three. Davis shared that Level Five was used for storage and that Lazarus was housed in diminutive Level Seven, but Level Three remained the mystery. Perhaps Level Three held an ugly truth about the Crypt.

After resisting, Davis fashioned Susan a military identity card that allowed her access to the level, though he warned that she would be on her own from the time she exited the Level Three elevator. JR's girlfriend in housekeeping had risked possible elimination from the Crypt in order to provide Susan a military uniform. And so Susan managed to get to Level Three on August 3.

It had every appearance of a full-scale military operation. She saw Pentagon types and Washington suits, she saw captains and colonels, and she even saw a general. When she passed by the office of the Air Force Research Laboratory Space Vehicles Directorate, headed by Dr. Thomas Ross, she was surprised to see only Dr. Matsumata and two other persons on duty. It made her wonder who was watching the Ark and put into perspective the importance to Level Three operations of sustaining life on Earth.

Through the windows of another office, she saw a series of computer monitors. She moved closer to the glass to see what was on the screens. Removing a pair of binocular glasses from her purse, she put them on and peered into the room.

On the screens were mountainous landscapes from various countries: the United States, Great Britain, Canada, France, Germany, Italy, Russia, Japan, China, Australia, Turkey, Greece, Nigeria, South Africa, Brazil and Argentina. Panning the room, she fixed her attention on a separate screen. On that screen, a specific line stood out:

MISSILE DEPLOYMENT

The hand that grasped her shoulder from behind was strong and firm.

"You do not have authorized access for this level, Miss Whitmore. Come with me. Now!"

Chapter 30

"It seems here that he's come up with his own mythology. The five masculine deities he mentions correspond to the five men on the Ark, and he's made himself the supreme god. He calls himself Nimrud. Layla Reed is the Great Goddess of life, fertility and the harvest, or the Great Mother. Isabel Benoit is the High Priestess and the other six or seven fertile women represent the lesser feminine deities."

Davis studied his wife as she pored over Alan Chan's black book. He wagged his head.

"It doesn't make sense, Asia. Mythology became useless when man discovered science, when man developed technology. Ancient people used mythology to explain things they didn't understand, but that was due to primitive thinking. What do you think Chan hopes to accomplish by creating this mythology?"

Asia closed the book and sighed.

"When this Life Ark returns in four hundred years and the volunteers start repopulating the planet, do you think anyone will understand how an all-powerful God could have let an asteroid destroy billions of people, including billions of people who prayed to him and believed in him right to the end? All these along with the rest of life on Earth? You think they'll look for a *scientific* answer to that question?"

Davis, who had been leaning toward his wife, sat back as he considered her comment.

"I don't know."

"Humans have an innate need to worship something. Do you think many of these volunteers will want to believe in and worship a god who allowed something as horrible as Nostradamus to happen?"

He sighed and shook his head, allowing her to continue.

"Of course they're going to look for answers, Davis. Regardless of the technology they'll possess, they're going to be just like the ancient, primitive people you described. They'll use mythologies to explain the things they won't understand. So what happens to the supreme deity the Christians, Muslims, Jews and other religions worship now? What happens to God? And what happens to man's great savior, Jesus Christ?"

"He will have failed?"

Asia stood.

"I don't know what's going to happen here, but it scares me. I discounted it before, but maybe God *is* going to intervene at the last moment to save humans. Maybe this is the ultimate test of our faith. It's hard to imagine it any other way."

"What do you mean?"

"I mean if God *doesn't* save humans, and the people from the Ark begin to repopulate the planet, Alan Chan will succeed in his new mythology as he rebuilds civilization. He will become the supreme god, and he'll deny the Christ as man's savior."

Davis's head snapped up.

"So Alan Chan wants to be *God*?"

She nodded.

"I've gone through every page of his black book. Although he left a lot of clues and mini-riddles, there's no way of knowing whether or not he's your Misanthrope at this point. But one thing's for sure— either he's trying to *reinvent* himself as the antichrist..."

She raised her eyebrows as she considered the thought.

"or worse: Alan Chan *is* the antichrist."

****

She had been lying prone in a state of sensory deprivation for three hours. Her arms and hands were restrained at her sides. Cocooned in a starched bed sheet, she could not flex her shoulders, elbows, hips, knees or ankles. There was something over her face, though she had no problem breathing. She batted her eyes, hoping to catch a glimpse of light from somewhere, but there was nothing but darkness and total silence.

She felt anxious and almost panicked. Remembering her childhood yoga classes, she performed breathing exercises to remain calm. When she heard the men's voices outside the door, she knew her time had come. She was prepared to die.

She felt strong hands grab her waist. Someone carried her for a short distance and placed her on a chair of some kind. The man who pulled the hood from her head seemed angry as he glared at her face.

"Susan Whitmore. We knew you'd be trouble. How much did you see?"

She squinted in the bright lights. Gradually, her surroundings came into focus. There were six large security guards stationed in the small room. The man who interrogated her wore a black suit, a black shirt and dark glasses.

"Enough to know you guys are a bigger threat to the world than Nostradamus ever was."

He grabbed a handful of her hair, pulling her head back.

"I don't have time for your games, Girl. You need to tell me what you saw."

She cringed in pain and clenched her teeth, her eyes defiant.

"Or what? You'll kill me? You'll kill me so I can't tell people about all those missiles you're going to launch at the other shelters?"

The interrogator sat, flicking open a large, sharp, switchblade-style knife. The keen edge glinted in the light as the knife danced on the tips of his deft fingers. Abruptly gripping the handle, he stabbed right through the white bed sheet that bound her.

She screamed, closed her eyes and held perfectly still, not even breathing. He smiled as he began to cut with the blade. She could hear the sheet ripping. She could feel the cold blade moving next to her bare skin. Initially she thought he had stabbed her, but he was actually cutting through the duct tape and sheet between her right elbow and her waist. He laughed.

"Not so tough anymore are you, little girl? Believe me, I'd love to kill you, but I can't. They won't let me do it. But they *did* say, if you say anything or try anything like this again, they'll let me come get your husband. Dexter? The young black guy? I haven't killed anyone since I've been down here, so I'm really looking forward to it. I hope you won't let me down."

Her hands free, she tore at the fabric binding her legs.

"*Who* won't let you do it? Smock? I want to talk to *him*. Where is he? Standing on the other side of this glass?"

She stood, walked over to the mirror and knocked. She shouted toward her unseen audience.

"Listen, if you let this ape kill my husband, I'll kill myself, so you'd be killing me all the same. Come in here and talk to me!"

She could not hold back the tears any longer.

"I just want to know the truth, Dr. Smock. I'm in no position to change anything. *Please* come in here and talk to me!"

The door opened and Dr. Don Smock eased into the room.

"Hello Susan."

She was crying.

"I thought you were one of the good guys. Do you know what they're doing down here? Are you a *part* of all this?"

Smock wagged his head.

"This is Level Three, Susan. It's run by the military. On this level, I have no authority. It was part of the deal I made to get the Crypt funded. I have no idea what they do down here, and I don't want to know. I never come down here."

She took off her shoe and threw it at her smirking interrogator.

"And why do they have people like *him* down here? He's an idiot!"

She focused her breathing again.

"But he did say *they* wouldn't let him kill me, and I know what that means. It means my father is still alive somewhere. Where is he? Cheyenne Mountain? NORAD?"

The interrogator answered.

"President Whitmore is dead. He died in a suicide bombing."

Smock raised a hand in protest.

"No, he isn't dead. I talked to him just this morning."

Susan squinted as she closed on Smock.

"I don't believe you. Why are you telling me this now?"

Smock looked toward the interrogator and the guards.

"Gentlemen, if you'll excuse us? I'll take it from here. She's one of mine."

Alone in the room with Susan, Smock sighed.

"I'm certain they're listening in, so I'll get right to the point. I wasn't lying. Your father is alive. He's at Cheyenne Mountain. I have the power to let you talk to him, but I'll only let you if you make some assurances to me."

Her eyes narrowed as she studied his every expression and gesture, as she analyzed every pause, as she considered his word choice. She nodded.

"I'm listening."

"You'll have to promise me you won't discuss anything you've seen down here with anyone, not with your husband, not with Asia Franklin. You'll also have to promise you'll never attempt anything like this again."

"And you'll let me talk to my father? And it will really *be* my father?"

Smock placed a hand on her shoulder.

"Yes. He had planned on contacting you on the 7th anyway. It should be no problem moving the call up a few days. Can you make me those assurances?"

Susan took a deep breath, savoring the prospect of hearing her father's voice again. Finally, she nodded.

"Yes. If I can talk to my father, I'll forget everything I saw down here, and I won't come down here again."

"And we can trust you at your word?"

She wagged her head and sighed.

"Trust me? Of *course* you can trust me. *I* don't work for the government."

****

Bourbon, scotch, vodka, gin, tequila, brandy, wine, champagne and beer, all short on supply. It was next to impossible to keep store shelves stocked as people readied themselves for August 7. By August 4, no one could buy marijuana, cocaine, Ecstasy IV, GHB II, heroin or methamphetamines. The drug dealers were dry.

They called them "Lights Out" parties, and these fetes had been planned in cities across the nation. Most were set to begin at 1:33 p.m. EST on August 6, exactly twenty-four hours before Nostradamus was projected to slam into the Earth in northern Romania. Revelers planned on partying for twenty-three and a half hours straight. Then at 1:03 p.m. EST on August 7, millions across the country would take a "pink pill to paradise." They would sleep through *the end of the conclusion*.

At Christian churches across the country, in auditoriums and stadiums, millions of other people would assemble at 1:33 p.m. EST on August 6 to begin a twenty-four-hour prayer vigil. There would be food for the hungry, speeches, testimony, readings and naturally, prayers, supplications and petitions to God.

National organizers of the *Let This Cup Pass* campaign left it to individual leaders to format their services, but every organization involved had agreed to recite the Lord's Prayer at the top of each hour and Matthew 26:39 at the half-hour.

The last twelve hours of the vigil at Jonah Williams' Greater Faith Church would be broadcast live in the U.S. and to affiliate television stations all over the world. The leaders of synagogues, mosques and temples in America would hold similar prayer vigils.

On August 4, many of the underground facilities, bunkers and shelters owned by world governments, military agencies, wealthy families and private individuals began to seal their doors. The Crypt was also sealed on that day.

Lazarus shut the thick, heavy doors and pumped the huge lock bolts into place. Then Lazarus began to execute a series of security protocols that would constantly monitor the facility's hull and keep it sealed for four hundred years. Under two thousand feet of solid granite, the futuristic Crypt was the most secure place on the planet.

Many others, who could not afford to build or pay their way into shelters, fled to the mountains for protection. Laden with pallets of foodstuffs, water and blankets, they took up living in mountain caves and grottoes, cut off from the world. Bereft of technology, their existence was simple, tenuous, primitive.

And still others, in small communities and rural enclaves, had decided to adopt a business-as-usual policy. They lived their lives, day by day, pretending the President had never gone public with the Nostradamus threat. They sought to live out their lives without worry, focusing instead on the joy of each day, on the miracle of each minute, on the pleasure of each second.

Chapter 31

"Is she any better now?"

Dr. Helen Hernandez looked up from her place beside the bed.

"Still the same. I warned you this would happen if we brought her out from cold sleep too fast."

Smock approached the bed and bent over, peering into the patient's eyes.

"Look at her—she's a drooling idiot."

He waved his hand past her blank expression.

"Helen? Helen, can you hear me?"

The doctor shot Smock a look of condemnation.

"Another ten days and she probably would have been okay."

Smock sneered.

"We don't have ten days, Doctor."

"Well you do now. *She* won't do you any good in the next ten days."

He stood.

"So you think there's a chance she might get better?"

"We can put her back in the chamber to repair some areas of her brain, but what's gone is gone. Maybe she'll recover, maybe she won't. Either way, she won't do you any good for at least a month."

Smock's eyes narrowed in anger.

"I don't have a month, Doctor. I need answers, now!"

He went back to the bed and spoke into the patient's ear.

"Helen, if you can hear me, I need you to fight to pull yourself back. I *believe* you now. The government is up to something and you know what it is. I need the answers you have locked somewhere in that head of yours."

He touched her cheek.

"We need you to come back to us. So fight your way back. Help us. Please!"

****

She could hardly believe her eyes and ears. The monitor's resolution was outstanding, assuaging her concerns that the encounter would be a government-manufactured deception. It was a face she thought she'd never see again. And his voice—its tenor and tone had been of greatest comfort to her even before she was born.

"Daddy! How are you Daddy?"

She was crying.

"I, I thought you were dead. I thought you left me again."

He was also crying.

"I promised you I wouldn't leave you ever again. And that's why I'm here. I agreed to come to Cheyenne Mountain because I knew I'd be able to talk to you from here. It was the next best thing to actually being with you there."

"I don't get it. Are you still the president?"

"Yes. I'm here. Jack Bray is here. I've got Cabinet members here. What you see up top is just a shadow government."

She had so many questions racing through her mind that she could not decide what to ask first.

"So what's going on? Is Nostradamus still going to hit? Is it smaller than we've been told?"

Whitmore hesitated.

"As far as I know, it will still hit. As for its size and whether or not it'll be a glancing blow—I've heard what you've heard. If for some reason someone could and is in fact manipulating the telemetry data, I'm out of that loop. I don't know. I'm just serving my function according to protocol."

He smiled.

"It's great seeing your face, Susan."

She was unsatisfied with his answer.

"Well, do you know what they're doing over here? On Level Three? They've got missiles pointed at countries that are supposed to be our friends—at their shelters! You're the president. If you're not making the calls on matters like that, then who is?"

Whitmore's face and tone expressed fatherly disapproval.

"Susan, you have to let it go. You have to stop all this digging. You have a husband now, and you'll have a safe life where you are. Don't concern yourself with Level Three and who's running the government. Make a life for yourself while you can. You don't know how lucky you are to be there with someone to love—and with someone who loves you as I know Dexter does. Love is the important thing."

If he hadn't looked and sounded so much like her father, she would have doubted his identity.

"But so is the *truth*, Daddy. You taught me that. You told me that life itself is a never-ending quest for truth. You said the search for truth was the duty of the brave and wise. Did you forget *telling* me those things?"

Joe Whitmore bowed his head, realizing that his daughter had, in such literal terms, embraced the lessons of life and philosophy he taught her as a girl. What he spoke in rhetoric and theory, she was applying in practice. She lived her life by the words of an idealistic father. As he looked at her distraught face on the monitor, he realized she could not be changed.

"Yes, I remember. It's just that I *love* you, Susan. You're all I've got. And your quest for the truth puts you in grave danger. There *are* things going on I don't know about, and I don't know who's responsible. I only know it's bigger than me; it's bigger than the U.S. government. I'm afraid that if you keep digging, you'll get yourself in a place where I won't be able to help you."

She smiled, realizing her father's concerns.

"I understand, Daddy. I'll be careful. I might even take a hiatus until the smoke clears, but at some point I have to find out what's going on down there. I have to know the truth."

She laughed.

"I'm younger than ninety-two percent of the people down here in a shelter that's sealed for four hundred years. That means those goons on Level Three will get old and die before me. If worst comes to worst, I'll just wait them out. As long as I'm down here, I'll never stop searching."

"But you will take a break... for now?"

She nodded.

"Yes."

Whitmore sighed, relieved.

"Thank you. You know, Susan, in the confusion I never got you and Dexter a wedding gift. I thought about it, made a few arrangements and came up with something that I think you'll both love. It'll make him happy, and I hope that makes you happy."

"What is it?"

"Tomorrow. I'll make sure he gets it tomorrow."

Chapter 32

They had agreed to meet at Liberty Summit on August 5. Like waking reptiles, they crawled out from caves, from makeshift tents, from holes in the ground. Many were injured, some were emaciated and still others were suffering from radioactive poisoning. In May, approximately eight thousand soldiers and their families had embarked on the journey into the middle Rocky Mountains to escape the U.S. military. Four months later, there were less than fifteen hundred people left alive.

The majority had perished as a result of the July 17 missile attacks. When addressing the nation, erstwhile President Chuck Bentsen characterized the assault as one that employed conventional bombs dropped from high-flying aircraft, but Robert E. Lee and hapless New Republic soldiers were victims of a much more sinister reality. The twenty to thirty Lance missiles that peppered the mountainsides were armed with neutron warheads.

Neutron warheads, or "enhanced radiation warheads" as they are called in scientific circles, are basically hydrogen bombs without the uranium-238 jacket, which absorbs neutrons to increase the force of the blast.

By eliminating the uranium jacket, the full fusion emission of neutrons is released, making the radioactivity more deadly with less destruction to physical surroundings. A one-kiloton neutron bomb could spread a lethal dose of neutron radiation to exposed people over a one-mile radius. Originally conceived as an antitank weapon, the warhead's greatest advantage lay in its ability to barbeque hiding soldiers, while preserving structures intact.

More than half the New Republic Army died during the nuclear weapons attacks on July 17, and no one, not even Robert Lee and Captain Clyde hiding farther up the mountain, knew until many days later.

While the thickness and mass of the mountains shielded some, many others had no protection from the penetrating neutron radiation. For many, foxholes and trenches became graves, and for others, caves and cracks became tombs and sepulchers.

Only after the bugles began to play the reveille on the morning of August 5, and only after the still-surviving soldiers assembled at Liberty Summit, did Lee and his motley group of followers realize the degree of death and devastation exacted by the missile attacks of July 17.

And thus with tears in his eyes, Robert E. Lee climbed to the top of a crag on the summit. The setting sun created a fire-line impression on the serrated horizon. As Robert looked out over the survivors, battered, broken, hungry and huddled in the clearing before him, he wept.

"We're all that's *left!*"

He raised his hands to the dimming sky.

"Out of a nation of more than three hundred million, we're all that's left! We are the last true Americans on the planet, and we will survive."

He wiped his face with the filthy sleeve of a long robe. In his hand he held a large staff that he used to support himself while walking. Injured during bombing raids, he walked with a noticeable limp. Long, graying, unbound hair flowing over his shoulders, he seemed like a tattered Moses.

"They thought they could ruin us, they thought they could wipe us out, but here it is August 5th and we're still standin. In two days, we will be able to look ta the heavens and proclaim ta our misguided brothers and sisters across this great country that we was right—that there ain't gonna be no asteroid. And when those millions of fooled people realize they can no longer trust the lyin U.S. government, they'll come ta us then."

Sporadic shouts of agreement and hesitant applause interrupted Robert's speech. As the cold closed in, the shivering men, women and children inched closer to the crackling bonfire.

"And they'll come ta us in a great crowd. They'll swarm ta us by the millions. And together we'll assemble a great army ta fight in the last great battle of good against evil. Together we'll save the heart and soul of America an rebuild the New Republic. The only question we need ta ask ourselves is this: Are we *ready* for that great and glorious day?"

The crowd responded with lukewarm enthusiasm. Robert could sense that the spirit had departed from his people. They were broken and demoralized. Sighing, he raised his right hand and continued.

"So for Earl Krebbs, for ma wife Becky and ma boys Dayton an Tyler, for the forty thousand men, women and children murdered by the U.S. government of America at Echo Valley, for those who died in the evacuation of New Lexinton, for those who died in the mountains and for those brave souls who died defendin us—those of us who live after ya owe ya a debt of gratitude, a debt we will repay in the weeks to come. We—"

An excited, stentorian shout interrupted his speech.

"Look at that! Look at the sky!"

As Robert's eyes searched the crowd for the man who yelled, he realized no one was listening to him. His people had turned away and were murmuring and gesturing in another direction. They had all raised their faces toward the east, where in the sky, an ominous object shone bright in the heavens.

It didn't matter to anyone that the object was not Nostradamus. People all over the world had been looking to the heavens for signs. Even more eerie, the fine dust dispersed into the atmosphere by the July 17 nuclear bombs cast the nearly full August moon in a deep crimson hue.

No one remarked aloud, but the entire audience, including Robert, had heard the scripture so many times in the last year that it had become imprinted in their collective psyches: the moon truly *had* become as blood!

****

"*Est-ce que t'as vu la lune ce soir?*"

The pilot pointed out the window at the blood-filled moon. The man seated to his right leaned forward for a better view.

"*Elle est rouge, non?*"

The men were unfamiliar with the prophecy of Revelation 6, but both were religious. They saw the sign of the darkened moon as a favorable omen from Allah. The pilot checked his instruments as his passenger said a last-minute prayer.

"*Merde! Ils nous voient! Ils viennent!*"

His partner finished the series of exclamations.

"*C'est fini. Nous sommes morts. Louange à Allah!*"

They could not see the air-to-air missiles launched by the incoming F-15 fighter jets, but they knew impact was seconds away. After all, the small prop plane was flying in unauthorized airspace just outside Philadelphia. And yet, despite their imminent deaths, the pilots had accomplished their mission. They had managed to get in the air with it—something no one thought they could ever do.

David LeJeune and Farouk Contier were American citizens with valid pilot's licenses. Both were born on U.S. soil to immigrant parents. Both had attended American schools and had become involved with anti-American groups during college.

After graduation from college, LeJeune went to Saudi Arabia, where he continued to study religion and history. Contier spent six years in Cairo, where he first became involved in al-Qaida sponsored terrorism. LeJeune and Contier met in Kandahar, Afghanistan, while attending al-Qaida sponsored training camps.

Shortly before the Twin Tower attacks on September 11, 2001, al-Qaida leaders ordered all the organization's American-born members to return to the United States and to wait there for further instructions. LeJeune and Contier were sent to Philadelphia.

Living as roommates, LeJeune taught Arabic at a mosque and Contier drove a cab. They waited on orders, even after Whitmore's announcement, anticipating their chance to give their lives for the cause.

The radioactive waste came from Europe through Mexico. The Americans did their best to protect their southern border, but a group of guards had been susceptible to cash bribes during the waning days of July. Al-Qaida recognized the opportunity and exploited the breach. The bomb was fashioned in Philadelphia, custom-designed to carry its radioactive component and disperse it upon detonation.

Sixteen months earlier, Contier purchased a used Cessna Caravan 675 and had stored it in a barn on private property outside the city. He chose the 675 because, according to Cessna, the model was "specifically designed for the abuse of 'unimproved' airfields." During July, he and LeJeune toiled sixteen hours a day to fashion a makeshift runway long enough for take-off. The finished airstrip was rough, but Contier was sure the 675 could handle it.

The engineers arrived with bomb components on August 1. They worked fifty-one hours creating the "dirty bomb" and loaded it into the cargo bay of the airplane. They gave the pilots instructions about how to manually discharge the bomb, but no one believed the small plane would reach its targeted detonation point over metropolitan Philadelphia.

The entire team prayed for success shortly before take-off at eleven p.m., and everyone on the ground cheered when the Cessna took to the sky just short of the runway's end. Contier, the acting pilot, flew low, hoping to avoid radar as he approached the city.

He did realize, however, that in order for the bomb to exact maximum contamination, it would have to be detonated high over the city. Ninety seconds after he began his final ascent, his radar screen showed the approaching fighter aircraft. If Contier could have continued another five minutes, he would have been directly over the metropolitan area, but he didn't have five minutes. He didn't have five seconds.

There were two explosions in quick succession. The blast, as the F-15's Sidewinder missiles slammed into the Cessna's fuselage, triggered the bomb's detonation device, creating a huge fireball that almost consumed the lead fighter. Reeling out of control, the fighter, trailing flames, spiraled toward the Earth where it crashed and continued to burn.

****

Jonah rolled over at 6:30 a.m. He stared at the clock, calculating the time.

"Thirty hours and three minutes."

He stood and stretched. The asteroid was supposed to hit in thirty hours. In six hours, he would go to the church, where he would stay until it hit or didn't hit. He thought about what message he would relate to his congregation and to the world watching. He didn't want to think about it. He wanted to give himself completely to the Lord, to be directed by the Lord. He didn't want to share his own thoughts and words; he wanted to share the Lord's message.

On a television special report, President Donovan Scott and military commanders briefed the nation about the nuclear bomb explosion over the town of Bustleton, in Northeast Philadelphia, where an estimated sixty thousand of the area's four hundred thousand residents were subjected to radiation from the crude weapon. At least seventy were already confirmed dead. President Scott urged people not to panic, assuring Americans that no non-military aircraft would be able to approach the nation's metropolitan areas.

Reactions from Americans interviewed ran the gamut. Some announced fears of an all-out terrorist bloody war on the morning of

August 7. Others expressed anti-Arab and anti-immigrant sentiments. One man praised former President Bentsen for nuking Iran and Iraq, suggesting the country would be better off with a man like Bentsen in charge.

Jonah sighed, turning off the set.

"Not as I will, but as *thou* wilt."

He went to the bedroom door and looked at Aaliyah sleeping. He smiled. He loved his wife. Would this be the last time he would be able to watch her sleeping?

"God's will, not mine."

When the phone rang, he figured it was his driver, confirming departure time.

"Eleven-thirty, Cedric—I'm already up."

"Dad?"

Jonah looked toward the heavens and closed his eyes, praising God. He had prayed so many times to hear that voice one more time. He worried it hadn't been God's will for him to hear from his son again.

"Dexter?"

"Yes, Dad. I wanted to call you to tell you that I'm okay. I wanted to tell you that I love you. And I wanted to tell Mom."

Jonah was so excited and nervous that he dropped the cordless phone. Fumbling to retrieve it, he returned it to his ear.

"Dexter, are you there? Your mom! I've got to wake up your mom!"

He rushed to the bed and pounced on Aaliyah, pushing the phone to her ear.

"Liyah, it's Dexter! Talk! I'll pick up the other line!"

She was already in tears.

"Dexter? Is it really you? Are you okay?"

"I'm fine. I love you, Mom."

"I love you too, my Baby, my sweet Baby Boy."

Jonah's voice interrupted Aaliyah's doting.

"Where *are* you, Son?"

"I'm in a shelter deep in a mountain. I wish we could be there with you."

His mother's intuition was keen.

"Dexter, who's with you? Are you with Megan?"

"Her name's actually Susan Whitmore, or *was* Susan Whitmore. She's my wife now. She wanted me to tell you she loves you both, and she wishes we could be with you tomorrow."

Aaliyah was crying, her right hand over heart, as if by patting her chest she might slow it down.

"Tell her we love her too and we're happy you two have each other."

"Thank you."

Dexter paused. Both he and Susan were crying.

"Mom and Dad—I have to go right now. I don't know what's going to happen tomorrow, but I promise I'll try to call you again. Thank you for everything you've given me. I love you so much."

Both parents responded at the same time.

"We love you too, Dexter!"

"God bless you, Mom and Dad. Goodbye."

Chapter 33

"The Lord is my Shepherd; I shall not want. He maketh me to lie down in green pastures: he leadeth me beside the still waters. He restoreth my soul: he leadeth me in the paths of righteousness for his name's sake."
Ten thirty-three p.m.—exactly twelve hours before the expected impact. Jonah led the congregation in scripture reading. The church was full, as were the majority of the churches around the world.

In a convalescent hospital in Billings, Montana, eighty-eight-year-old Dale Clark, a bitter racist all his life, read from his Bible along with Jonah; he held his six-year-old grandson's hand. In Vancouver, British Columbia, the members of a Chinese Baptist church were watching Jonah on three ninety-six-inch television monitors stationed in front of the pews.

In Richmond, Virginia, thirteen-year-old Katie Shepard, who had no Bible, read the words from the text at the bottom of the television screen. An hour earlier, Katie's parents said their tearful goodbyes, leaving her in charge of her siblings, who were eleven-year-old Justin, ten-year-old Natalie, six-year-old Chandra and five-year-old Tatum. Her parents told her they were going to a party and would not be coming back.

In the West Bank, the early morning sun was not yet warm, though smoke rose from the ground. In the distance, rubble from a disintegrated house littered the street. A puddle of drying blood had congealed in a depression in the pavement. The blood trail to it streaked from one of the night's casualties, a nine-year-old girl with brown skin and a doll tucked under one arm. Because the back of her head was gone, her still-open eyes had sunk into her skull. Flies crawled in and out of her mouth and nostrils.

In the distance, a flatbed truck laden with corpses was stopped to let workers restack bodies that had spilled off one side. August 6 had been one of the bloodiest nights in the history of the region, the ultimate result of animosities reaching back four thousand years to a conflict between the sons of Abraham.

During July and August, many former enemies on Earth had resolved to settle differences and to forget old grudges. The mantle of peace and safety had settled securely on most of the planet. Yet in Israel and Palestine, the wounds ran so deep that the entire world realized any mending or lessening of hostilities in the end was impossible, even in Earth's final twenty-four hours.

The night's death toll: three thousand and counting. After years of brutality and bloodguilt from both sides, the world had become inured to the savagery and inhumanity of the opposing peoples. The world had at last realized that the violence of the region had become one of Earth's natural cycles, as natural as the eternal conflicts between lions and hyenas, between ants and termites, between cats and dogs.

In America, the panic and unease that resulted from the dirty bomb explosion over Northeast Philadelphia had subsided, though there were television news rumors of similar attempts over San Francisco and Chicago. The reports suggested that the Air Force had shot down other bomb-rigged cargo planes outside those two cities, but the government denied knowledge of additional attacks on American targets.

American cities became violent on August 7, as people became more and more desperate. By 12:01 a.m., the streets and alleys were filled with murderers, thieves, drug addicts, drunken people, freaks, lunatics and insurrectionists. Conspicuously missing were the federalized National Guard, who had been effective at maintaining peace for three hundred and sixty-four days. They had deserted their posts to be with their families.

Most decent people were indoors. Some had lamb's blood smeared on the two side jambs and on the upper door jamb of their houses. Many were in various churches. Others were spending special "last moments" with loved ones and some were watching television, hanging on Jonah's every word, awaiting his last-hour message.

"Yea, though I walk through the valley of the shadow of death, I will fear no evil: for thou art with me; thy rod and thy staff they comfort me. Thou preparest a table before me in the presence of mine enemies; thou anointest my head with oil; my cup runneth over. Surely goodness and mercy shall follow me all the days of my life: and I will dwell in the house of the Lord for ever."

In stark contrast to the chaos and fear that dominated the surface of the planet, the community of the Crypt was peaceful, though concerned. Most television sets went back and forth between Jonah's church broadcast and a science documentary about the crash of Nostradamus and impending cosmic winter. On a separate channel, a few watched a rerun program from January in which proponents of the glancing blow theory urged people to keep their senses and to conserve resources. They conceded that a great tribulation was imminent, but it would be nothing on the scale of cosmic winter.

Days earlier, Don Smock and Davis, at last employing Calypso, had determined that the American government had the means to alter incoming telemetric data on a global scale. They had discovered sophisticated programs hidden in all data collection software. The U.S. government could access those programs to alter data input even before computers worldwide could begin analysis and interpretation.

Data received from the corporate-funded *Helios* were especially suspect. If changes were made at the data collection level, if the government had altered the initial input that computers received worldwide, then all the results, regardless of who ran the analysis, would be flawed.

The questions were disconcerting. *Had* the government used its hidden programs to change the way instruments around the world received input about Nostradamus? If so, how had that input been altered? And still more troubling, *why* would they do it? What was the government's hidden agenda?

At 6:30 on the evening of August 6, Davis decided to stop working, even though many nagging questions remained unanswered. Smock insisted on continuing, but Davis refused. He told Smock that, while the questions at hand needed to be resolved, nothing on Earth was more important to him than Asia and Blake. He said he was going home to spend time with his family.

"I've never been able to say this before, but I'm quitting. I realize we still have a lot of work to do, and we might not figure this out for weeks. But my family needs me now, and that's where I'll be— with them. You should be with yours."

Left alone in his office, Smock considered Davis's words. He and Davis were alike in many ways. Both were busy, thinking, driven men. Neither had ever put family before work, especially Smock. And while Davis Franklin recognized what was perhaps his last opportunity to change his life and its priorities, it was too late for Smock.

Don Smock had been married for twenty-five years to a beautiful and patient woman named Ally. Ally loved him, fought for him, catered to him. And what had he given her in return? Nothing. She had a comfortable life, and they had a son together, but he had given her nothing of himself. The best of his time, the best of his energy, the best of all he could offer was spent pursuing his life's ambitions, his dreams and his life's work. Ally got nothing. Only then, on August 6, did Don reflect on how lonely she must have been over those twenty-five years.

She complained sometimes. On several occasions, she even threatened to leave if he didn't start paying more attention to her. When Adam left for college, she became desperate. One night, she confessed to Don that she had had a brief affair in a weak, lonely moment.

Don was livid. He felt betrayed in the worst of ways. Although Ally begged his forgiveness and swore she would never make the mistake again, he left her that night. He acted in anger. He left her and proceeded to take everything from her. He sold the properties and the cars. He hired lawyers to persecute her and disgrace her until she was just too humiliated and tired to pursue spousal support and community property.

When Ally landed in a halfway house, Adam tried to intervene with his father on her behalf, but Don threatened to disown and disinherit his son if he continued. Don did not talk to Adam again until Ally's funeral seven years later. By then it was too late. It was too late for Don Smock to change anything.

Only after Ally's death did Don realize she was the best wife he could have ever had. He realized too that she was human, and that humans needed affection. What he refused to give her, she took from someone else in a weak, lonely moment.

For that, he should have forgiven her. The affair should have been a wake-up call for him, and her death should have been a pronouncement shouted from the heavens. His priorities were all wrong. He should have changed his priorities back then and he knew it, but he was too busy. He just... let the time pass.

His relationship with Helen Engstrom started out differently though. Initially, he took time off work to spend with her. He included her in some of his personal plans. He even spent a week assisting her in her work. And yet after a year, he had gone back to his old ways. She complained, but she loved him. She loved him right up until the moment she went into one of the Refugium's cryochambers to hide from the government.

And what had he done? Before she went under, he refused to listen to her theories about the asteroid's size and its earthbound trajectory. And then when he himself began to doubt the government, he ruined her by bringing her out of cold sleep too quickly. Again, he realized his priorities were wrong, and yet there was a shred of hope.

Taking a deep breath, he knocked on the door. The large man who answered seemed angry for the intrusion, though he called his wife. Seeing her face, Don smiled.

"Helen! Helen, I need you to do me a favor."

She seemed confused.

"The wedding was *yesterday*. It was on your invitation."

"No, I, I was working. I'm sorry I didn't make it. Congratulations."

He sighed.

"I need you to check on Helen. I need to see if she's come around yet."

Her expression was disapproving.

"First of all, you made me rush her revival. We don't know if she'll *ever* be right in the head, but that isn't it. It's August 7th, Don. I'm not *going* to work today. I have a family. I'm *lucky* to be spending time with my family today."

Instead of returning to his private residence on Level One, crestfallen Don Smock returned to his office on Level Four. He was the only living soul on the entire level, an ironic portent of his lonely, static hell ahead.

Sitting at his desk, he called the command.

"Television."

He recognized the man who spoke, and yet for a first time, he listened to the message.

****

"Over the past year, we've heard volumes about August 7th. We've dreaded it, imagined it, debated it, renamed it—we've had a hard time just *dealing* with it. And now that it's here, what do we see? The sun rose this morning just like it has every other morning. It's just another day. August 7th is *just* another day. So what we've been fretting and dreading hasn't been about August 7th after all, has it?"

Jonah smiled with confidence. He didn't know where he was going. Speaking extemporaneously, he tried to let the Lord direct him.

"No, it isn't August 7th we've feared. What we've been *fearing* is Judgment Day. So what exactly *is* Judgment Day? The dictionary calls it the end of the world, or doomsday, but we know better. The Bible describes it as the time of God's final judgment of all people. It is the day when each of our lives, each at its own time, is taken into account. All our deeds, private and public, all our thoughts, all our motivations, all the good we may have done, as well as the evil... are called into account."

He paused for a drink of water.

"We've been fearing an August 7th Judgment Day for the past year, when in actuality Judgment Day is a different day and separate judgment for each of us. Judgment Day for Martin Luther was February 18, 1546. For Abraham Lincoln, it came on April 14, 1865. On January 30, 1948, Mahatma Gandhi arrived at Judgment Day. On the day we die, our lives themselves stand as our record. The lives we have lived stand as our testimony before God. We are judged according to the lives we've lived."

He looked for Aaliyah in her usual place, but he saw an old woman there. Aaliyah had surrendered her seat in the overcrowded church. She smiled at Jonah from where she stood in the aisle nearby.

"If we have lived reasonably good, though imperfect lives, there is nothing to fear on Judgment Day, whenever that might come for us. If we have lived wicked, evil lives, it still might not be too late. On Nisan 14, 33 C.E. at Calvary, as our Lord Jesus faced his own death, his own Judgment Day, one of the malefactors, or evildoers, hanging next to him rebuked the other who had taunted Jesus, saying, 'We receive the due reward of our deeds.' By this, he meant that he and the other thief deserved to die for the evil they had done, but he went on to ask, 'Jesus, Lord, remember me when thou comest into thy kingdom.' And Jesus replied, 'Verily I say unto thee, Today shalt thou be with me in paradise.'"

He looked toward the main camera.

"By this, our Lord Jesus demonstrated his willingness to forgive truly repentant sinners, even in the last hour. There are no doubt malefactors who have found their way into churches tonight. There are evildoers who have turned on their television sets and are watching at this moment. Seeking the Lord is a good first step, but Jesus urges you to repent from your sinful ways, to turn back from all wrongdoing. Unlike the malefactors hanged next to Jesus, you are not yet on that torture stake. We don't know *what* will happen at 10:33 this morning and thereafter. In a world of chaos and lawlessness, you have an opportunity to demonstrate your repentance. Therefore, do all the good that you can do right now, before it's too late. Set matters right, while you still can."

Chapter 34

At six a.m., the Space Needle party in Seattle was still going strong, though couples were beginning to peel off to spend their last few hours enjoying sex, drugs and rock and roll in private. Bob Taylor was drunk, but he was ready to go. His date Lisa, however, still wanted to dance. The DJ was playing two full hours of Jimi Hendrix, and she wasn't ready to trade such an electric, incredible last-chance experience for a so-so one-timer with drunken Bob. She told him to have another drink, which he had along with two additional rails of cocaine.

Bob wandered through the vast room, hoping to pick up another chick for his last-time romp, but he wasn't getting any action, even though he offered drugs. Lisa was his best bet, so he went back to her and waited. The last song in the set was *The Star Spangled Banner* by Hendrix.

The instant that Bob heard it, he began to cry. He was a former Marine, and that song on that morning was the most beautiful thing he had heard in all his life. Hearing it, he felt pride, patriotism, nostalgia and love like he had never felt before. Drunk and drugged though he was, he felt sober through the song. When it was over, he was a changed man. He was glad he had stayed, because Hendrix had been born to change his life that very night. And yet when the song was over, he realized Lisa had left with another man to finish partying in private.

****

At a church in Evansville, Indiana, an entire congregation sat in their Sunday best, waiting for the moment that God was going to snatch them into heaven. Their leader, the Reverend Clayton T. Bowes, seemed a little uneasy as he sat on the stage. He had gotten up on several occasions since midnight to lend encouragement to nervous members, but he had run out of things to say.

"We shall not sleep, but we shall all be changed, in a moment, in the twinkling of an eye, we shall be raised up incorruptible, we shall be changed, the wicked will suffer and burn on Earth while the righteous will be caught up in rapture and transferred instantly to heavenly life."

In the front row, pretty Jenna Gilbert looked toward her husband and smiled. She had always been such a dutiful wife. She never talked back. When she looked over, her pious husband nodded, approving her humble attitude and bowed head. He had no idea what she was really thinking.

She awaited the moment. She had imagined it many times. They would all be sitting there, waiting on the Lord, and when he came, almost everyone in the congregation would be instantly snatched up. As she left her seat, she would see her husband, still sitting there. His expression would show surprise, shock and horror when he realized he hadn't been raptured. As he looked up and reached for her as she departed, she would slap his filthy hands away and say what she had waited a year to say.

"Thought you was goin somewhere, didn't ya Billy? Well, *now* you can have her. She's the only other one *left*."

Then guilty Billy would turn around and he'd see her—Tonya Butters, the tramp he went to Chicago with behind Jenna's back. Jenna would fly off to heaven, leaving the two of them to burn in Hell on Earth.

Though the seated Reverend Bowes smiled at faces he recognized from time to time, he was having second thoughts about *how* it would happen. He had imagined it all his life, but there, in the last few hours, doubt had begun to invade his former fantasies. What if he had been wrong about the rapture?

What if that Jonah Williams was right? What if it wasn't going to happen? What if he and his congregation were stuck on Earth after the asteroid hit? If that happened, if there was no rapture and the Earth was on fire—everyone would no doubt come to him. They would close in on him. Panicked and angry, they would blame him. They would demand answers. They would want to know why had he led them down the path to destruction.

Closing his eyes, he leaned forward and fell to the floor on his knees as he prayed to God for salvation. He prayed for his fellow ministers around the world who, like him, were having last minute doubts. And then he prayed for his congregation. If they all died, their blood would be on his hands.

He found himself praying for the asteroid to hit, praying for the destruction of the Earth, praying for the rapture. And then, in the midst of all his praying, a scripture came to him. It just sort of popped into his head. *Not as I will, but as thou wilt.* And hearing it, he stopped praying at once.

When he opened his eyes and looked up, he realized that the congregation had followed his lead. They had all fallen to their knees and were praying for the rapture and the destruction of Earth.

****

"I know y'all saw it. I saw it. Maybe it *was* a sign from God. But I submit he was tellin us we got a bloody battle ahead."

A year ago, Robert E. Lee was virtually unknown. He was the leader of a band of ignorant men, a lone fanatic voice crying out in the wilderness. Within a year, he had become a household name, a national hero to many, the leader of a movement that had threatened to rip America apart at its seams. It had been a good run, but the federal government proved to be too powerful.

His rise to national prominence came at great personal cost. He had lost Becky, his wife, and son Dayton. He had lost his mother and his Uncle Earl. He had lost son Tyler during the July bombings. He had lost eighteen thousand soldiers. And just that morning, he had lost Captain Clyde, his spiritual teacher, his friend and his father figure.

"We're still almost a thousand strong, but that'll change tamarra. Tamarra the people of America are gonna remember the New Republic! Tamarra we head back down the mountain! Tamarra we'll bring all the confused masses together and organize an even greater New Republic army! Tamarra we begin the great American Liberation!"

Only four hundred people had shown up for Robert Lee's hastily convened assembly. Many of the missing had found caves near the summit where they were determined to hide until the worst consequences from the asteroid's impact had passed. They already knew the New Republic's plan.

Lee said Nostradamus was not going to hit, but he hadn't offered any scientific proof. No one trusted the federal government, but they all had seen the sign in the heavens with their own eyes. If Nostradamus did hit, they hoped to be safe in the caves of the summit, in a strong and steady mountain range high above the Earth. If it didn't hit or if it was a glancing blow like Robert had insisted, they were prepared to follow and help him liberate America.

****

Rabbi David Blum read from the Pentateuch in Hebrew. His synagogue, like other synagogues and temples around the world, was full. He read from the second book, about the condition of the Hebrews in Egypt prior to their deliverance by God. Alternating between Hebrew and English, he detailed the circumstances of the first Passover and the significance of its tokens. He encouraged his congregation to reflect on God's qualities and on their relationship with him. He reminded them that with God, all things were possible, even things that seemed impossible, like miracles.

He had spent August 5 with his close friend Jonah Williams. They had prayed to God for salvation together and had discussed the content of their final messages to their respective congregations. Before Jonah departed, David hugged him long and hard. They wept in each other's arms, whispering blessings and words of encouragement.

David was no longer gaunt as before. His health had been restored. During July, he and Dr. Levin traveled to Jerusalem and to other Israeli cities, bearing witness to the power of faith when facing trials in life. Dr. Levin described David's cancer as one of the worst cases he had ever encountered. He admitted that he had exaggerated David's odds for survival when he estimated the rabbi had a ten percent chance of pulling through. Tears in his eyes, he spoke to television audiences.

"I never believed in Hollywood endings, but nothing I've seen has ever come close to this. This ending could have only been written by God."

David's story had tremendous appeal all over Israel and beyond. The Israeli television broadcast was replayed all over the world and embraced by people of many faiths. After a brief tour of American cities, David insisted on stepping out of the spotlight to spend time with his family.

His wife, Lynda, and son, Stephen, had returned from Rhode Island in April, and they brought Lynda's mother, Claire, much to David's discontent. He called her his nemesis.

Whenever he related his story to eager listeners, whenever Jews or anyone else praised him, Claire was always there to point out his imperfections. Even as he outlined the talk he planned to give on August 7, eighty-one-year-old Claire was sitting across the room, telling him he needed to stand straighter and speak with a little more chutzpah.

He thought of Claire as he stood before the congregation, straightening his back. In a sedate tone, he called on his audience to remember the story of the man Job. It was the story of a dedicated servant of God whose faith was tested.

In rapid succession, Job lost his possessions, his family, his social status, and finally, he had lost his very health. From a condition of profound suffering, he wondered *why* so many trials had befallen him. He wondered why God had *let* such tragedy come upon him.

Little did Job know that, though he was just a lowly man, he was the central figure in a great spiritual debate. He did not know his actions, or reactions, were being scrutinized by a vast audience seeking to resolve a significant spiritual issue. He did not know that his trials would provide instruction for billions of people thousands of years later. What we learn from Job, David insisted, is that we waste time and energy questioning God and what he does.

"A much more profitable thing it is to *trust* him, to rely on him."

****

"It seems fitting that now we return to Calvary. We are followers of Christ, so each of us, as we face the trials that lie ahead, can look to his example. As Christ faced his death, he wasn't afraid. He wasn't angry and he didn't blame his father. No, despite being up all night, being falsely accused, being whipped, being ridiculed, being beat and spat on, Lord Jesus maintained his focus about his mission on Earth."

It was nine a.m. in Los Angeles, where downtown, the streets were empty. The landscape seemed an ashy gray. The same scene was playing in cities across the country. In Europe it was the same episode. People had locked themselves in homes, apartments, shelters, caves and hovels as they counted down Earth's final ninety minutes.

In the East, Nostradamus was visible through binoculars in the dimming sky, though it would still take another sixty-five to seventy-five minutes before it reached Earth's outer atmosphere. The whole world was in mourning.

He had only heard them over the course of an hour, but Jonah recognized the cries of the newborn twin boys. Brenda had the babies at 3:30 and 3:55 a.m., and though she was exhausted, she insisted on being in the church that morning. She sat in a wheelchair in the front, patting one boy's back while Aaliyah sat in a folding chair next to her, rocking the other on an elevated thigh.

Jonah sighed and continued.

"Never once did Jesus let fear or anger or anxiety cloud the sight of his earthly mission. And yet, when I was younger, I always wondered about two sets of the seven last words he spoke and why he spoke them. If you remember, the first set is found in the first two gospels, where Jesus says, '*E-li, E-li, la-ma sa-bach-tha-ni?*' Matthew translates this as, '*My God, My God, Why has thou forsaken me?*'"

He paused to let his audience consider the question.

"Now I just stood here and told you that Jesus let nothing stand in the way of his earthly mission, and here we have him, in his own words, asking his father, 'Why has thou abandoned me?'"

He smiled to put his listeners at ease.

"Perhaps some of us feel forsaken by God today. And perhaps some of us are letting that feeling of abandonment cloud the sight of our respective missions on Earth. But the truth is: Jesus didn't call that question to the heavens because he had lost sight of his mission. Quite the contrary. He said those words because he was *remembering* his mission. He was remembering Psalm 22, where the persecution he had endured the night before had been prophesied by David. He was remembering biblical prophecy had been fulfilled when they pierced his hands and his feet. As he watched the guards dividing up his clothing, he was mentally recalling that David prophesied they would part his garments among them and cast lots upon his vesture."

He nodded.

"Yes, even as Jesus suffered on that torture stake, dying, he never lost sight of his mission. His reflection on Psalm 22 confirmed the fulfillment of Bible prophecy. And which Psalm was that? It was the one that begins, 'My God, my God, why hast thou forsaken me?'"

As he scanned the front row, he could see his message was registering on some of the faces.

"His actual *last* words are found in Luke and John. Luke says Jesus cried out with a loud voice, saying, 'Father, into thy hands I commend my spirit.' John recorded the same words. Those were his very last words before he gave up the ghost, his last affirmation before he died."

Glancing at his watch, he decided to conclude. It was already 9:30. He wanted to spend time with Aaliyah before the next message. He hoped to resume at 10:15 and speak right through the predicted impact.

"So Brothers and Sisters, if we truly seek to imitate Christ as we face whatever trials lie ahead, we will go forward without anger, without fear and without anxiousness. We will seek not as we will, but as God would. And *whenever* that day comes, the day we give up the ghost, whether it is today or fifty years from now, let us live our lives in a way so that each of us can say with great confidence, 'Father, into thy hands I commend my spirit.'"

Chapter 35

"Hard to believe it was just a year ago—one year ago today, exactly.

"What?"

"It was exactly one year ago that my father went before the world to say it was coming."

Dexter bowed his head, remembering.

"I was sitting at the table with my parents. Things were normal then. Seems like a lot longer than a year."

"Tell me about it! My mother and sister were alive. I could wake up and see my father... usually."

Dexter and Susan sat on a couch in the cozy, little living room. Her feet were in his lap. The television was on, though muted. After a while he sighed, patting her knee.

"You ever wonder if he did the right thing?"

"Who, my father? You mean do I think he should have told the world that day?"

"Yes. If he hadn't, do you think things would have been better, or worse?"

Susan crossed her arms, responding in a pensive tone.

"I don't know. Things would be *different*. Maybe Mom and Beth would still be alive, but then maybe not. Some things were just bound to happen. I mean, the world was going to find out at some point. By coming out with it, he may have saved the country from mass chaos."

Both sat thinking in silence for a few minutes. Dexter glanced at the countdown clock on the television and nudged his wife.

"Less than thirty minutes."

She hadn't stopped considering his previous question.

"You know, I'd like to believe there's a lesson in everything that happens to us, and I've been thinking about what we're supposed to *learn* from this. Maybe we need to learn you can *never* know whether or not you've made the right choice. It doesn't even matter. There are no do-overs. The only choice that matters is the one you have before you now—the one you're *just* about to make."

She stopped to smear a tear from her cheek.

"Mom—that's what she meant."

She nodded.

"The important question is, are we strong and smart enough to make our *own* choices and live with them, or do we sell-out for whatever reason and let other people make those choices for us?"

Dexter listened, surprised that his wife was speaking so profoundly. She sounded like a grown-up. Then he realized what she was trying to tell him.

"So if you had a *choice*, Susan, where would you be today?"

Her response was immediate. She pointed toward the television.

"There, with your parents, with people I love, placing my faith in God. And you?"

He smiled.

"I'd be there too, with you."

He turned away from the television because the countdown was distracting.

"Do you think we're sell-outs?"

"I think we're down here for a purpose, and I think we need to find out what that is. We need to find our mission here and accomplish it. It's the only way our lives will have meaning."

****

Around the world, families and close friends spent the dwindling hours in a variety of ways, with one commonality: the outpouring of love. Many had already finished elaborate feasts, featuring the finest entrees, wines and desserts that money could buy. They drank the last of the world's old ports and cognacs, sparing no expense. There was no reason to save anything, after all.

In some homes, as many as one hundred people were crowded in, all hugging one another, crying in each other's arms, begging forgiveness in some cases, and confessing love in others. Many were weeping, saying final farewells.

Other places had fewer people, but the spirit was the same. A few read poetry and tearful speeches. Video slide perspectives of family photo collections, all set to favorite songs, played in thousands of dwellings.

In other apartments and homes, it was just two people, sharing a last meal and precious moments. Some danced to love songs, some just held each other to feel secure and others made love.

And then in some cases, it was just a single family—parents and children or a parent and child. In religious homes, families read uplifting Bible passages, prayed or watched Jonah Williams on television. In other homes, parents shared encouragement from world literature and explained Earth's predicament in calm, positive, philosophical terms. All over, parents held their children and reaffirmed their love.

Five-year-old Blake sat between Davis and Asia on the couch. The television was off. She held her favorite book in her lap. It was a book she usually asked her parents to read to her, but she was learning quickly. This time, she insisted on reading to them.

"Once upon a time there was a dear little chicken named Chicken Little. One morning as she was scratching in her garden, a pebble fell off the roof and hit her on the head.

'Oh, dear me!' she cried, 'The sky is falling. I must go and tell the King,' and away she ran down the road."

****

"One year ago, we all found out that this eight-mile-wide asteroid was supposed to be headed our way. For many of us, it was paralyzing news, the equivalent of a doctor telling us we had exactly one year to live."

Jonah had begun with his final message.

"When I was in college, I remember reading a book that dealt with the psychology of death and dying. In fact, one expert explained that people who know they're going to die go through five stages in the process. These five stages are denial, anger, bargaining, depression and acceptance. Over the past year, we've seen the entire Earth go through these stages.

"Right here in America, we've seen the denial from New Lexington, the anger and frustration from right here in California. We've seen and participated in organized prayer as a way of bargaining our salvation, and recently, we've seen an epidemic of pink pill deaths, the result of profound depression the world over. So now, as we watch the final drama unfold on our televisions, we've come to accept the fact that something *is* definitely coming our way. We can look out there and see it."

He believed he could feel the spirit of God flowing over him, overwhelming him.

"The only thing missing in the equation, is faith. Faith gives us the power to create miracles. In fact, Jesus said if you have faith as a grain of mustard seed, you can say unto this mountain, 'Remove hence to yonder place,' and nothing will be impossible to you. If you have faith, Brothers and Sisters, now is the time to make that faith evident. If you have faith, now is the time to look to the skies and welcome the glorious return of our Lord Jesus Christ!"

****

Lisa flicked on the television and checked the clock.

"Only twenty minutes! Get your clothes off! We don't have much time."

The young man looked at the countdown box at the bottom right corner of the screen and then he looked toward the ceiling.

"Nineteen minutes. Oh my God!"

"*Oh my God!* is right! We've gotta get started."

She was already nude, except for her clear high heels. She eased back onto the bed and struck a pose. Fumbling, he removed his clothes and climbed on top of her, kissing her neck and breasts. And yet, three minutes later, she was sitting up, annoyed.

"What's wrong? What is *wrong* with you?"

He sat up.

"I'm sorry. This has never happened to me before."

"Yeah, right."

He tugged at the unresponsive source of her frustration.

"It's performance anxiety to the extreme. I've never had to do this with a giant meteor aimed right at my ass, either."

"Here. Take this. What's your name?"

He answered as he swallowed the blue, triangular pill.

"Steve. What was that you gave me?"

"Viagra."

"Viagra?"

Sarcastic, he laughed.

"That's rich, Lady. You know how *long* those things take to kick in?"

"No."

"At least thirty minutes under *normal* circumstances."

He smirked as he watched the realization and disappointment flood her expression.

"We've only got fourteen minutes left."

****

"*By and by they became tired, and sat down to rest, when out from behind the rocks jumped Foxy Loxy.*

'Where are you all going?' he asked with a sly grin.

'The sky is falling and we are going to tell the King!' they all replied together.

'You are not going the right way. Shall I show it to you?' said Foxy Loxy.

'Oh certainly!' they all answered and at once followed Foxy Loxy, until they came to the door of his cave among the rocks. Just as the little feathered folks crowded around the dark, na—narrow hole, eager to follow the sly fox, a little gray squirrel, with very bright eyes, jumped out from behind the bushes and whispered to them: 'Don't go in, don't go in, all your little necks he'll wring, and you'll never see the King.'"

Chapter 36

"Good afternoon, gentlemen."

They answered in a chorus.

"Good afternoon, Mr. President."

In Cheyenne Mountain, a room full of military men and women watched the monitors. One feed was coming from *Helios*, but it was breaking up as the probe, along with Nostradamus, neared Earth. The other feeds came from the Hubbell Space Telescope and from telescope cameras on the ground.

At a table near the bank of communications computers sat *The Eight*, a shadow organization of men representing the most powerful interests on Earth. According to guards, *The Eight* had been in the mountain for some time, but their group's rules prohibited any contact or association with the general population.

Naturally, the government scientists, astronomers, engineers and military experts hard at work were shocked when they were told *The Eight* would watch the impact from the control room. They sat quietly in a section near the largest monitors, occasionally whispering among themselves.

President Joe Whitmore took a place at the head of the table and sighed, loosening his tie. He stared at the screen, wagging his head. Next to him sat Vice President Jack Bray. After a brief conversation between the two, Jack rose, walked over to *The Eight* and grabbed one man by the collar, turning him.

"You know, I think I've been left out of the loop long enough. I'm the Vice President of the United States of America."

He took a .38-caliber pistol from his waistband and placed the barrel at the man's sternum. The two guards at the door reacted by drawing their own weapons, but they pointed the barrels in the air rather than at the Vice President. Soliciting support for his bold move, Jack Bray spoke loud enough for everyone in the room to hear.

"Now I'm an old man with a bad heart. I'm not afraid to die today, which means I'm not afraid to kill you and as many of the others as I can. So you're going to tell me right now: Exactly how big is that thing and what's going to happen when it hits?"

****

"But the sharp ears of Foxy Loxy heard the warning, and quick as a blink, he turned and caught Gander Pander. Just as he was about to twist Gander Pander's neck, the little squirrel threw a big stone and hit the old fox right on the head.

'The sky is surely falling!' groaned Foxy Loxy, creeping into the darkest corner of his cave."

****

For two minutes, the moon was directly between the sun and the Earth, causing darkness in the moon's broad shadow. People in the East stared at the skies in horror, watching as Nostradamus, shining bright, closed on the Earth.

Jonah read from the Bible.

"There shall be signs in the sun, and in the moon, and in the stars; and upon the earth distress of nations, with perplexity; the sea and the waves roaring; men's hearts failing them for fear, and for looking after those things which are coming on the earth: for the powers of the heaven shall be shaken. And then shall they see the Son of man coming in a great cloud with power and great glory. And when these things begin to come to pass, then look up, and lift up your heads; for your redemption draweth nigh."

Placing the Bible on the podium, he walked around it and off the rostrum toward the congregation.

"The world trembles in fear, Brothers and Sisters, but we who have faith in the Lord Jesus welcome his return, a return his Christian followers have anticipated since the day he left. As prophesied at Revelation, every eye shall see him, but while for those of the world, their hearts fail them for fear, we faithful Christians lift our heads and eyes in joy, for our redemption draweth nigh!"

****

"Time's up."

The man's body stiffened as blood and bone exploded from his back, spraying two of the remaining seven. The man next to the victim stood, looking toward the guards at the door. Bray pointed the gun at his throat.

"A volunteer? You're next. Same question. How big is it and what are you guys up to?"

The tall man, defiant and arrogant, answered in English distorted by a German accent.

"You're crazy. You can't kill us all."

"Dead wrong."

Without warning, Bray pulled the trigger.

"Now you're *The Six*."

The man fell. And yet as Bray moved for his third victim, he felt a gun barrel pressed against the side of his head. The nervous guard appealed to the old man.

"Killing them won't change anything, Mr. Vice President. In a minute, we'll *all* know."

****

"By and by they came to the beautiful palace in which lived the wise King, and upon being brought before him, they all shouted at once, 'Good and wise King, we have come to warn you that the sky is falling!'

'How do you know the sky is falling?' asked the King.

'Because a piece of it fell on my head!' said Chicken Little.

'Come nearer, Chicken Little,' said the King, and leaning from his velvet throne, he picked the pebble from the feathers of Chicken Little's head.

'You see it was only a pebble and not part of the sky at all,' said the King. 'Go home in peace and do not fear because the sky cannot fall; only rain falls from the sky.'"

****

"Our Father, which art in heaven,

Hallowed be thy name."

Jonah held Aaliyah's hand. Aaliyah held Brenda's hand. Brenda, babies sleeping in bassinets next to her, held her mother's hand. The entire congregation held hands as they recited the Lord's Prayer in the last minute. Throughout the world, the Lord's Prayer was being recited in churches and homes.

In the East, the asteroid shone like lightning as it trailed toward the Earth. Its cloud-like glory was so great that it could even be seen in the West.

"Thy kingdom come. Thy will be done in earth, as in heaven."
In the Crypt, Dexter held Susan as both watched the television. Davis and Asia held Blake and each other. Weeping together, Helen and Reggie held Gala between them. Don Smock still sat alone in his office on Level Four, the coffin on a table against the wall looming large in the background.

"Give us this day our daily bread. And forgive us our debts, as we forgive our debtors."
President Joe Whitmore held Jack Bray. In the control room, no one was working at the instruments. All were standing, transfixed, watching Nostradamus on the monitor.

In the coldness of space, a red light blinked on the hull of a super space shuttle called the *Savior*. Inside, forty-four humans slept, awaiting the computer-controlled sequence of events that would return them to life and to Earth.

"And lead us not into temptation, but deliver us from evil;"
From other shelters, the fortunate of Earth watched the cloud of fire descend from the sky, unaware that missile launch orders were already set.

An act of Almighty God and a matter of sheer coincidence. Divine judgment and pure science. The great meteor crashed to Earth at exactly 5:33 p.m. GMT just as predicted, the completion of a mechanical cosmic event that had been ordained from the moment of creation and the Big Bang.

"For thine is the kingdom, and the power, and the glory, for ever, and ever. Amen."

www.ingramcontent.com/pod-product-compliance
Lightning Source LLC
Chambersburg PA
CBHW020205270626
47157CB00028B/1144

* 9 7 8 0 9 8 2 6 9 3 6 9 8 *